THE IRON Grains

JESS ZEPEDA

Brilliant Books Literary
137 Forest Park Lane Thomasville
North Carolina 27360 USA

CHAPTER 1

A Sun in the Valley

Thank God I'm free at last

The crying was loud, monstrous. Tears were blinking and shimmering in the traces of sunlight, and an acapella of the crowd was crying. The blades of grass were crying; the skies were crying. The birds mimicked, and the wind moaned. The people huddled next to a mariachi band, which played music to a song "Haya en el Rancho Grande."

"Allá en el rancho grande, allá donde vivía," sang the musicians from the warm dressed-colored Mexican singing group. Viewing the crowd, one could see that many of the people were wearing black and white outfits of formal attire. The entire world appeared black and white, and the atmosphere dominated the celebration of the Easter Sunday. Yes, it was an Easter Sunday in a very placid, commonplace…hometown USA.

People began throwing dirt over the coffin.

They each individually had privileges with the honor of the cold earth. Two figures stood out from the crowd and were seen together toward the rear of the assembly. The sun began shining fiercely, and the public began to quiet. One of the distant figure took a large airmail-stamped envelope from his raincoat. He opened it and began to read the letter to his partner:

All was quiet. The spring frost had seized the valley floor that morning, and the sunrise reacted for a breath of freedom and cut through the icicles. An ice palace formed itself within the background and foreground of the countryside's terrain.

Black crows were flying low and sat on top of the vines as in congregations. Smith Mountain lay apart from the town nearly two miles hidden well within the fog. The valley lay still, and from the summit, one could see a long caravan plowing its way through the main road. There was a long line of cars, and a hearse stood out among the other vehicles like a phantom wizard leading an opera to its last opening. All eyes watched on as the motorcade assembled an orphanage troupe playing in a field of air harvest and searching for a patch of earth to plant a new seed bearing itself within its underarms. This was the resemblance of a very good harvest, and all appeared to show that the day would be a very good day.

This funeral ceremony did not look the same as other funerals, which were pronounced at its arrival during this time of the twentieth century. It was not ordinary even if the people had construed it to be so. The shops in the town were all closed. The church bells were ringing, and the American flag waved freely as most flags stood over the front door of the houses. Yes, all was quiet.

The fog began to lift. The motorcade carved itself a path through the front gate of the cemetery. As if a rehearsal had taken place, all at once the cars emptied. There were townspeople seen walking from the town and children riding on their bikes. Several of them were climbing over the mountain and running through the orchard. The people gathered in masses around the tent as the priest delivered a sermon with his voice heard above the tears and moans of the crowd. The VFW cadre stood to south sides of the tent, blackbirds dispersed in bundles across the lawn, and the rifles were raised to the heaven in formal military fashion. The twenty-one-gun salute resounded and echoed a volley, which clamored throughout the east side of the mountain. The crowd began to walk away.

"He was the revolution," cried out one man.

"Let's go have some beer," said another man.

"I never knew him," whispered one lady.

"Let's go have some menudo," spoke out an old man.

Several cars began leaving the cemetery, yet many people remained on the site as the fog continued lifting. The high-noon sun began shining through the blanched purity of the white clouds. The sunlight fell upon the grave. Instantaneously, four thousand figures walking about the lawns traversed staunchly with a rapid chatter while carrying flowers. With a majority of the group wearing dark robes and suits and several persons in common apparel, the scene would remind you of an army of dark-clad ants crawling about and searching for their leader. The queen was dead.

Yes, at first, I could not believe it, but it was true. The country was behaving as if to a woman going through child labor. Two hundred years after, the revolution had matured over in the East Coast. America was indeed a different America, and I felt like the American who was still very much a part of that revolution. The pains of pregnancy had long been overdue. No more recalcitrant tribulations. A new child was indeed on its way. And if I dared to detour, dared to deny myself, to fool myself, to shun and pretend at hiding, I seldom found myself. Now, I would not retrieve from the fact that I was an American. I felt it more so now, and I accepted it with total honors.

I felt the roots were mine, in the soil, the earth. I felt comfortable. The silence entombed me with reconciliation, and I received it with negative feelings of a betrayal from an unpaid debt I felt I had not relinquished. And all of this I believed. All of this I accepted. Isolation was mine to keep, at last.

America's isolation was not hers to keep to herself, however. Instead, she revealed to the world the monster she had been during the major period of the twentieth century. Yes, this was the glorious, monstrous hypocrite the people had created for their celebration of bicentennial happiness. Only a narrow outlook on life and those illusions were necessary and at once revealed to us a truer picture of this particular type of happiness. Assuming those premises dealing with the basic freedoms of our individual lives, those dealings of a democracy contrary to the pentagons of communism, socialism, and rules of inherent satellites, let's follow an understanding of the remorse regarded in those of religion and personal imbue. As I have accepted, let us all accept the feelings of being an American.

At first, the entire cemetery seemed to characterize the makings of an oversized chessboard cluttered with memories and tribulations as the only opponents of the game. It was just as though he could have planned it, the funeral. This small world couldn't have shown a better reflection or carbon copy of the community he had once known. Most people acted out the roles they knew expected of him. Nothing had changed except for the eerie mood of the day. After some time, the ceremony would remind you of a carnival filled with children running about and dogs barking wildly. The air during the harvest was a good one, and the townspeople had good attitudes about the pastoral goods—orchards and vineyards. Most of them wore dark hats and smoked cigars as they huddled among themselves, separated from the other crowd. A mariachi band stood to the west of the grave near the entrance and played several last tunes from their repertoire. The majority of the people who were remaining were younger in age; the young and innocent were those who stood around the grave.

The crowd was celebrating more than a eulogy of a man. The year was 1976; two hundred years had passed after the American Revolution. This was the celebration about a rebirth of a nation that was, by this time, the greatest the world has ever known. Yes, it was truly a celebration. There were shouts of laughter, quaint giggles, and clapping hands. The younger people began to dance in circles as if a trance had been cast over the graveyard, and quickened insanity had overpowered the gloomy celibacy, which at first had characterized the ceremony. There was no better time that these so-called Californians could have gathered to discuss whatever politics and the kind of rumors and backsliding they always had among themselves. For now, at last, there was no one to hear of their reminiscences about their own wars, which through all this time they had hidden to themselves and within their minds. What glorious hypocrites…cowards. What glorious fools. Inside each and every soul was a cancer decaying the agony of each of their own deaths and menial destinies. This was the only way they could be loved, the only call in which they could be commended. How terrible was the feeling of despair existing within their souls, a sharp clenching despair. Their consciences were now free and unbound. They were no longer the slaves of the past and memories of a Peyton Place with clinging imprisonment. A chessboard appearance became the scene of this cemetery, and the lawn began taking the resemblance of statuettes that stood above the tombstones and monuments placed around the mausoleum. The funeral had come to an end and had finished at last.

A cold wind began to cover the valley in an uneven gust. The breeze could be seen pushing through the cemetery as their coats began flapping and goggling back and forth. The people put their hands into their pockets and then huddled closer together. The sounds of the cars diminished as the padre could be seen leaving last in his black Mercedes Benz. He smoked his cigar as he drove up and down the mountain to the other side and into town with his radio on full power. You could hear the music as he left the area. The roosters and chickens carried on haplessly in their boredom at a ranch next to the mausoleum. And further down the field, cows could be seen dragging their hoofs toward the ditch next to the orchards of orange trees that lined the mountain on its side. How carefree was the evening. How subtle was the look of the gigantic canyons of the Kings and Sequoias to the east, glowing as fiery diamonds, like burning wood in a fireplace. They stood proud and shined against the light of the sunset on this middle date in April. Julian Solbriozo's body lay in peace, *por* última *vez*, and the sun began to sink behind the purple horizon of the Sierra Madre Coastal Range. The final rays of light breathed for freedom as the sky turned to an emerald green, and the wind from the south faded away as the mariachi began to play "Haya en el Rancho Grande."

"For heaven's sake, David, turn off that damn transistor radio, for not even that kind of *musica* will wake up the dead, much less stir up the hearts of the townspeople."

"Come on now, Ramon. Please don't feel so downhearted. You act as if all is lost, as if it was all your fault. You should have seen the expression on the faces of the VFW cadre as the mariachi placed its last refrain."

What was that supposed to mean? thought Ramon to himself. Just then, the last chunk of square piece of grass was shoved atop Julian Solbriozo's grave. The cemetery's yardman gathered the hoes and shovels and climbed into the truck and drove away. The yard became quiet. David and Ramon walked away to the edge of the road to where the entrance of the cemetery stood. The '57 Ford parked there looked as somber as a praying mantis as if it were praying and carrying on its own religious cult, waiting to be awakened from a deep sleep. And as the car moved away, the mountain lying to one side of the graveyard looked like a naked woman stretched out above the plains, protesting her chastity, protecting her make-believe children, and guarding and keeping her newly born.

"I'm alive, alive at last," whispered the sun, and the world is free to touch, to feel, to burst with passion, to turn with ease…and to cry a tear. I'm truly myself now, for no one can destroy me.

Signed: Julian Solbriozo
April 14, 1976
Good Friday

At first, there was shock, amazement, a sudden pause, and at the end, a sigh of breath.

"I don't believe it," said Ramon Grijalva. "It can't be! Today is Easter Sunday, and the letter is dated the 16th of April, the Good Friday. Julian's body was taken to the morgue Thursday night, the night of the 13th."

"You talk as if you know something, as if someone told you a thing or two. Do you?" asked David. "Do you?" He paused a moment and gazed with a jury's smile into Ramon's eyes. "Are you the author of this yourself?" he shouted.

"But I swear on God's name, the man who gave it to me at the bar last night told me to read the letter in the morning as soon as the ceremony had once started. I was drunk, I didn't know. I mean, I can't remember who he was."

"Shut up, Ramon. And for heaven's sake, don't swear on God's name. You're no more a good Christian than that of the atheist." His eyes began turning a red color. He gasped. "Oh my god. Can it be?" All of a sudden, David looked puzzled as he stared into Ramon's eyes. "Could it have been Julian last night? We must not speak a word of this to anyone," he whispered into Ramon's shoulder.

"Well, cry if it makes you feel any better, you fool!" David's voice ascended.

"I don't know if I can now," muttered Ramon. "I really don't know if I can."

"We will come tonight when all is quiet," said David. Ramon just stared back with frigid horror at David. "Hey, you're the one who's crazy now," stated Ramon.

"After all, it was closed casket during the ceremony. No one saw the body. They say it was burnt beyond recognition. We'll dig it up tonight about midnight. And you'll come with me, you damn atheist," commanded David, who was at this time mad with rage.

"I will, I will!" cried Ramon, as he splendidly gave in to David's sermon. "You've got to be some kind of a communist," he resigned.

"This is no time to discuss and argue religion. Why, you hypocrite! You're going to come with me tonight!"

That night, the crickets and frogs could be heard having their evening tea parties. The cemetery was lit up with the lamp lights which surrounded the fence. A car was on its way from the town as it detoured through the small roads that branched themselves from the main highway, a road leading into the city limits. The sky was crisply clear that night, and the stars shone with an overwhelming character, trenchant, and glittered with an omnipresent brightness. And they all appeared to be attracted to the powerful portrait of the moon as it showed its face over every object and living thing. The car arrived, and two figures left the vehicle and carried shovels and flashlights. They crossed the lawns and came to a halt. Next, they began digging furiously.

"Are you sure we're doing the right thing?" spoke Ramon as if holding himself back. "I'm not sure I can live with myself the rest of my life. What do you expect to find, David? Money, jewelry, a will, or perhaps more broken dreams of yours? David, what the hell do you want with Julian's body?"

No answer.

"You mean you're telling me that Julian wasn't buried after all?"

"Very possible," answered David, covered with dust and sweat and panting very heavily.

A half an hour had passed, and the shovels' tips had hit the cover of the coffin. The dirt was still soft, and the pit had taken the shape of a tomb very readily. They continued removing the dirt surrounding the coffin. Reaching the handles, David unlatched them one by one.

"Give me more light," he asked. Ramon pointed the flashlight into the pit toward David. He watched on as David lifted the cover.

"You fool!" cried out Ramon. "It's his father." Only a skeleton appeared with bits of embedded flesh covered the bones and draped with traces of clothing. As they both stared in horror, David closed the cover to the golden box and jumped from the pit wildly examining the tombstone. It read: "Julian Solbriozo 1900-1966."

"How could we have not noticed this," trembled David. "I don't know," answered Ramon. Grabbing the flashlight from Ramon's hand, David ran about, examining the lawn and reading to himself the other tombstones. He gazed in futility, amazed, for there was no other tombstone or landmark to be found with the same name.

"I swear on God's name that the ceremony took place in this area," spoke out David.

"Yes, I know, I know!" yelled out Ramon. "We must work fast and assemble the grave. It is already three o'clock in the morning, and the sun will be rising soon. I don't know what to think," commented David. "The ceremony seemed so real, and this is sure not a dream nor fantasy."

"But then, what of Julian, and where is he?" asked Ramon.

"God knows where," answered David.

CHAPTER 2

Highway Soldier, Iron Rainbow the Birth of an Artist

"Rebel, oh dear rebel, if not for your fight, then how would you show me the revolution?"

To be nineteen years old and a young stud in America during these times of adolescence meant a very rough period of a go for any young boy learning to become a man. This was only half the story according to the people coming from the valley in California. The hottest days had just begun, and it was a warm third of July of perhaps the most controversial season. The war in Vietnam had just subsided, and most of the troops who were at that line called lifers by civilian standards were being shipped back to the homeland. The politico-savor front of the valley had quieted down; however, the standstill was not yet dead. Remnants remained intact, especially the ill feelings that lay within the conscience of Julian Solbriozo's soul. And by this time, most of the people knew about him being drafted into the US Army. Most of these ill-fed characters felt it a shock.

For the majority of people who were less concerned, Julian was just another young adolescent, mixed up, confused, and very wet behind the ears. Any young man from a small country town who was being drafted into the US Army could have fallen under this category. It meant no more strange situations created by Julian. It meant no more having to tolerate a mysterious young man, a man who had the town believing that he was a mentally sick young man, mind you! No, they probably just couldn't have cared less.

For Julian, it meant no more classes at the nearby Junior College, no more being able to renovate his friends, perhaps no more painting, which was the love of his life. A serene figure he was, a secret boy thought most of by his female acquaintances.

The morning was crisp, and he arrived at the induction center at eight o'clock with curiosity and amazement. A strange new world appeared to him, which seemed like the beginning of a long theatrical play. Yes, a long rehearsal for Julian. He could not see himself in such a situation, giving up one's own freedom while taking an oath to the American flag.

But why shouldn't I? he thought again. *All the other guys are doing it.* And once he was in line, he waited. It came his turn…he gave his oath. "You are now a member of the United States Army," stated the sergeant with cynical complacent eyes as to that of a raven's.

"Looks like we're all in the same boat!" yelled one of the younger fellas. The group consisted of young men entering the Coast Guard, Navy, Air Force, Marines, and of course, that of Julian's Army.

After complete physical examinations, there would be lunch and bus time preparations. The doctor who was soliciting that day was a young man, loud, and would walk into the room, saying, "Everyone, pull down your pants and shorts. Bend over and open those cheeks wide. And spread them as wide as you can." Of course, it was like any other day at the induction center.

She was a Greyhound express. The time was eleven forty-eight, and all those civilians boarded the bus one at a time. And everyone was there to wave goodbye—relatives, parents, girlfriends, and enemies. Julian's salutations had been taken care of back in Lumber town. With all the commotion and noise, and of course, crying, the wheels began moving from the city, Raisintown. Julian felt as if he would never see home again. "Next stop, Fort Ord!" yelled the driver. With a sudden jerk, the bus's wheels began moving, rolling, and the city disappeared in a few minutes. Julian looked back for one last time, debating yet unreluctant to those things he was last remembering.

I've become a victim of a bureaucratic democracy to become a soldier. But of what type? he first thought. He was nervous, and his hands were shaking and trembling.

"Hey, you, green one," said a voice from behind him. It was an older man sitting next to a woman. "Where are you going?"

"I'm going to the fort like most other young guys here." The old man just grinned and laughed. "Keep to yourself. You'll like it," he said.

"I'll do whatever I'm supposed to do," replied Julian. There he sat, quiet, nonchalant, as the bus crossed the desert. He stood not near six feet in height, 150 pounds to weight, dark-brown wavy hair. A Mexican American he was, but he preferred to be called Mexican by most of his friends. Asunder from family hang-ups over cultural ethnicity, he knew who he was deep inside himself as most of us do in times of revealing our true identities. Yet this entire realm of conscious thinking raptured his mind, for entering the army had left him confused. What else was one to conclude during a time of centurion adolescence brought up in an ever softening of moral values in a society such as America? This parasitic dilemma wasn't only Julian's personal battle but, at the then present state of affairs, everyone's battle.

The bus began climbing the Sierra Madre Range, the hills known as Pacheco Pass. The speed on the wheels slowed, and everyone began taking notice of each other for the first time. The glorious boulders of ice began to break one at a time. Everyone began taking deeper breaths, and respirations became less superficial with ears popping and perspiration building up by the minute.

There were close to thirty of them sitting all from different parts of the states and others from different areas of the union. They awaited their survival—timid, green-horned, anticipated, suspicious in mind, and awed. Julian sat toward the back of the bus next to a large-sized black older fella who was very quiet. Everybody else called him Red, Big Red.

"My name is Bill, Bill Reed," he spoke to Julian in a very righteously self-assertive manner.

"Hello, my name is Julian Solbriozo."

"I'm glad to know ya, Julie," the big man replied, smiling complacently. And soon after, Julian shook the man's hand.

The bus began to cross the Peninsula of Monterey, and Julian stared at the point where John Steinbeck had once written about Tortilla Flats and stories about the Fisherman's Wharf. The bus approached the fort, which appeared like the portrayal of a prison surrounded by tall iron fences lined with barbed wire, and the guards stood up straight, looking like toy soldiers at the gate. They suddenly reminded Julian of the ones he used to play with when he was a child. To the west roared on the Pacific Ocean. The clouds rolled above. The time was now 2:59 past noon, and Julian was the last to leave the bus.

Four more bus loads rolled in. There they were, 240 civilian green necks standing around in front of the entrance station, waiting to be plucked, processed, and geared to become an American fighting machine or a group of flunk heads thought by Julian, as did many of the other guys. This was not his attitude at first. This new life was indeed a new experience for Julian. This new entrance was not his ideal nor his hope. Neither was it to be a game. However, this new stage would become his near destiny.

"All right, you bunch of sassy shitheads, line up, line up!" yelled the sergeant major. His name was Martinez.

But this is supposed to be an ethical institution, thought Julian. He was left speechless, as were the rest of them, amazed at this act of capital punishment and government blabbering.

"Stop smiling at me, Solbriozo! I'm not your mother!" yelled the sergeant. Embarrassed, Julian withdrew, and the standing figures smiled. Being a mixture of ethnic groups from different countries, they came from the Philippines, Guam, Mexico, Africa, New York, and of course,

California. It was a universal army, a company of youth from all over the world.

How strange, thought Julian. *How strange for America's cause.*

The remaining hours of daylight were spent getting heads shaved, uniforms, assignments, and more instructions from the military cadre. After the first meal was served, the day darkened with overcast, and quarantine had been ordered to all the companies. With barren silence and enduring patience, one could hear the retreat.

"But it's only a record player," said one of the Guamanians whose name was Jingo. The phonograph played throughout the entire fort. "It's a phony setup!" he exclaimed again. "It's all phony!" yelled out Julian. "It is as phony as you want it to be." The voices quieted, and the barracks became tranquil.

The academy area was as old as the hills. The buildings and the chow hall, including the headquarters unit, were built of wood, painted a light-green color dating all the way back to 1938, a time during the prewar years of World War II. She looked like a museum, and the old war spirits were ever yet present and could be felt throughout the surroundings and in the atmosphere. You could swear to God that everything was old, very old for these young rebels…perhaps too old yet one at the same novice and new.

The time was 9:00 p.m., and an entire company of men could be heard marching with the usual chant. Several moving trucks could be heard nearby amid the roar of the ocean.

"Left, left, left, left, right…left, left, left, right." And then the marchers' feet began to move away. The chant grew fainter and fainter. "Left…left, right." The day had gone by, and the barracks became the social hour of the fort. Tdeas spurted forth. For Julian, it was only the beginning of an acquaintance.

Throughout the night, the chatter continued and grew louder. The Guamanians and other foreigners began politicizing and chastising the American boys with religion and politics, and they showed very much jealousy at times. Julian was calm. Being the philosopher that he was, he soon joined in the argument and defended his position.

But I'm only defending my land, he thought, *I have nothing else to defend.*

"You're all jealous because of the land we live in," he told them. The frolicking continued until the morning low sunrise. Soon the atmosphere took on the character of a summer camp.

Despite the civilian influence handed to this particular class of young men, they truly were from a crop of young adolescents from different racial personalities consisting of a group of college men, including Julian and others such as ex-cons, criminals, runaways, derelicts, and bums. And there were the very educated with many institutional degrees but carried no viable status worth talking about. It was the year Cesar Chavez was fighting over the grapes in the San Joaquin Valley. Jane Fonda was coming back from Vietnam with the troops after entertaining the war-torn. The president had passed a law diminishing the draft, doing away with it once and for good. All of this happened only several days after Julian was drafted by the draft board.

Oh, but how lucky I am, he thought. *To be in such a depressing, blasted institution, I'm to become a killer and a notorious criminal. That's what! A notorious what? A notorious bald eagle, that's what!* This soon became the entire attitude from the entire company of the Third Battalion, Second Brigade, Company C, Charlie Company.

The next nine weeks were spent as a boot camp, which featured rigorous training, physical. This proved to be a mental strain for many of the members of the company. The military ethics and legal brainwashing techniques were introduced during the first two weeks, and the passions began to rise within the various platoons of the company. Many of the men began to break in physical and mental stamina like flies in a poison trap. Sure, the war was over, but this one had only begun.

Most of these lifers, as they were called, and controllers of the fort began to show their withdrawal symptoms brought back with them from Vietnam. Here they would take out their feelings on Company C. No, it wasn't a persecution complex. It was a group of some of America's rebels reuniting together for a confrontation against a mother image called the US Army. It couldn't have been a better place for the gathering of eagles. After all, the Monterey Peninsula had been known for a reputation as a rowdy area of California because of the servicemen who live there. This military world took on the character of an X-rated film. Exposure of these conditions to the outside world meant unbelievable and wishful thinking.

The local community had always been that kind of a community. It had every reason to stay that way regardless of how many generations were going to come along to try to change things. And this was final.

The cadre was a rough and tough group from the start; however, the entire disciplinary system seemed more lax than the earlier lotteries. This is what Julian had learned after several days had passed. One night before a bivouac, Julian sat down and wrote a poem and mailed it to an old friend (girl) the next day. He hadn't been the only one to receive "Dear John" letters.

His poem went as such:

> I looked out the window, curiously, from the second floor, sandy beaches stretched below the ivory blanket. Monterey appeared as a mural, and I still felt like that lonely prisoner from the universal Alcatraz in the cage of my mind.
>
> I am an emerald mercenary dressed in green, like an alert praying mantis praying for tranquility, training for a ruined battleground somewhere across the ocean or perhaps in the poppies of my backyard, paid well, fed well by the zookeeper of the museum.
>
> I am a young man, but they say I am a boy. My teachers, the leaders whose lives were destroyed, they teach us the ethics and the morals of war and make *militarism* a word that sounds with remorse. They hand me a gun and tell me to kill children and women whose souls race so still.
>
> Discipline is the name of the game; confidence, unity, our names sound the same. We fight for perfection, God willing, and might run like the tiger when the time yields to the right.
>
> Camaraderie, camaraderie, where do you come from? You seem like my brothers I left way back home.

We're all faceless strangers from places far away. Yet our world seems one and the same. We speak and act different with each other. Yet our feelings and hopes remain like those brothers.

I'm a prisoner in a prison, and the one in my mind keeps fighting and shaking like the bells in a chime. We need not leave this home, for the true war lies within each of us. Our true enemies become our own reflection. I hope to God that this universal soldier keeps his own Vietnams to himself and never again passes my shadow.

"Better luck next time." Big Red smiled as he heard the news during a night guard pull with Julian. At that instant, Mike Davenport, who was a platoon leader at the time, walked in.

"What do ya say, nigger lover?" he asked sarcastically and walked up the stairway toward Bill and Julian.

"Go to hell," spoke out Julian.

Red smiled and said, "You cats all ready for tomorrow?"

"Drill Sergeant James is gonna make you carry the first aid box, Mex," said Davenport.

"Yeah, well, if your gut happens to spill, I'm going to walk right past you, mother——" replied Julian.

"Come on, Solbriozo, you'll have plenty of time to beat the shit out of me tomorrow night up in the mountain." Davenport laughed. "You're good at painting pretty pictures and writing poems, sweetheart. I'd like to see how good you are tomorrow night."

Red kept smiling.

"Hey, leave him alone, you asshole!" yelled out Joe Mendoza, an ex-con from San Quentin. "Can't you see I'm trying to get some sleep? Hey! Why don't you wait until the morning to put on your pitchfork, Davenport? Then you could preach to us more about West Point, soldier boy."

"Knock it off!" yelled back Davenport. "Tomorrow morning at four thirty. Everybody understood?" He walked into his bunk quarters and closed the door behind him. Two other privates, Tom Lance and Jingo, relieved Julian and Big Red from the night guard watch. "Take her easy," said Lance.

Julian jumped into his bunk bed and closed his eyes, and his dream that night was like any other dream of his.

"Tomorrow we must perform for sure. We play the game, camp out, and then it's POW training for one entire day," his dream appeared to be telling him. Everybody gathered for this big day. It would be a day when all would have to prove themselves, and Julian's nightmare would be over for good.

What could everyone be doing back home—my brothers, my sister, my friends? he questioned himself in his thoughts. *I wonder what the world is like outside of this fort, outside of this living hell, this impeccable maelstrom, this trial of a monster from an impeachable destiny. It was as if Hollywood were shooting its last film:* An Army War Picture *or* From Here to Eternity. *But where is eternity? Life ends here. Either you do or die! I won't question it any further, for there is too much pain to ask why. I'll play it by ear. Yes! That's it! I'll play it by ear. This nightmare is not that bad after all. I'll rest now and get some sleep. It's a long march in the morning.*

The thoughts withered, and the bunkhouse became a sonorous lullaby. The wall clock was ticking away loud in resonance, and some of the bunk beds would shake because most of the men did not want to masturbate any other way. The female foldouts hung on the walls, and the snoring continued. Yes, everybody for certain wanted out, out for good, out of this sidetracked nightmare, this game of slaughter and a test for roles to be played. Julian thought it best to let everyone go first on the stage so that he would be last in the game. However, he was certain to be the first to go through the lines. He slept.

The morning arrived, and the sun rose in a bright hue above the mountain range that lay behind the fort. The fog lifted, and the signs of a hot summer day were showing everywhere. The company's four platoons were fully geared, lined up, and ready to march the seven-mile run to the mountain range. Lieutenant Perez was in the front, Sergeant Major Martinez on the flank, and Drill Sergeant James stood beside the fourth platoon. Julian was behind the formation and toward the rear. He carried the first-aid box. The whistle sounded, a blow from Sergeant

Major Martinez. They were off again and seen marching over the ridge. The company area lay quiet at last while the marchers could be heard singing their song about Jody's girlfriend. The group looked like a pack of untrained juveniles not fit to fight anybody's war. Marching up the sandy roads led them to the canyon where many of the men began to drop out one by one. There was no letting up. Fire bombs were thrown at them, and empty grenade caps followed with the sound of machine gun fire. Everybody hit the dirt. It was a simulated ambush and very real in nature. There were many laughs among them, including Julian. They all waited beside the road, crouched down like an army of timid ants, for a period of twenty minutes.

"Did you hear what's going to happen to Lieutenant Perez, Julian? The cadre at Fourth Brigade Headquarters is sending him to another company," said Joe Mendoza.

"But why?" whispered Julian.

"They say he's getting too friendly with the men here in the company."

Just then, Sergeant Major Martinez came walking up to them after he heard the conversation. "Okay, Solbriozo, since you're a medic and since you're the big mouth, Mendoza, lead the charge. Both of you! Well, what are you waiting for? Move it!" he yelled with anger. He then picked up Julian's rifle and fired two rounds toward the mountaintop. He threw the rifle back into Julian's arms.

"I said lead it, Solbriozo!" he stated once more.

Julian looked at Joe and whispered, "We'd better move it. He's liable to have a nervous breakdown."

"Charge!" yelled Joe. "Move out!" yelled Julian standing alongside him.

And with every four steps, they all fired one round of blanks. Davenport was enraged at what took place. A faceless expression in jealousy was his anger. Lieutenant Perez was at the top of the mountain, waving his hands back and forth.

"I'm over here, you bunch of sissies. Look! I'm over here." Everybody in the company fixed their Canadian buffalo sites on him with great care. Then they let him have it…3,840 rounds aimed toward his chest. It was terrible fun, they all thought later. The men liked Lieutenant Perez. This was to be his last week with them.

Man! thought Julian. *Perez has been lenient with us, and he's a liberal all the way. What's going to become of the company's moral once he leaves? This is bad for us…very bad.* More flashes ran through his mind. Sweat ran down his face. He was tired and worn out. The original group stayed back in the brush area where they would camp out for the night.

Everybody pitched their tents at dusk, and at 11:00 p.m. the entire camp was hit by tear gas. As everyone did, naturally, Julian also placed his gas mask on his face during the rainstorm of gas molecules. He felt his skin itch. A burning sensation spread throughout his body, and tears ran from his eyes, but he managed to maintain his composure. Yelling could be heard throughout the camp. It was Drill Sergeant James giving instructions to line up in formation. The gathering was to begin a march to the camp toward a hidden valley where POW training was to take place. It would be a four-mile march to the unloading area. This was an area where they would be turned loose on a three-mile obstacle course before being picked up by the trucks and taken over to the prison camp where the ex-Vietnam Green Berets training ex officios were waiting for them. Everyone had the option of being captured by a make-believe enemy (Green Berets), tied up, loaded onto trucks, and stacked like dead logs or getting through the obstacle course and passing the test. Success meant reaching a large platform with a huge floodlight that lay three miles away from the starting point. Soon, away they would be hauled like civilized human beings over to a prison camp to watch the remaining theatrical scenes with comfortable seats.

The time was 12:32 a.m. The company of Charlie reached the foot of the canyon and was set free. Like wild rebels, they danced, jumped, and ran as if scared jackrabbits would be when trying to escape a threatening fox. There were flares hovering over the sky and dud bombs being thrown throughout the brush, their faces shown within the dark-lit greenery. The sky was clear, and the stars were visible. So were the trainees' egos.

"Now was the time to leave and go away," whispered Joe Mendoza to Julian and Mike Davenport as they huddled against some large granite boulders with the sky above them lighting up like a high noon in midnight.

"You do whatever the damn hell you please," cried out Davenport. "It's your ass, not mine!"

From the top of the mountain, above the canyon, M-60 machine guns were firing blank rounds at them. The gunfire lasted for one hour. After the first barrage of shelling had diminished, the brush became quiet. Burnt gunpowder and smoke were the only remnants remaining. Toward the lower grounds, everything remained quiet and pitch black. Soon crickets could be heard doing a morning awakening with their sharp chirps and signals. Rustling of the brush could be heard everywhere. The entire company had separated, and everyone had each gone their own ways.

Julian, Joe, and Mike were running the course close together. They crossed streams, climbed small cliffs, and crawled through embankments. Next, they came to a large grassy field with dead oak trees scattered about the terrain. It was at this time that the tables turned against them. Upon reaching the grassland, the large light projector tanker could be seen at the bottom of the slope one mile away. A hand suddenly grabbed Julian's ankle. He kicked and freed himself. Several more figures jumped from the brush and began wrestling with Joe and Mike. Julian ran off with one wild leap while Joe managed to escape the attackers. Mike had become a captive. He'd been wrestled to the ground and tied up.

"Wait up, Julian, wait for me!" cried out Joe. Julian paused for a few seconds. Their steps became equal. Now they were running. Julian had never run his fastest in all his life. They were both being chased all the way to the light platform. The berets faded out; they both had made it to the platform. They had won. Members of the remaining few who had reached the platform were waiting for them. Both out of breath, Julian and Joe fell to the ground because of exhaustion.

"Now, that wasn't so hard, was it?" asked Drill Sergeant James as he spoke out casually and discreetly. "Don't you feel lucky, Solbriozo? Now you can ride the cattle's truck to prison like a normal person with the rest of these human beings. Okay?"

Muddy, brandished, and tired, they all jumped aboard the truck and were driven away, huddled like domesticated cattle, smoking their cigarettes and others with reefers of marijuana. Most of them awaited their turns with a calm repose. Big Red was also among the group who survived the obstacle course. It couldn't have been a better group or a worse group.

The trucks traveled through the canyon for six miles, came to a grade, and reached the top of a mountain. The lights in the town of Salinas were brightly lit and could be seen from the ridge. The caravan rolled over the crest and came to a stop a mile down the road. The time was 2:45 a.m.

"We've arrived at this prisoner-of-war camp!" yelled out Jingo, anxious and impatient. A member of the group from the Philippine Islands (and proved to be a fast long-distance runner) was also one of the lucky ones.

The Green Berets were walking around the trucks, shouting at the group and laughing at times. These open-bed ten-ton trucks moved alongside the cattle trucks. Sight of laughter, false humility, and the rush of complaints were all that could be heard in those very first moments. There they were, all those from the company of Charlie who had failed to cross the obstacle course…yes, all of those who were tied at the ankles and tied with their hands behind their backs. They were tossed on top of one another like beets on a farm truck. After being unbound and set loose, they joined the other groups who were soon led down a small path to the entrance of the prison gates. A melancholy-looking fort stood there surrounded by barbed-wire fences that were ten feet high, and there were sentries and light towers armed with guards at every corner. It reminded Julian of the wooden fort by Daniel Boone or whoever built the damn thing from the American history literature he had read in elementary school.

What brainwashing, he thought. *What a total brainwashing*. He was laughing inside throughout the game.

Once they were escorted into the main grounds surrounded by those walls, everyone was lined up, pushed, jeered, and some of the figures were beaten. It was very real.

The first prisoner of war to be captured in Vietnam was presiding over the majority of the trainers. He was a tall, slim man, and he carried a large whip, wore his head beret and baggy pants (pantaloons), which met his knee-high boots. His name was Captain Jacques, an American of French-descendant blood. He yelled at everyone with a sharp tongue, like a twentieth-century Napoleon. Everybody seemed to fear him as they stared with wide-open, frigid eyes. Standing on top of a platform located in the center of the yard, he delivered a long speech in a radical way by waving his whip back and forth when he spoke. Threatening them all, he said, "This is the way a communist would do it. This is the way they did it to me." After some time, he began sounding like a preacher who was delivering a sermon on the mount, and Charlie Company became his private congregation. His altar boys were the meanest Julian had ever witnessed. After all the captives pushed into a formation and lined up, the captain would walk slowly by each man seeking only one question, "What is your last name?"

"Solbriozo, sir," answered Julian in a dignified tone.

"Go over to the corner, sit down, and shut up," stated the officer. Everyone who sat in this one particular corner was all those people whose last names ended in anything other than English descent. This group included Latinos, Chinese, Orientals, blacks, and everybody from the stereotyped Third World. They all huddled in this one corner, smoked their cigarettes, and in a hilarious and paradoxical fashion, were allowed to eat their rice and chicken like privileged human beings, like a guest at a concert and given the front seats and handed down a taste of freedom—a breath— by the captain. This captain looked and smiled at Julian and had a certain weakness in his eyes.

"All dem white boys, gettin' thar asses kicked," said Big Red with his deepened Southern accent.

"They're crawling to eat their rice," whispered Joe Mendoza. "Check it out! It's crazy." They were all laughing inside. Anyone who had rank received the worst treatment. All of those who had fallen in love with power fell in love right then and there with their comrades. Julian remembered that this was the way the morning had ended.

The final week of boot camp had diminished far from a happy note. During a shooting exercise on the range after marching toward the beach, a trooper and one of the drill sergeants killed one another in a shootout. In another instance, one of the men hung himself from the top of the stairway in the barracks. But there were incidents in other companies, and Charlie Company managed to maintain its composure and moral.

After the company's graduation ceremony, Julian received orders to stay on base. Most members of the company were shipped to Germany or Korea. It was the last time Julian would see his old friends as they soon were separated and each went their own way. Julian channeled himself throughout the base, and in the end, he landed a position with the Fourth Brigade Headquarters, the most prestigious command post. Here, he would be working for all the brass, such as the chiefs in command, the biggest honchos of all the lifers put together.

For once, he felt at home. He felt as if he had been grounded. Julian had built his solid reputation by now. They knew of him. That is, the cadre knew of him. He was welcomed by everyone the first day he arrived. Most of the men were mechanics, draftsmen, engineers, and truck drivers. The women were just as good. There were these car drivers who drove the lieutenants about the fort areas; they were all blonds. However, Julian began to reject fitting within the realm of matters and situations. His attitude began to change as the days went on. It was at this time he felt that he should leave the fort. It was a feeling of lonely despair, inward resentment, agony. *I must leave*, he thought.

His actual planning had begun before his basic graduation, and it was a fantasy that overtook him. Julian had become a rebel. He began fighting the military system, fighting himself wild and vicious. This lonesome figure was no longer the ambitious trainee who had pronounced military ethics months earlier.

After buying himself a pickup truck with army pay, he drove home—a two-hundred-mile drive down the coast. Julian was not that kind of a young man to go AWOL. He did everything the hard way. The winter was well present, and it was Christmastime. He arrived home to find that the house was empty. Loading several of his large painted murals onto the bed of his new truck, he drove back to the fort.

That same night, he met one who would encourage him very much and become a good friend he would not forget for some time. His name was David Segura, who had been shipped back from Vietnam. He had arrived at the company that afternoon before Julian had returned back from his home visit. They both met upstairs in the barracks. The time was 9:00 a.m. The lights were still turned on, and most of the men were preparing to call it a night. The room was noisy, and people were talking. David's bunk was across the floor from Julian's.

All of a sudden, a familiar figure walked into the room. It was Mike Davenport, who was married to the colonel's daughter after basic training ended. And much to Julian's song, he received orders to stay on base. Everybody in the barracks knew of Davenport, and they couldn't handle him, much less put up with his false pride character, a very raw character indeed. He laughed as he approached Julian. The room quieted.

"Well, if it isn't the hot Mex. How does the colonel treat you these days, Mex…still painting your pretty pictures? What's the matter, don't you talk any more these days, or are your paintbrushes getting to you?"

David looked at Julian and smiled. Everybody took sides. Davenport took the first swing. Julian blocked it. And in a sudden fierce and flurry of arm throwing and swinging, Solbriozo pushed Davenport toward the stairway until a surrender of verbalization had commenced.

"Okay, Julian. We're living off-base. She already wants a divorce, but I'm trying to get it back together again," said Davenport. Everyone broke out laughing.

"The colonel will be very happy," said Jim Wies, one of the company's engineers and a bomb expert. He always talked about the fact that he had a plan on how to burn down the entire fort with dynamite. The majority of the soldiers were former criminals and street fighters bred all the way from Chicago, Harlem, and other areas of New York. The group consisted of many Puerto Ricans. They all sided with Julian.

David Segura, back from Vietnam, carried with him a killing-machine attitude! He was short, built very stalky, sturdy, and was feared by many of the cadre, including the Fourth Brigade Headquarters. In Vietnam, he went before a military trial for murdering his lieutenant in the field after disobeying an order. After that, he had been released, innocent, despite his consequences. He carried a .38 special revolver with him wherever he would go. He and Julian would spend time together, on and off base, in the clubs, the hall, and friendly beer occasions, which included juggling around with the prostitutes of Monterey. These women would come over to the base every day.

Two other characters soon massed with them. They were Gino Vagarte, a Portuguese from New York, and Ramon Grijalva from Bakersfield, who at that time was prime minister of the Brown Berets. The Brown Berets were a radical Chicano group during the turbulent agricultural times in the late sixties. They soon became a picked bunch on the fort, but it was a saintly wickedness created by them. And this is what everybody began to fear, including the headquarter psychiatrist. By this time, it was obvious that they all wanted out of the service, including Julian. An unreal Christmas present it was.

A week later, the base allowed Julian to display his murals at the NCO club. All seventy thousand pairs of eyes closed on his colored messages as the painted boards showed themselves with great brilliance.

After work and at times even earlier, Captain Ames, a company officer, would allow him to go paint at the craft shop until the closing hours of the night arrived. His reputation as a painter was at last established on base. The only members of the company who began thinking twice about him were members of the cadre. They thought him to be a small amount crazy. Julian only felt he was showing his sanity.

It was a warm March afternoon one day, and Julian had received orders from Captain Ames to go to the company next door to give the lieutenant transfer slips. Julian approached the entrance of the headquarter door and walked into the old office occupied by the Guamanian official.

"Say, I have some slips here to give to you from Captain Ames's company next door," spoke out Julian. "You what! Trooper?" slammed the Guamanian, who was so fat that his belly stuck out over his belt. "You don't talk to me like that."

"But, sir!" Julian exclaimed.

"You think it's funny, don't you?" Julian was losing control this time around as the lieutenant questioned him. The fat lieutenant stood up from his chair and, with enough force, pushed Julian out the front door. The immediate company's captain and the troopers peered on with patient stares and large grins on their faces as they looked out the windows of the barracks.

"Stop pushing me, you fat mother——!" spoke out Julian. This lieutenant pushed him all the way out to the middle of the street pavement that crossed the front of the company area. The world fell apart. Julian landed his left fist on the foreigner's right cheek.

"C'mon, fat boy," he cried out, taking off his hat. Members of the company area were stepping outside of the barracks, and Julian could be seen skipping back to his own company area. The lieutenant chased him into the office, and the next moments were silenced by faces staring at each other.

"Keep him away from me," cried out Julian. "Keep this animal away from me." Members in the room separated them. Julian was in one corner, and the Guamanians were in another. As the fat, short-circuit, tempered lieutenant entered the captain's office, the door slammed behind him. Yelling could be heard. Everyone outside the captain's office was laughing except Julian. A large discussion followed.

"Leave that man alone. He's a professional artist," Captain Ames could be heard. Sixty seconds passed, and out walked both of the instant-made gentlemen with their mouths shut and their chins tucked in. They both walked out of the captain's office like a couple of pregnant ducks. It was a disastrous site. After the calamity had calmed itself down, the captain walked out of his office and asked Julian to come inside of his room and have a talk with him. This time, everyone crossed their fingers. The door shut.

"Okay, Solbriozo, I've had enough of your crap. What's the main problem with you, kid?" he gestured in leisure attitude. A big man with a mustache and smoked a large cigar lay back in this chair and his feet on top of the desk.

"What's the matter? Don't you know how to get along with anyone?"

"I did not tell him anything which was degrading, Captain."

"How do you mean?" asked Julian. "I mean, why are you trying to get out of the army? Why did you sign up for it to begin with?"

"I didn't sign up and was drafted."

"Do you have any personal or social problems, Julian?"

"Yes. Of course I do. You see. This is the social problem!" yelled out the tall, dark-headed youth. "How long have you been in this outfit, Captain?"

At first, the captain managed to chuckle. He paused and stated with a sharp answer, "Seven years."

"No wonder your mind is so corroded," said Julian with a chuckle. And his laughter was that of despairing, relentless solitude. The captain picked up the phone and dialed, "Hello, Doctor. I'm sending him over to you right away. Yes…yes, he says that he must go home to fight a war. He looks desperate."

Everyone outside the door was standing close by, listening. They backed away from the door as soon as the captain was beginning to escort Julian away from the building.

Julian was taken over to the main medic's building on the base where he met Captain Poor, who was the head psychiatrist. He entered the large two-story wooden building, walked up a flight of stairs, and trammeled down a long hallway. His footsteps came to an end. He approached a door which read: "Dr. James Poor, Captain, 4th Brigade Headquarters."

"Come in," a voice from inside the room could be heard. He opened the door, walked into the light, and sat himself down on a large wooden seat in front of a walnut-coated desk. The doctor had a large mustache, and short hair covered his partly balding head. He had a large physique, tall, stalky, and very gentle in his ways. Pulling a large wooden pipe from out of his desk, the cheap kind of pipe that was sold at the PX stores, he lit it with a lighter.

"What is it about the army that you don't like, Julian?" he asked as he spoke in a soft and complacent tone. "I heard about what you told the colonel and his wife the other night at the craft shop while you were working on one of your paintings. You remember! They had been visiting. What did you tell the colonel that night, Julian?"

"I had been painting when they walked in. I began explaining the meaning of my painting, and they began asking me questions."

"But didn't you threaten him, Julian?"

"I don't feel I did. He did conclude in asking me one question."

"And what was that?" asked the doctor.

"He asked me, 'Well, are you going to finish it now that you've started it?'"

"And did you answer him?"

"Yes, I did! I told him that I would sweat it out. I would finish it." Julian paused a moment. "Are you implying war, Doctor?"

"That's not what I said, Julian. Do you feel that you're fighting a war?"

"At times. At other times it's a game. As I've said, at times I feel that it's a war." The conversation ended in this manner of tone. Julian received orders to return to the company area. And at once, he continued.

The morning came, and Julian failed to show up to work at the fort's Special Services Division. He had left for the mountains above the fort to a place called Point Zero. The area was given this name because it was used as a target zone for artillery and war games called "maneuvers." After picking up David Segura and explaining to him where he was going and why, they both rode in Julian's truck through a six-mile stretch of windy, curved roads, brush and sea type of jungle. This was Point Zero. They had heard of it many times mentioned from some of the lifers and regular personnel working on base. The rumors and stories had created an illusion centered on this area of land of unknown territory, better known as "no man's land"…every fool's dream, every general's rainbow, every trooper's highest goal.

"There are various penalties for pretending to be boss," said David, shaking his head and glancing over to Julian with inquisitive eyes.

"You got out of your pit. Well, didn't you?" asked Julian.

"Sure, but that was different, Julian. It was in a land where I was forced to kill somebody and not in a land where I had lived all my life."

"Then what's so different about this situation? Isn't it the same thought, the same manner of speaking?" asked Julian. "Isn't it the same war, David?"

"No, no. It isn't the same war, Julian." David shrugged. "It's your own private war. That's all. That's all it is."

At that instance, the truck was passing through an area where large armored personnel carriers and tanks of various sorts and types were stationary throughout the landscape. Several jeeps were parked on the sides of the road. All the men and women's personnel were staring and laughing as the truck moved on by. A modern-day Don Quixote could not have painted a better picture. Only this time, there were no windmills. The truck continued moving through the mountain range like a bowling ball on free flight over a chessboard table, knocking everything down in its path. The truck reached the East Garrison, an old abandoned training camp that had not been in use for over twenty-five years—a serene graveyard-looking ghost town.

The general's relic, perhaps his past! wondered Julian. After they decided to stop at the NCO club, one which the controllers had closed, they both arrived at one of the company's beer clubs and soon drowned themselves into utmost drunkenness and forgetfulness.

And it was a great time, thought Julian. At once, he began to follow his created illusion, his naïveté, his stubbornness, or perhaps what was his thoughtfulness.

That night in the barracks, everyone seemed to be in some merriment, jolly or blinking drunk. Yet the company area had been placed under strict order for curfew by the general. If you were vulnerably walking alone through the company area after 8:00 p.m., the night patrols would commit their acts of arrest. Everyone was under the impression that the entire base was being spied on because of new formalities being created by the company commanders. The curfew became a foreign etiquette never before used at the fort.

The light from exploding bombs could be seen on the mountain, resembling fireworks to celebrate Fourth of July. Several companies were conducting maneuvers before daylight. The company next door to the 4th Brigade had turned into a riot as the cooks and truck drivers went lunging at each other in a large gang fight created by both barracks. Havoc became the centered characteristic throughout the night. Too drunk to discuss foul play about scheming, Julian and David fell fast asleep. "Sweet dreams, you lonely rebels, sweet dreams."

The morning had followed, and David left the barracks for work. But for Julian, it meant another visit with Captain Poor, the base psychiatrist. As soon as he received his orders, he jumped into his pickup truck to leave to the doctor's office. Once again, everybody simply stared at him as he drove by the company's headquarters office.

"Good morning, Julian. How are you today, my friend? Are you still fighting the war? Are you winning?" the doctor spoke with whimsical questioning as he smiled. "Are you painting more these days, Julian? By the way, how are your paintings coming along? Do you still paint, Julian?" And he continued with a multitude of questions.

Julian nodded with a yes and no answers. Then he spoke, "I don't believe in this war, Doctor. I don't believe in politics."

"Never mind, Julian. You're doing a good job." He smiled. "If you want to leave, you can. I will have arrangements made with your company commander in the morning." Julian sighed, at first not accepting to believe what he had heard.

The next morning was spent signing papers and loading all his gear and paintings onto his truck. And from the time the truck passed the front gate onto the freeway, he had been cursed at, teased, and jibed by most of the people on the fort.

"We will meet again someday," he told David Segura just before leaving. And he was like a wild horse running from its trainer. *I'm leaving the peninsula for good, once and for all, never again to be kept jailed from this monster, this demon*, he thought. The truck sped north on the freeway toward Capitola, and there were rainclouds rolling in furiously from the ocean. He could be seen from one of the overpasses still wearing his army greens and boots. The rains came.

But this entire situation couldn't be possible, he thought. It was as if good luck had the full house this time, for the entire deck that Julian was playing with was not filled with instant miracles. Was it only yesterday that he had arrived at the induction center and had given an oath to this monster, to this nasty mother——? Wasn't it just recently he had met foreigners who had become like brothers to him, like weather-beaten pillows enslaved with agony, somebody to cling to for support and companionship? Who were they? Who were those strange faces who looked like war, like hell, like linen that had been washed thousands of times and left out do dry in the weather? These faces had become wounds of remnants of wars untold, a world forgotten into itself from an emasculation of a modern society that had lost itself through the doldrums of an institutionalized pentagon...a collector's item. The situation had become a museum managed like a carnival intrigued with jeering spectators.

Nine months fighting the government was too short a time to call it an escape dream. It was more like a nightmare. Could this have been an illusion sublimated into the obscurity of everyday living? No! Julian was too naive for this; he was too fragile, too inexperienced, too youthful and a novice at many bouts and tryouts of unplanned rehearsals. But he had won. He was out of the army, alone, away and free from hell. He had been thrown out into the mother of hell, a home for rejection...a black sheep!

For he himself looked like hell—nervous, tired, and anxious. Looking much older, his face took on a rigid character—conscious, awake, and anticipating the unknown. Three thousand dollars richer was the stipend granted to him by the military department, and he wondered what he would do with the money and how he would spend it. He remembered the events with a clear mind. And after leaving Capitola, he turned the truck around and drove southward along the freeway, which clung alongside the beach and water's shores.

"Solo, bien solo," he remembered of his partners on base telling him that he would soon rough it on the outside. "Things get harder when you're alone and you become alienated." He paid no attention to his thoughts, yet he pondered on the tomorrows. The waters clamored onto the cliff's edge, which supported the roadside. The clouds above began to disappear in a slow and serene fashion, dispersing themselves away in the sunlight.

Alone, the truck moved through rolling green grass-covered hills while sea doves hovered above the road. The air smelled of unique freshness and of seaweed with wet sand covering the ocean's water. The eucalyptus trees stood stretching out across the landscape. Whenever he made stops on the roadside, people would look down upon him with raging eyes filled of hate and envy. After one final stop, he quickly changed his clothes, and he dressed himself into civilian Levi's, a T-shirt, and a pair of PX sunglasses.

The valley looked vast, and smog dominated the Sierra Madre ranges. Soon, the hot air could be felt, and he began to feel at home again. The fort seemed like a huge dream, something which could never have happened. However, much damage was yet to be felt. The day was April 21, 1973, and he already had written several months earlier to his oldest brother, telling him that his discharge would soon be coming over the hill and that he would be driving home. From one war to another, from one maze to another. This was Julian's pace. He was no longer the same figure of youth he was once known to have been. The sun began setting into the Pacific Ocean as the evening came.

Into the valley, the truck rolled, down, down, to the bottom of the floor, the San Joaquin pit. Home at last. He passed the Highway 99 freeway and was soon seen moving through miles and miles of vineyards…Steinbeck's grapes of wrath and Chavez's homecoming. Back he drove into this dreadful isolated little town—this haven, a place made for creatures who thrived on playing hide and seek and a toast with a bottle of gin for this so-called Peyton Place. Once he had arrived on Main Street, he drove straight to the cemetery, three miles east of the town. He entered the gate and drove to the central lawns of the yard. He turned his engine off, walked twenty yards, and threw himself on the grass. He stretched his body out in a prone position and gazed toward the sky. First, he thought about his dead father. Then women came to his mind. Afraid to go home to his mother's house, he thought about last.

"What a fool I must have been! What a fool I am," he thought aloud, once again to himself, "to think that I could be in Korea at this very moment, next to China, or in Germany somewhere, supporting the communist movement with my mouth shut like a dry mop, all the way. Instead, I've ended up jacking off like an asshole, like a culprit for ten months. Where did I go? It wasn't too far from here, up the road and above this valley. Yes, it must have been a dream." He left for home.

"I should kick your ass in," spoke out Julian's brother, Rafael, while walking into the bedroom where Julian was changing his clothes to go to bed.

"I should beat you up for what you did," repeated Rafael. Julian only laughed, turned over while pulling the covers above his shoulders, and closed his eyes. "Never you mind," he answered. Even after Rafael had turned off the light, he continued staring with angered eyes. Envy appeared to overtake him. It was certain. This was no time for brothers to be fighting even if they were only acting like brothers.

The room became dark and quiet, and Julian could hear his family arguing—loud voices, laughter—for the hour did not seem like a welcoming homecoming. It sounded more like a conspiracy to oust him.

But this could not be so, he thought. *I am only suspecting. I'm skeptical. My insecurity, perhaps? Of course, it isn't true. Wait. My mother! She called me a coward. She actually told me that I was scared to fight. A coward. An illustrious coward! My brothers, my sister? No. Of course not! I'm only imagining. But wait. This is for real, very real.* Yes, the walls felt real. The bed he lay in was real. *The darkness. Oh, such dreadful hidden darkness.* And all at one time, he could feel it closing in on him, smothering, bothering and chastising his sensitivity. He began to accept and witness an obscurity of defeat, of self-renunciation. This overpowered him. A deep, enthralled, mysterious monster, a sense of alienation nested itself about him. This was not the home Julian had come to know before going into the service, for his world had changed overnight, as well as the family's. But most of the situations had become pure trivia, for the entire valley where he had lived in was changing, as was the texture and landscape of the mountains and the valley floor. Soon, news had touched the passions of the townspeople, and everyone knew about Julian's fight with this compassionate government to the north of the valley. He had become unmasked.

It was early the next day that Julian had awaken and left the town in his truck. He headed southward, not being able to bear staying near his mother's house because of the withdrawn feelings that still existed. He felt it better to get out and see the valley, breathe some different air. After two hours had passed, he stopped at an office twenty-five miles distance, an office where life insurance was sold. Julian met the agent. A husky, gray-haired man of dignified stature spoke like a preacher, but this time, this agent was selling a different story. Julian was in search of some good life insurance for himself, a transfer of policies, a continuation from the service.

At first glance, the situation seemed ecumenical in the religious sense but highly businesslike.

Another ludicrous devil, thought Julian. *Another naive communist*, he rallied with himself. *Perhaps.*

"I cannot insure your life," he spoke out to Julian.

"Why not?"

"Only because you've displayed misconduct and resentment in your lifetime. You told me you used to experiment with various drugs and narcotics, and now that you've committed these so-called high crimes while in the service and against this government automatically disqualifies you from attaining one of my policies. You're a high risk, Julian."

"Yes, but I was used. I mean I never wanted to take drugs. I was pushed into it," Julian began pleading. "I don't understand, sir. When you speak of high crimes, which high crimes are you referring to, sir?"

"I'm talking about your conduct. You're trying to be somebody that you're not in reality. You have admitted to me that you were accused of trying to start a revolution, inciting party members, and attempting to overthrow the government of the United States of America."

"But I've explained to you that I was showing my sanity, that's all!" asserted Julian.

"During peaceful times!" shouted the businessman. Julian looked down and nodded. "No matter where you go, Julian, no one will insure your life. You are a risk, my friend." Julian looked on with great distress and distrust, not knowing what to say next.

"However, you do have one choice, my friend."

"And what is that?"

"You can join my church and become part of my segregation," he answered.

Julian gasped and looked at him, and he remained quiet and paused. *He must be the devil*, he thought.

"Therefore, you'd come to my segregation next Sunday, and you'd join my church by becoming baptized during our ceremony."

Boy! What bullshit, Julian continued thinking to himself. *He, no doubt, runs his clientele this way. First, he propagandizes them, they join his church. In the end, he collects the money. A big crook running a Christian community. What a laugh. He must have all these people under his thumb, and I'm to become another one of his lost lambs. It's hard to see myself in this predicament. He wants me to become the catalyst for acting like a savior to his people and preaching for his behalf.*

At the moment, a plump man walked in with dark glasses and said that he was Cesar Chavez's cousin and one of the agents' clients.

"He's really particular about making friends and who he chooses to meet, isn't he?" he asked the question to the insurance agent. Next, he laughed and walked out of the office.

Julian was not himself as they both continued speaking. And the sun just as well should have fallen into the ocean, and that well-known predicted earthquake should have tumbled its way into the valley. But it never happened this way. There were a great silence and pause.

"I want you to live with me and become my son, Julian," said the insurance agent.

This is impossible, thought Julian. *His son is the one unwilling to grow up to become a preacher man like his father. And now he wants me to fulfill the role. It looks like they really want to hang me this time,* Julian rationalized. *They're looking for a guinea pig. They're looking for me.* And sure enough, Julian fell for this carnival act, this merry-go-round. His weak heart had grown weaker, fallible to their commands. His conscience was folding and had become defeated to this religious-political trap, as if a black widow had built her nest on a plan of attack. He had become the bait, the prey, a sucker. *They really expect me to go around telling all these criminals and prostitutes that they are wrong and I am right—I am here to save them, to capture them from corruption, from their own corruption? That I'm pure? That I'm supposed to be holy, perfect, and all of that kind of Holy Roller brainwashing bullshit? The damn hypocrites. They just want to use me…the lazy bastards,* thought Julian. And this soon came to be true.

The initial action was executed; the initial shock was portrayed in this fashion. It could not have happened any other way. This time, the place, this history, this vainglorious history of ours created life this way. The world has always been looking for a fool to lead other fools, other arrogant, indigent, derelict rejects. Only a reject could fulfill this empty stall for strangely two-legged animals. This was a youthful idealism for radical hypocrites. The time could not have been a better time, for what greater destiny could there have been for a thoughtful child.

Disillusioned, Julian arrived back in his hometown, and he was disturbed about what had happened. It was a late summer night, quiet, and crickets and frogs could be heard in the nearby ditch. The streets of the town were very still, empty with no movement. Julian opened the front door to the house where his mother lived, and there she sat in her bedroom, counting out several bills and sorting out envelopes. His brothers and sister were not found at home. His oldest brother was married and had moved up north. His younger brother, Rafael, was out gallivanting that night, while his sister had gone on a date with her boyfriend. He entered his mother's room, and she was reading. She wore a nightgown.

"Hello, Mother," he stated.

"Where have you been? It's late. Look at the time…it's two o'clock in the morning."

"You didn't have to wait up for me. You could have gone to sleep."

"Sleep! How in the hell am I going to sleep with the way you've been acting lately?"

"So what! I'm no different from my brothers and sister, that you should be worrying yourself sickly."

She became angry. "You're malice. You've become a monster, and you're nothing but a coward. And I'll say it again. Yes, you're just a coward!" she yelled out.

"Mom! I've come to ask you a favor," he asked as he trembled.

"A favor!" She paused. "What do you know about favors?" she blurted. "You've never done anybody any favors. The only favor you've ever done was to yourself. If only your father were here. If only he were alive. He'd turn in his grave. He'd whip you! The things you make me go through and the things you put me up against. Fine examples you set. What will the people be thinking in this town?" And she rumbled onward, hardly giving Julian a chance to talk. Oh, yes, but she was beautiful in her deliverance. Being a woman of much stamina and education, because she had gone to school at several universities, she would power herself outward, bright, like a chanticleer in its fullest potential and end like a storm in the winter. She was a woman respected yet feared by many of the townspeople. This was Julian's mother.

"I only want to borrow your King James Version of the Bible," he asked.

"My what?" Her eyes were as fire, and Julian felt a great emptiness.

"What is it that you want with my Bible?"

"I am going to join this Baptist church group—"

"And do their dirty work," she answered quick and sharp, cutting him off. "Look, I am a Catholic, and you're a Catholic. Now, if you're so damn unhappy, go on, get out of this house! Just get the hell out of here, if you're so unhappy."

Julian was hearing those bells again, the somberness of the morning, but he wasn't going to stand there and pretend to be a perfect little angel. No, he was too much of a rebel to do that, too much filled with life, yet a great curiosity surrounded and captured him. He was a young gentleman, to say the least, to not respect his mother on most occasions, he thought. However, providence had established that it was he who had always fought his mother so much. He would challenge her. And all seemed so right for the time, a perfect game for a family battle of filial enchantment—the only way of doing things. This was perhaps normal, as normal as the summer heat or winter's cold, like a day filled from activity and rabid thoughts. Oedipus Rex could have been at show. The birds cry because they are also lonely.

When the morning came, Julian was off driving in his Ford van with all his junk and murals loaded on the top of this white-painted four-wheeled machine. A large eagle with giant wings and claws painted in bright colors showed on each side of the old '61 wagon. It was an ugly sight to watch after a time being; nevertheless, it seemed to capture the attention of most road people. He drove south toward the mountains, passed a small town and a large Armenian church, turned right and continued driving toward a bridge that blanketed a large irrigation canal. He stopped the vehicle at that point. The sun was setting, and the vast fields of alfalfa and watermelons lie before him. He could feel the valley breeze. The clouds stripped high above over a ranch in the distance, and the large oak trees, which surrounded the old shacks danced to the gust of the wind as the innocence of the evening mixed in with the quietude. The only sounds heard were barking dogs, crying peacocks, and the calamity of a few chickens.

The old-looking, rundown appearance of the ranch and forty acres was an archaic sight in view. A house built of old wood was surrounded by a decaying fence and pomegranate trees. There were two old decayed outhouse-type restrooms next to where an old truck stood aside a tractor. Most of the peacocks nestled themselves on the roof of the house and on the outstretched limbs of a large walnut tree that stood in front of the doorstep. The umbrella appearance of her limbs covered the entire yard, which was gutted with dead, dried leaves and nuts not yet ripe to eat. A very solemn place indeed. He parked the Ford van next to an abandoned white wooden house, which sat to the right side of the sandy driveway. After walking over to the larger ranch house, he approached the doorstep and knocked gently upon the wooden door. An aged, short, heavyset woman wearing a purple shawl came to the door and peeked out after opening it ajar. A large brown fur-coated wolf-like dog jumped through the door and began tugging at Julian's clothes.

"Off! Get off, you damn dog. Get off my clothes!"

"Come in, come in, my child," she spoke in a soft tone and was glad to see him standing in front of her. He walked into the large parlor-type room and noticed his grandfather sitting on a wooden chair next to a heater. The old man wore a large dusty hat, the ten-gallon-body style.

"How are you, my son?" he spoke out.

"I'm fine, Grandfather. I'm fine. I came to ask you both permission if I may use the old abandoned house across from the drive. I want to paint. I need a place to paint." They both looked into each other's aged eyes and felt in their minds that he was running away from something.

Yes, he is a strange one, they thought. "Why?"

This was the character Julian carried with him, a technique. This is why he stayed with older people even to a desolate place as a ranch. There, he would burrow himself in the old house and paint his mural in one last solitude. In solace and silence, he would begin moving his brushes, and the wind called outside, luring itself against the outside walls of the house. The breaks in the windowpanes whistled with the wind's roar. The limbs of the rose bushes could be heard scratching along the wooden walls with help from the slashing arms of the wind.

A feeling of entrapment encircled Julian's mind, a feeling that the walls began closing in on him. Harsh, rigid and arbitrary. A deep, enthralling feeling shook him. Sweat and perspiration came, and next a pause…shocks. He heard it again, and then he froze. "Julian, Julian," it called out. And the voice continued calling. Julian began walking to the front door. His steps were slow and cautiously executed. He put his hand on the knob and turned it. A fast wind, growling, unmasked itself upon him as he pushed the door open. The voice stopped, and the voice quieted. Turning around with his back facing the wind and hearing the voice again, more loud, he faced the wind once again, and closed the door. He walked back to the room where he had been painting. And each time he neared his mural, the voices would cease.

It could be possibly that my friends back from town are playing tricks on me again, he thought. And as the time passed on, he became less skeptical. After circling the outside of the house several times by foot, he had convinced himself that he was either going insane or was truly hearing voices.

Once more, he was like a hermit, like a pauper in disguise, alone and away from inner civilization and all of it's ludicrous offerings. At times, he would take long walks to the bridge and back. One day, the old man came to the doorstep, and soon they both began talking. Both figures sat down; the old man pulled out some cigarettes from his pant pockets and began smoking heavily. Smoke all around the room.

"What do your paintings say…what are they speaking? They seem to be full of passion and bright colors but too wild for my imagination. Are you disturbed, my son?"

"I'm only bothered when I paint," answered Julian.

"But why do you come all the way out here to paint? Isn't town good enough for you? Why are you running?" he said with large open eyes and with a smile embracing his jaws. Julian did not answer that one. He only paused and kept quiet while keeping his head down.

The next day toward evening, there were knocks at his door. Julian opened it, and in walked David Segura.

"How did you know that I was here?" asked Julian, wiping off the paint from his hands onto a towel. "I went to your mother's home, and she let me know where you might be, someplace where no one could find you or bother you. And sure enough, I was right. I had remembered about you telling me that the ranch was always a good place to lay down one's passions in a most quiet way."

Lay down one's passions? thought Julian. He turned on the volume of the transistor radio, and they both sat and listened to the music all night and drank Coors beer until they no longer could stand on their feet. "And you should have seen when I shot my lieutenant that day!"

David laughed. He continued laughing. This was the real David Segura, perhaps the only true way that he could become himself. He called on Julian, "Hey you, kid, you could never kill a man. Right?" His body rolled across the wooden floor, his smile set heavy on his face. Julian had been knocked out cold by the beer. The lights in the room were left on that night, and they both slept across the floor.

There were many days that had passed since that one summer night at the ranch. The crops had all been picked by now, and most of the workers from Mexico were traveling south to the border. The winds of the winter were beginning to show, and Julian's truck had driven under a large arched gate that read, "Veterans Hospital, Menlo Park." He entered the large beige building that was surrounded by large pillars, and palm trees stood throughout the lawn. A large chicken-wire fence separated the hospital from a nearby elite semi-commercial district neighborhood. It was the subdued, clinical atmosphere, a world within a world, which drew him all the way from the valley. He acted as if his perceptions were still cloudy in his mind, a very rancid and perplexed mind. Many people on the outside thought him to be definite crazy this time. But he had volunteered, much like the draft board. He spoke to a psychiatrist, Dr. Sands, whose legs were the prettiest objects to look at, besides the others that consisted of the staff. She directed him to a therapeutic home called the Happy House, a community therapy experience and only a step away from the asylum. She walked him across the lawns and to the entrance of the building that was surrounded by three-story maple and oak trees. He walked into a large-sized room, big enough to be a small house, where there were chairs lined up against the walls to every corner. In the center of the room, there was a long line of chairs lined up in a row, back to back against one another. A slim-bodied, ball-headed man walked in from a flight of stairs located in the southwest corner of the room.

"Welcome, Mr. Solbriozo. We were expecting you. Won't you please have a seat?"

Julian sat and waited several minutes. There was a large clock piece on the wall that read 2:52 a.m. The clock was inoperable. A large-boned, muscular black man walked in, telling Julian to go upstairs to the office where the doctors were waiting. The man was wearing a blue crash helmet at the time. Upon entering the office, Julian was once again asked to sit. The doctors began interrogating him and asking him harsh questions.

"What did you come here for, Solbriozo? You belong out in the streets, creating and making revolutions." At that same instant, another doctor walked in with discharge evidence papers from the army. "Just fits this character, right? We always get creeps like you!" he said, pointing his fingers at Julian.

Julian stood up and yelled out, "And I got to know a lot of the CTA idiots looking for me in the service! They would stare for hours at a time, like your…lying eyes." The man left the room, walked down the hallway, and could be seen leaving the front door from the two-story office window. Julian returned to the main receiving office, where Dr. Sands was waiting for him. She was smiling with a bright glare on her face as he entered her office once again.

"I'll send you to the asylum," she said.

But this fulfillment, however, was the most preposterous of events, according to Julian's vision of the advice that the Veterans Administration was feeding him. He did arrive for a purpose, and he at last found it.

It was another large room that he had entered, with many different paintings hanging on the walls. The chairs were all scattered in random fashion, and there was a large Wurlitzer piano set in one corner. Toward the center of the room was a large canvas-covered punching bag, which hung from a chain attached to the ceiling. A six-foot blackboard mounted on a pedestal stood toward the front of the room, and there were chalks covering its shoulders. He prodded into the room, and there was a radio with its music playing very loud. He sat, and a nurse passed by him with a large smile on her face. She continued walking toward the bedroom ward. Julian grew restless, and he began to stand himself up from the chair. A large hairy hand touched his left shoulder, forcing him to take his seat.

"How do you do?" spoke out a deep voice. "I would like to introduce myself…My name is Adolf Hitler."

Julian was afraid to turn around; he rotated his body with a cautious jilt. There stood a tall man with a patch on his left eye, dark hair, and carried a shiny wooden cane in his left hand. Nor did he even take the resemblance of the Führer, much less to that of a well-known incognito. Another man walked in, calling himself Winston Churchill. Next, a Mussolini walked in. At the end of an hour, there was six Jesus Christs who had revealed themselves to all of them.

And in the corner sat an elderly woman who showed very many years. She wore a young girl's dress, and her hair was made up in pigtails tied about with ribbons. The redness of her cheeks balanced the red color of her socks, which hugged her legs up to her knees. She held on tight to a medium-sized ragged doll and clung to her with staunch nervousness. She acted and behaved like a three-year-old girl. Leaning herself over onto Julian's chair, she began hugging him and kissing him about the cheeks and neck. Most of the other men called her Babylon and jeered her constantly. She called Julian Alexander the Great. Everyone sat around, laughed, and jeeringly stared holes through Julian's conscience, which at this time was being revealed. Horrified and embarrassed, he was at a loss for words. That great overpowering feeling of loneliness overtook him, and simultaneously, a sense of false identity and humility uncloaked him. Toward a dark corner of the room, a large group of lame handlers huddled among themselves.

CHAPTER 3

The Struggle to Be Camino Real

"Oh, dear God, for it is such a long war, and my public has at last abandoned me."

The way of Julian's was not necessarily one of renunciation, although he seemed the type of young man who behaved so. Nor was he happy when people told him how to live or what to do, even though rarely at times would he be sure of a certain way. After leaving that day from Menlo Park, he realized that he wasn't a total loss. When the psychiatrist had told him that he belonged in the streets creating revolutions, the occasion wasn't every day that any person off the streets was told something in regard to this particular strange nature of events. Yet this adventure was not all that strange, as far as domestic issues were concerned. The glorious valley of plentiful began to take on a personal portrait, a portrait which had begun to unmask itself, clamoring with a pulsating life, a portrait that had opened herself to conversion, criticism, and a stage set for a new theater to be played. Her name was the San Joaquin Valley.

The weather was beginning to change as were the people and her lower life's inhabitants. The open air, outdoor, sunny-teaser appealed to Julian's taste, and he took to the fields where the passions were a rage and a domestic trial had begun to take place. This would be a working man's trial.

There was another face. Maria Andasola was actually a very ugly girl; however, nobody would ever admit it to her face, including Julian himself. Being of the same age in years as Julian, background, and having met in college earlier, they were at times more than friends passing fun hours together, but near lovers. He had always thought of her as a plain, wholesome girl, intelligent and having an inner beauty within her. All this attracted Julian. Above the tribulations, she wasn't exactly a saint either. Many times, she was like a sister to him, only when he wanted her to be. Even the times before Julian had gone to the fort, she had played tricks on him by using many antics of a childish nature. She built him up, made him feel glorious, and in the end, tossed him out the window in an old-fashioned sort of way. He remembered the time she had told him how she would escape from paying her traffic debts by showing her legs to the judge during her court appearances. She was very good at hiding herself but poorly displayed her round plump body at the wrong times.

"I'll have to ask you to leave now, so you'd better take me home while it's still early," she spoke to Julian.

Julian veered the car downhill and began coasting the vehicle through the winding highway that cut through the forest and the canyons to the valley bottom. And Julian remembered how they always took those rides through the mountains and countryside. They were very long rides at times. Many of the evenings were spent together by the river, which met itself about halfway from each other's house. And he remembered the grass that they sat on as they would chat and reminisce for hours at a time next to the water's edge. Oh, if only he could catch those youthful, carefree moments of happiness and gaiety again; he would surely cherish them forever. A boyhood's fantasy had matured, and these times could never have changed his first true love.

She was ironic. "But you have no heart at all, Julian. You're heartless," she would openly attack him. "You are senseless and heartless, and most of all, you care nothing about anybody but yourself. You're in love with yourself, and you're a coward." And that was that.

Julian liked her much for her plainness, simplicity, and practicality and because she was old-fashioned in many ways. She always bragged to him about her working habits and her family's background of struggling in the fields, because they were poor. She lived in a poor neighborhood where the project homes dominated the street corners next to the central valley's largest freeway. And this freeway cut through the vineyards of raisin and table grapes.

"You're just another Mexican," he would tell her. She would turn and toss her long dark-brown hair, and her green eyes would sparkle.

The weather seemed as hot as an agrarian rejoice, the rage of the people during those summer days. And this heat, along with Julian, took to the fields where the politico-rancho war between the farm laborers and the teamsters was ablaze. Cesar Chavez's caravan moved throughout the valley like the crusaders during the European religious wars. That same year, his army grew in numbers about the grape vineyards and orchards throughout the state, and red flags were waving.

"Viva la huelga, que viva la huelga" was resounding verbally by the field workers and shed across all channels of communication, like a wind out of control and on fire.

The time was 6:00 a.m., and Diego Luna was arriving from town in a small gray Ranchero truck loaded with buckets, pails for water, and paper for laying out the pans. The sun was rising, and Julian leaned against the vineyard post as many of the other workers amassed themselves against the vines, waiting for Luna's orders.

"Go ahead and start picking. Soon the sun will be settling, and you'll all begin to feel sorry for yourselves." He began writing down names and social security numbers on a small notebook. One-half of the crew were women, but from a distance, one couldn't tell because of the pants and working shirts they wore. Their hats and scarfs disguised their appearances, and they looked like the men who were the handfuls of eager-to-work Mexicans as Diego had explained to Julian over the night before.

"It will be hard for you to keep up with them," he told Julian. As time passed along, the situation proved quite different. Julian continued to set the pace, and the other workers began to wonder and asked him why he did not look for a job back in town like other young men who have better sense to save their elite-ridden bodies from the drudgery of uneducated labor and wasted time. This toil was not in vain. Julian proved himself to be quite complacent with the matter until the hands on his wristwatch showed one hour before noon. He saw two sheriffs' cars parked across the street at the corner of the field to where the rows headed in that particular direction. Exactly as he was cutting the stems, he could hear yelling and shouting. At first, he thought he was hearing things, perhaps the sun or some of the workers slacking off from the rows. Diego would make his rounds, inspecting everyone's footsteps.

"Perhaps I'm tired, exhausted," he continued thinking. A large blue-and-yellow bus pulled alongside the road in front of the sheriffs' cars and came to a dead stop. Several cars followed in a caravan and parked behind the workers' bus. People were leaving this foreign bus, yelling and stomping the dirt, carrying their pickets and flags. There were tall ones, fat ones, all wearing sunglasses. Women too.

"Traders, traders, why do you work? You fools, stop working!" yelled the distant voices from the bus people. A few rocks were being thrown. Julian stared at the projectiles. The deputy sheriffs climbed from their vehicles and walked over to the field. The bus people began running into the vineyards from a walking chant and gait. They charged the rows in one large human wave attack. Diego began yelling for everyone to take cover and hide themselves in the vines. And they hid as the intruders passed through the fields. The only ones who were stopping their tracks and turning back toward the main road were the Catholic priests and nuns. They had been marching back and forth with members of the townspeople. They had been lined up in a straight line and were cajoling on the road. The priests were praying out loud and urging the crowd not to start any violence. It appeared, however, that the church was making matters worse, and everybody knew it too. And situations were very similar to this one, whenever one would go into the field where most pickings were taking place. The world was indeed fighting over peaches, plums, nectarines, and of course, the grapes…as were her ego.

"Such audacity, such amateurishness, what devilish hypocrites!" Julian's thoughts rolled over and over as he looked at the fading opaque moon in the daylight.

Fifteen minutes had passed, and the entire field was surrounded by pickets from every corner of the road. It was here that Julian showed his greatest weakness, his infallibility toward his own demeanor, his capriciousness toward taking ideas seriously, which is what he did in the face of domestic strife. A truer tone of a personal war soon became revealed. Yet these times proved to be the greatest conflict of his life: the beginning of a fight, a lost cause of another venture in searching for an identity. It was a settling of a gripe, as was everyone's! He noticed and recognized the familiar faces in the crowd. They were the faces of some of his own friends back from town.

What a surprise, a first confrontation, he thought, *of knowing who we were.*

The day was nearly over. Exhausted as was everyone else, Julian picked up his lunch pail and bags and drove off to town only because Diego had begged him to do so. And so he left the "Song Ranch" on a happy note that day, neither worrying nervous nor caring about what was to become of the situation.

Like everything else, it will all be shown in the end, kike truth. "Let it become discovered, but without me. Let them celebrate the festival of an unwanted spoiled child," whispered the wind.

All the way back to town, the roads were lined with pickets, and crowds dispersed from the caravan's trail, emblematic of the movement built up by the laboring disillusioned or another plot created by a group of naive radicals who was being controlled by somebody's next-door neighbor. This was truly the irony of Julian's problem. He felt that he'd become a slave to a wasted conflict.

Nighttime came, and Maria Andasola was busy washing dishes in her mother's kitchen. Her long brown hair hung down to her shoulders as she worked very snobbishly. Her mother came to the door, asking who the caller might be. Julian pounded on its front side with his fists, begging her to let him in.

"It's me, Julian. I only want to talk a while with Maria. Please let me in!"

"No. I know who you are by now, Julian," the old woman projected with a stern look on her face. Maria could be heard walking to her bedroom. Julian began forcing his way in, but the woman lodged his head in between the doorway's entrance and the door itself.

"We've worked all of our lives, hard, in ranches and fields, and we are proud of it," she said, shutting the door on him. He continued knocking on the door for several minutes more. At last, she yelled out and threatened to call the police. Julian left the house and hurriedly sped away in his truck. Discouraged and very disappointed with the day, he vigorously drank away his troubles after stopping at the nearest bar. This character was always a major downfall to Julian. The female gender destroyed his feeble gentleness, his disowned conceit. His love for her was of a strong taste, like to the love of a sister. He sat there and waited till the bar closed.

The winter months had come, and Maria Andasola was no longer seen around her home, nor did anyone see Julian taking joyrides with her on the weekend afternoons as they used to. No, not a soul was watching her nor Julian any longer. Then the rains came, and a cold wind overtook the scenery. Maria had run away with an older man who had more money, status, and age than Julian. But Julian was so surprised as to see that the rain was falling. So he took his hurt with him to the mountains, and he fought the pines and the snow clouds all at once, all together. And it rained, and it snowed.

The world had no time to listen to such pettiness and gossip, much less give Julian advice on how to conquer the female. Becoming a "do-nothing, know-nothing" was not an easy task to do in this situation, and especially in this American society during these times. Julian was not a true isolate, but people had him considered as one.

Society was indeed a different breed of mass. It was no longer a mature society built from a younger generation that grew with respect toward the older, mature system. The streets, even the country streets, were beginning to show signs of loose ends and untidiness. Yes, Julian was the typical isolate of commonplace, according to the younger generation.

David Segura was drunk, and he knew it, as he knocked on Julian's front door to the porch of his mother's house. Julian opened the door with a big smile, and he noticed a car that was smoking under the hood.

The driver of the car was pouring water down the throat of the radiator, and he was using the hose to the front yard. David threw his arms around Julian and gave him a big hug. A black patch worn on his left eye gave him the look of a bandit.

"Hey, Julian! Hush. Let's go for a ride and look for the mamas. What do you say, huh?" David asked with a persuasive tone of voice. And David's other companion, the driver whose name was Ramon Grijalva, encouraged him. And the car sped out north toward the mountains. These heads could be seen slouching back on the cars' seats, and they were tipping quarts of Coors bottles. The weather was very hot that day. Las Mananitas, an already picked dried nectarine orchard, lie baked in the sun, and the old Oldsmobile made its way up the road, passed the Kings River bridge, and out to the lake below the dam. They were drunk.

The sun was beating down fiercely, and the coolness of the lake's water was a refreshing reliever, indeed. Julian, David, and Raymond sank their bodies into the water near the shore. The depth was at least four feet at that point. Beer cans and old junk items resting on the silt bottom could be seen from the surface. And the lake stretched for a quarter of a mile to the other side where boulders mounted themselves in formation.

A couple of young girls in bikinis soon joined them, and the area took on the appearance of underwater orgy. And they played, and they drank.

David began challenging Julian to stunts and dives and, at last, to a test to see who could swim the farthest out across the waters. Julian won the first several spars as his confidence grew. Soon, they were both seen standing on the water's edge with their hands behind their backs. Raymond yelled out to go, and they dove out of sight head-first into the water. David was seen emerging yards out; however, Julian was seen nowhere. Raymond ran quickly to the shore line as Julian dragged himself onto the edge, grasping for some grass thicket. And the blood ran down his head, onto his face, and down his body. They carried him to the car and began pressing together his broken head with towels. The onlookers watched with patient eyes. Darkness and all consciousness left on a silver wing. Julian opened his eyes and saw a surgeon dressed in white with two pretty nurses holding his arms down. The sutures stabbed his head, one at a time, and the pain that he felt was the greatest thing that could never have happened to him. Terrible. "I'm right here next to you. Don't worry." Julian could hear the voice of David. The lights above his head were bright, very bright. Sweat rolled down his face, together with his attitude about David and Ramon. Yes, Julian was beginning to feel he was losing something. His image had become of a losing-character type. And how quaint was it that acquaintances and people made fun of him. Rumors had spread throughout the town, whispers of his jumping off the bridge that stood over the river below the dam. *A country clown. I've become a country clown*, he thought. And his head was sore for many days and nights. He had dove onto a large rock at the water's bottom, and he had forgotten to snap his neck upward on his last dive.

The next morning, Julian was awakened by the footsteps of his sister, Anna. "I'm going away with some friends of mine for a few days. Tell mother, would you?"

"How in the hell do you expect me to do that when she's never around?" he yelled. "Damn it, go ahead. It's all right with me."

"But, Julian, your head! What has happened to you? Stitches? You look like someone who has been crucified. I know…you got into a fight. You stupid idiot." And she slammed the door shut. Everything was quiet, and the house was empty. And as always, when going to his mother's parlor, he sat using the love seat while he played the old piano. The music drooled and was depressing most of the time, and it continually drooled on. He thought of Anna.

These were the events that happened before the time Julian's world had changed. This was his life that came to be. The rainbow was truly of a different spectrum, and the colors were growing harsher in hues. His dreams were shrinking to the ground. But his personal situation reflected the world's situation, the situation he pictured the world to be at that time. Even the large time or "big time" governmental accusations made by Julian in his earlier years began taking a change, a change for independency. This would be Julian's next move. It was a sure time to leave his mother's womb and into the black sheep's nest. He was not yet defeated, and the valley was now livelier than ever. A new battlefield for novice and youthful passion had begun to blossom. The song of solitude began to take on a deepened personality:

Please tell me the story of the nine dead-end dudes, and I'll tell you about a mirror of realistic friendship, about a street lamp which cried with the brightest tears, about the scavengers who dwelled through the garbage cans, about a fight which had no heroes, about a "trip" sprinkled with hard colors.

There were no leaders, there were no cowards. The bravery, the honesty, the passions were never lost. Between bullies who were pussycats to the straight kid who defended a friend available in need.

The petals began to fall away, one by one, with roles of the painted alleys we had to play, and filtered Halloweens making the scene again…those were the days…those were the days. Where are such friends? For they've gone away.

CHAPTER 4

"Too much to be seen"
Older Women

"The hallways seemed endless, and the doors were unlocked."

The time it takes a man to stand on his own two feet is more painstaking than that of a giant redwood enduring a thousand years of nature's beating of storms and rain and the great fires that sweep through her sequoia forest. Perhaps a small rose bush with many growing thorns and falling petals of youth could tell the story of a young man becoming a virulent root overnight.

During these times, international instability was at its great peak on the biorhythm. The nation was screaming for a new government and a president. The Mars satellite in the outer space sent us back pictures of entertainment, and China's Mao had at last croaked dead in his old age. Domestically, men couldn't decide on being men, or women, women. Many lovers of attention continued their streaking causes for sports, flying balloons across the Atlantic, racing cars, or trying to cross the Grand Canyon in a rocket cycle. Others continued their patriotic ways yearning for international wars as "old soldiers" who never die and sailors trying to conquer the Nautilus's route made a century earlier. Most human species, according to Julian, forgot about what a man truly was or who we as human beings were on this dreaming space-age earth of ours. Julian left home, but he didn't go far to find this cancerous dream, less than sixty miles round trip, and there he anchored. Heroes know who they are. Realistic wars are fought close to home. *Kindness* becomes another word for an allowance in accepting a role which was meant for your own self, the one role you could play the best. For Julian, there wasn't much of a world to conquer, for there wasn't that big a world after all. Al was rather a stubborn old fool, yet very open and down to earth about a good many things, except his very personal life. But all in all, he was the landlord who most people knew, most people passing through the valley that is. His motel would be Julian's key in the months to come, and time would shape the corner of the county fairgrounds where Julian landed a job as an orderly working at the old County General Hospital.

The time was 10:30 p.m., and while on his way to work from Raisintown, he entered the old trailer park, which was poorly lit, and walked up to the front door of the old house, a business office, in his white uniform, quietly and very nervous. The sign read, "Vacancy."

"Yes, sir," and the elderly man stood with an eager inclination with gray hair. He was muscular and stalk.

"I need a room," spoke out Julian. "I can afford it. I'm working at the county hospital at the corner."

"Number seven is the best I have. I'll let you have it for thirty dollars a week, no deposit charge, and it has a kitchen, a shower, and a black-and-white television," he said.

A black-and-white TV, thought Julian. *Who does he think I am?* He didn't argue with the man. He conceded with him. "I'll return in the morning after work. I need to pack the rest of my items."

"Bring in whatever you have, but don't start hanging paintings on the walls. I can't stand paintings on the walls."

"Don't worry," answered Julian. And he walked away and left the scenery.

Upon arriving the following morning, he discovered the small shack that looked like a very small one. It resembled a minute-sized house and stood in the middle of the trailer park that was in front of the county fairground stadium and almost between the welfare office and the hospital. After making several trips back to town and with the help of an old friend, Julian managed to park an old '57 Ford, his truck, and at once, he moved in his paintings, drawings, and murals. An old drunk named Nick lived to one side of him while an older woman named Dorothy rented to the other side of him. A retired detective from Chicago, whose name was Ben, also lived close by. Julian was among an older generation, the one big generation he had been hiding with yet fighting against.

The summer of '76 was not Julian's only surprise. Certain people had moved to this small country town, Dairytown, which lay between Delano and Raisintown. This was a crossroad type of haven for persons who were migrating from the eastern states and the old south, Tennessee and Oklahoma. Dairymen, ranchers, farmers, creameries, and real estate ranged the spotlights. Work was the reason most people flocked to this train town. While all this domestic habituation continued, Julian burrowed himself inside at this county's bottom dump—a fifty-year-old building where sheriffs, police, and the remainder of a populace gathered for local "county war," the General Hospital. For the first time in Julian's life, he could visualize what he lived in. And he was able to discover the reasons for coming alone this far away from his mother's home, reasons that would soon frighten him as the months passed on.

The railroad to the Southern Pacific crossed Julian's backyard from the court he lived in. The train would pass by as loud as thunder, blowing her horn as the morning sun rose, and Julian would enter his cabin. And it rumbled with this train passing, trenchant, desperate. He had been walking home from work, exhausted, tired, and forlorn from the Saturday morning. He unlocked the door and fell onto the large bed. Seconds later, there were knocks on the door, and the voice of a woman spoke out, "Hello, is anyone home. Can I come in?"

Julian, being timid in character day in and night since he had arrived, did not leave his cabin very often. Many people at the hospital thought of him for being paranoid. However, a new leaf had turned and proved to be quite normal. And according to Julian's chronological calculations, he felt that he was only doing a normal thing as a stranger in a foreign town.

"Who is it?" he asked, going to the door half nude. The time was seven thirty in the morning. "It's me, Wanda. Let me in."

Then and there, many thoughts raced through Julian's mind—at first embarrassment, consequently a dignified resignation toward quiet complacency happened. He distinctly remembered meeting her several days earlier when his next-door neighbor Dorothy had introduced Wanda to him, telling him she had a good body to be a thirty-four-year-old white gal with a husband who did field work and had two mentally retarded children. Yes, Julian felt guilty at first and, next, privileged. In a humble method and display, he opened the door gently and allowed her to walk inside.

"I came to rob you," she said and smiled in a sarcastic faceless stare. "For twenty dollars, you can go to bed with me whenever I come over to see you."

Her hair was dark brown, and she had large green eyes. Yet she was a good many years older in looks than her age. Her left nipple was turned inside out, because of an operation she had after smashing her breast by falling off a barn as a young girl. Yet her smooth, well-balanced body was enticing to Julian's vulnerability. *She was worth the twenty dollars,* he thought. *To hell with what other people think and say. They really don't know who I am nor who this prostitute is, even though she works out from Delano all the way to Raisintown throughout the labor camps.* Queen of the Prostitutes, a reject, a sympathizer to Julian's cause, or perhaps just another person to help Julian in his depression times. An omen? All these shocking questions burned throughout his mind, but she was there, and he was there. The domestic dangers had vanished. And that was all that mattered.

"But I can't live this way forever!"

"But why not?" answered his shadow. His conscience. "Most married people do it this way. There is nothing free in a contract, for there is nothing free, ever, only the rains when they fall. Then we don't pay for it. We only run through the puddles of water and take for granted everything. We get our feet wet."

This arriving situation would certainly be a lot cheaper than supporting a cause as to that of supporting a wife or even a dog. The other elderly ladies who lived around Julian had become jealous, and their humored-nature took on the image of a good-natured clown. It was hilarious, but a good setup all the way. And soon, most strangers laughed with the idea that Julian was running a "cat house," better known as a home for prostitution. But of course he was! He neither let it bother him, because he knew they also had the same problems, only much worse.

"What you need is to shower with me, and then we'll go skinny-dipping," she whispered in his ears. A truck just then pulled over in front of his steps and stopped, and the gears could be heard grinding. The truck's door slammed.

"Sir, I'm ready to go home. Jean wants to go to the carnival. Come on, let's go."

"Who in the hell is Jean?" whispered out Julian. "Stop being such a big sissy. Jean happens to be my sister in law."

The door opened, and the sunlight shone over the bed. Still pressed to each other's bodies and under the sheets, they both turned and noticed the twenty-eight-year-old fat-figured female standing in the doorway and holding onto a medium-sized doll that was covered with dirt.

"I need some money for some rides. The tickets are seventy-five cents apiece this year."

"Why don't you just wait a minute till I get some money off this son of a bitch?" Wanda wrangled her words. "Come on, Julian! Hand over the twenty dollars." She began struggling for his wallet with a vigorous motion.

"Why in the hell don't you behave, you damn bitch!" cried out Julian. He laughed sarcastically.

"She needs money for the carnival you tight son of a bitch!" Wanda yelled with continued loudness.

Her younger sister, who had been driving the truck, walked in, smiled, and laughed. "I'll go down with you for five." She giggled.

"You shut up," cried Wanda, blushing with redness on her face.

There he was, surrounded by some foreign family, an Irish Western Anglo family, in his bedroom. He was in bed with a strange woman and handing twenty dollars to her. The carnival sounded full blast from across the street in the fairgrounds. The voices and screaming of children could be heard. The sun began to set, and it seemed as if a replay from one of Humphrey Bogart's movies was being shown. And the dust piled up with the rush of the cars passing by the road—old Highway 99. El Camino Real. This night appeared as in a fog. The truck had pulled away, and Wanda had left with the others in a noisy scant. Soon, the cabin became quiet again.

The Fourth of July came around, and the day was spent as any previous in her history. And thank goodness for that. The fireworks stretched themselves overhead of Julian's cabin. The sky was aflame, and the crowd was massive. Sitting on top of the fence next to the road, Julian leaned on the wooden frame and could see people on the other side of the street. They were calling him a trader for not joining in with them as part of the celebration that night, and they looked on with veracious laughter. He smiled back at them with a dignity that penetrated the crowd.

"Ah, you son of a gun!" came a coarse voice from behind. Sitting on his front porch waving some cans of beer was the short, husky man called Ben, a retired detective from Chicago—middle fifties, built with the physique of a marine colonel. They both laughed together along with the gulps of several beers. Ben reminisced about his detective stories and adventures in Chicago.

"The cops are screwballs, assholes—nothing, were always for the money, and nobody was ever for caring about people. Bad business, it was all bad business," he spoke out softly in disgusting gestures and expressions of wretched pessimism.

"You mind if I join you?" said a tall man of fifty years dressed in old rags. He sat next to both of them and quickly pulled out a bottle of whiskey from his pant pocket. "The name's Paul. I work out in Hanford…and I drive a tractor. What do you do?"

The next moment, Al, the landlord, came walking along with an established reputation for being a dedicated child molester. He grinned and waved his hands back and forth. "So what the hell's going on? What does the local mafia have to say these days? Any doorstep cookies passing by lately?"

And all these shepherd-rejected animals of canine species sat around until their shadows disappeared. And then, the night fell to the ground.

And in this lonely place, this colony of lost renters in the middle of nowhere, only a hospital was worth talking or mentioning about. Or was there? They've always said the strangest things happen in the most remote areas…"big packages." A big stick. The dawn of the morning came, and the eight-o'clock morning train heading south could be heard cutting the bolts on the rails with iron wheels and sheet of a heavy armature, rough, rigid, frightening, and lonely as thunder.

As the months passed on, Julian continued working at the hospital known by many from the county as the "gateway to hell." At times, he could be seen walking alongside the fairgrounds on his way to work, carrying with him his gunnysack consisting of books and a stethoscope, including several other secrets that he showed to no one. He walked on to this front, a corner clinic.

There was simply no way for this twenty-three-year-old stud to get ahead, working in such conditions. Do or die! He had no choice. Being out on a graveyard shift, he picked up the ropes of helping in the emergency ward, where he felt like a slave in despair as never before in his life. The job required patience and retrieved within itself the stamina and danger of any other quest for very few jobs existing. The hell! He was surely no exception, as for that type of sympathy called for. That's right! Nobody special, just another grain of sand on the beach getting wet and washed through the barrages of tides and aged with baking sunshine.

Another leaf fell from a maple tree, falling faster to the ground with matured life and hues of color unlike the piles. Perhaps, this would prove to be Julian's blessing in disguise and a chance to make up difference from what he had spoiled at the fort while he was in the army. This would be his chance to change colors, mix them, and then at arming himself with different brushes…a new canvas…a small world.

Burying yourself alive can be done in more ways than one, but facing reality can also prove to be a bereavement. This is true for everyone, every taxpaying earthling that is! These times were tight, economically speaking, and starting out alone proved to be enormously expensive. President Carter began to chop away his inaugural address. Nobody was, in actuality, offering the world a chance to breathe, a garden of roses, or a new national anthem whose title was "I've Seen the Light." I've seen shit or hell. The hell I have! No one's giving you a damn thing. It'll be up a hill all the way, and you'd better take whatever's there. And that's the way the rent ended on a political note. And that's the way Julian felt. All melody, yet no rhythm.

On the corner, from a distance, the hospital would remind you of a large white mansion that had belonged to a stout county millionaire. These large mansions were always typical in old films about the Old South. Its large white pillars towered between the ionic Roman and Greek designs. The large oak trees covered the ground to one side of its old annex and pediatric buildings. Yes, from the outside, the building seemed old, bleak, and aged with time: stale, silent, placid…a place where people would come only if they had to. And sooner or later, they would have to. For this was the end of the tow, the chain, the line. This place would finish all dreams, all hopes, all games…all needs. The personal milieu of any life ended. But where had Julian been all his life? Had he been blind all this time? Were people telling him that he had it made feasibly, economically, and that his world was the "lucky one?" This corner of anonymity, a nest of incognito, and the revelations would bring an end to all wishful thinking and start the beginning of hard reality. Like a lightning bolt, it was all very shocking, just the thought of it. This was truly a long way to nowhere, the beginning of an end. And whoever this millionaire might have been, he must have conceded to crudeness, shrewdness, and unselfishness. God bless him. Blame him?

When a man becomes a burden to the auspices of motherhood, one begins to think he's a "mama's boy." But when he becomes a slave to women only because they become the authority of being allowed to become a woman, there is nothing wrong with being that type of slave, as long as the man leaves the woman in a woman. For a young man whose style would be far removed from chauvinistic ways, the adjustment wouldn't seem so difficult. At the onset, it would appear as so, but as time passed on, so would Oedipus Rex and all definitions a man would have to know to understand a woman. Julian was a dreamer, but even his most absurd sexual fantasies were tied in between his love life and his mother. Again, this could be as normal to most young men during these times, for every young man has within him his struggle of breaking away from the womb, destroying the mother state, and declaring an independence unlike any other uniqueness of his gender. For to rebel against one's own mother meant to rebel against the wickedness that tries to hinder the love that wants love, the only passion begging and thirsting for more healing, defying catalysts that create a special beauty between a man and a woman and, secondly, between a man and his own mother. He may have arrived here because of a search for love, which is why many times the world changes and history becomes the catapult for moving the masses of individuals…and, at last, the stage for war. But what is war, and what is love? And with these thoughts of spider web-like character covering his mind, he concluded and resigned, for the first time in his life, his destiny. Oh, but this definitely was an expensive jewel to struggle with, a price that soared as did the utilities and commodities of the country. And the word *love* headed toward another depression. What pity, what tragedy! Humorous?

When the last time Julian had met his mother, it was in an exchange of last-minute W-2 forms and income tax checks as any economic-minded mother would for her child—pardon the expression, an exposed child. However, even in such working conditions, he could feel her presence, her tugging, her begging, a yearning that had always existed when even as a child. Don't nations experience this type of yearning, a desire to love the mother country, ending in a quick, sudden, catastrophic rebellion? Yet with every woman he had met and made love to, he could feel her body, her breast, a warmth that was securing. In all paradoxical merriment, he paid these women. These prostitutes of women were shedding ladylike features, yet still very much women. And he paid his way through with money, only because of the respect he carried for his mother. Such patriotic respect! Using curtains, which were blind to the eyes, revealed an animosity that could not be seen.

He was able to see again the image of his father as he walked up the steps to the sawmill. And the big, husky man with a helmet on and arms on crimson redwood would turn his face toward him, solemn yet always a mystery. And the levels of boards rolled on by as if never ending in movement while the pulleys of steel creamed and the noise of the factory became deafening to a point of despair. Julian would wake up as if in a nightmare, walking back downstairs with all the faces of the townspeople looking on. "Go away, fatherless child, go away. Go back to your mother." A tug pulled him down, the slap of a chain, and he was a slave once more.

This ancient building was actually a very new institution in many ways, the hospital that is. Where else could such lies begin their lofty unfeeling ends? It was as if the entire environment were waiting for him, feeling out his steps one at a time every inch of the way. He did the same to their steps. The railroad tracks were at times lined with the bums and tramps. This was next to where he lived. He would find himself taking to the relics of passerby, traces of humility, poverty, and the simpleness of freedom. And this precise character became embedded within the framework of the hospital, like a steel mold being cast time after time over. Even as the hours passed on, Julian began to feel this way. And the people around him began to feel these waves of feelings right along with him. As most similar to other times past, his reasons for loving were always simple.

He remembered the night back home with his mother as she dressed into her nightgown. He still felt very much near home as he worked in the hospital. He could see the face of a girl, her red hair and fair-skin body. And she was also dressed in a loose pink nightgown. He continued working with nervous patience and stamina while the girl on the gurney who was covered with blood on her face turned toward him. Soon the emergency room was crowded with police officers, and the head doctor, whose name was Wagner, entered with a smile on his face, asking Julian what it was that he was conspiring.

"Nothing, sir! I work alone. One who's alone, certainly, could not be conspiring anything. Surely! Only a conspiracy against himself," replied Julian.

The sirens and lights of the ambulance disappeared, and in a quick flash, he could see his mother's bedroom while stopping at her door as he walked toward his own room. And as he stood there, he noticed his mother, who stood near the bed with her back toward him, naked and holding onto her panties. She began dressing into her nightgown. This frightened him. Even as he turned away, he continued staring and weakened totally. She did not say anything. He swallowed with hungry, lustful eyes upon her naked figure, rounded, and with plump breast.

Trembling, he walked with a gentle gait into his room. And once he was inside, he closed the door, hugging the wall as he held onto the doorknob. She had climbed into her bed now and all the lights were shut off in the house. "Good night."

And he answered her, "Good night, Mom."

There were other times she would walk into his room at night with only a bra and panties being worn, and she would talk to him about her teaching job. He'd listen, as any son to his mother, but most of the time, he couldn't understand her. He could feel himself crawl in bed with her as she uncovered herself and stretched out, enticing him with sedulous passion. His hands were rolling over her body, touching her breast and hips, removing her fine clothing. They lay there both naked, and he began kissing her neck. Finally, his lips touched her round brownish nipples as his body fell onto hers. The warmth, the seclusion ended. "Oh, I don't understand this woman. Please help me!"

Her hands held onto his body while they held and pressed each other tightly. He sank into her flesh, and he felt as if this would go on for hours. He closed his eyes and thought about tomorrow as the dream would overpower him. A long dream. But it was just a dream, thank God! It was not reality. Julian winked with a jarred look on his face as the bloody face of the girl was cleaned up now, and she was soon being rolled out of the emergency ward.

"What's the matter with you, Julian?" asked Dr. Wagner, peering over his shoulder. "You don't seem yourself tonight. You're acting as if you're not even here. Is there a problem?"

"Oh, nothing, Doctor. Simply nothing," he answered. "I've never worked in a hospital before. I don't know about these things, that's all."

"You think too much orderly! That's very dangerous!" clamored out the doctor.

The clinician, dressed in white, walked upstairs to his bedroom, where he slept for the night. The emergency room was quiet, and everyone had left the scene except for Julian and a night-charge nurse whose name was Kathleen. The silence had roared along with the night hours. Kathleen's red hair sparkled against the lights hanging throughout the clinic, and Julian would stare into her glittering eyes. A security blanket? A mother image? The entire world appeared to be doing the similar "song and dance," a very minute song and dance. However, there was no time to discuss, analyze, and dissect the situation, the world's situation. The social and psychological changes were too great to handle at first. It was like a hammer hitting the skull of your head till the pain was so great that the loss of total consciousness became inevitable. Like a plotted-out destiny, the only choice to be taken was one route. This hospital became Julian's limbo, and as time passed on, a top to a cliff looking over hell. And it became a particular hell, which was at the time so personal, so close to home, yet so far away, seeming almost as endless as time racing through his mind. With all this happening in his dura mater, an overnight world had taken onto higher platitudes and humilities. Events became a change domestically shocking. People divided themselves into two equal sides: the rich, affluent running and controlling these cowardly minds to the right, while the poor, menial working bohemian slave jettisoned to the left.

Meek, hypocritical schemers, thought Julian. He noticed all the black people; he felt amicable among them. Yet there were many people who always wondered in the midnight of the sun why he never mingled around Mexicans and Hispanics…his own association, his own kind. But that was the way he was.

Seclusion became a large part of his life, and as the months passed on, he began seeing very little daylight. Julian met the crossroad in his life. In the middle of the San Joaquin Valley, a country etiquette is what it seemed to appear. He began trying to forget old memories and make new experiences come true. Surely, the hallways seemed endless, and the doors unlocked themselves one by one to a new world.

Kathleen lived down the road, about three miles in the direction to Delano to one side of the freeway in an old mediocre trailer park, which set aside the Sky Ranch Motel. And the municipal airport became a place where Julian decided to take upon a task too good to be real, too gruesome to be an easy one, yet another panacea for winning hearts. To fly an airplane was indeed an insane idea at first, everyone thought at the hospital. Kathleen agreed right along with them.

Yes, this is a beast from a rejected valley culture, she thought. *This spoiled brat.*

Flying once with an instructor younger than himself and covering the area of the city, he was able to catch a first-ever glimpse of the valley below the horizon, which overlooked the sunset setting below the coastal range. He felt free, and for a five-dollar fee, he couldn't have gone for a better ride. Taking off down the runway was easy, but landing the contraption was indeed a chore, and Julian soon let everyone know it too. Being confused, he convinced himself to the fact that he would take on such a drastic task as to play with his life in such a manner. And during this other time, he felt he was falling in love with Kathleen, the German girl, who was the strange nurse working at the hospital. His feelings were leading him to believe his piloting debut was executed because he wanted to conquer her in a way of acclaiming fear of himself. He began turning into an amoral animal of the lowest menial kind. A mole? No! Another child taking over his exhausted facade or perhaps another boyhood dream overwhelming his own adulthood became the result.

"It is time?" questioned the minds of the people at the hospital. *What do they mean?* asked Julian to himself. *Is it time? Time for what?*

The old abandoned airfield lay ten miles from the ground school where an old abandoned B-17 lay rotting to one side of the freeway for the onlookers to see. Yes, perhaps it was time to prepare for another war, a second chance for Julian's chivalry, or another escape into the world of lost dreams? But what a better way to fall in love, to lose one's mind over something so feminine, so delicate, so fragile, yet so very dangerous. All is fair in love and war. One must know when to stop when playing with only a queen and a duce. Perhaps solitaire.

It was true. The government was preparing to accept an oncoming war just as the people were learning to accept a new cabinet under President Carter. This kind of regimentation existed at every level of government throughout the country. A cold front, snow blizzard, had hit hardest in the Eastern states creating disaster for millions of people. Even the stories of the great storm came to the valley as people fled the snow all the way from Ohio. California was spoiled and the valley even more so. Everyone was grateful for this blessed meteorological reincarnation.

"We couldn't have had it better," recalled Julian. "Weather-wise, the only real problem we were faced with was the lack of rain, possibly an oncoming drought. This eventually meant a rise of cost in the commodity market of agriculture, which frightened the farmers and gave out heart attacks to those people who couldn't even afford to feed their own children. Living was indeed a very tight financial affair. One would learn fast how to live, how to survive, or either take yours of getting hacked with a hatchet. The heads would roll only because one wouldn't make the effort."

Living day to day was the only way Julian decided to live life for the time being, spending only what he had to, and being a loner meant that he had to. Looking toward the horizon meant looking at a debt that had to be paid as if being forced to drink more coffee just to stay awake to keep from falling asleep. Even its price, a jar, rose out of sight. You had to play the game by ear. Pity on those souls who had to drink coffee just to stay alive!

Julian lived as simple as he could make himself, and he continued to barricade himself in his small shack, trying to maintain a truck, a car, cooking, and paying one hundred and twenty dollars of rent. When Wanda would walk in, the twenty-dollar payment seemed like twenty thousand dollars every time she asked for it. For the one year that had gone by, his income tax return was enough for a month's shack up. Hell, living as simple and as poor as you can be meant the only way to survive. The lake of the valley's pastoralness was wide enough to give everyone the same problem: being caught and getting fished out or becoming a loser. Julian decided to keep his mouth shut and become a loser. *I've hit the bottom*, he thought, *and it is time!*

Yes, this time it was an unknown force conquering Julian's heart, and his passions were beginning to show on his work and especially on his paintings. It was one day, at two o'clock, that Kathleen sat on her front porch while posed for his weakened patience. And there she sat on her front porch while she posed for his weakened patience. And there she sat on her front porch in all her melancholy as the clouds moved overhead fast, and the wind rolled through her hair. She faced the airport, which lay across from Highway 99. Her expression showed a disappointing portrayal. She sat with a grimace look and had the appearance of a tired woman. He sketched her more daring than he had ever seen her.

And through more current times, Julian's mother, Juana, and Anna, his sister, were living with the stepfather, Joaquin, who had married Juana a year earlier when, at that time, Julian decided to leave home. Like most young jealous men, he was against the marriage from the start. His immaturity surprised him when he found out that other relatives of the family had also been against the marriage. This was a brass conclusion, for he was too young for these occurrences and didn't know any better. But like everything else, there was nothing he could do about it, not even intervene in the struggle of that marriage. He became prejudiced, but he'd always been prejudiced toward this entity. He began living this type of prejudiced life.

Joaquin, being of meek character, liked to drink; he was honest, and a demanding master mechanic in a very strange way became Julian's savior in emergencies of mechanical conspiracy. He was always there when Julian needed him. Mechanics was a large part of everyone's life in the family.

Julian would drive over to Raisintown to visit even if it meant emergency stopping to visit his brothers or sister along the way. Rafael was working to support his family at the sawmill where their father had worked for years earlier; and his older brother, Deamond, was frivolous at wasting no time to selling life insurance to half the valley. Julian felt somewhat in the middle of it all, losing toward a family life and being fast at increasing his profits while he collected the financial gains on that precise, family life.

The one character who influenced Julian's early life was his Uncle Samuel, the oldest of the brothers in Juana's family. His early military experience in the Korean War and having a talent to paint paralleled Julian's own boyhood and early adulthood struggle. A bachelor and living alone in north Raisintown, he painted there and worked his own life, fire, and home real estate business, a trade he had been pursuing to become successful for years in Los Angeles before moving to the valley. But he was aging, tired, and still shell-shocked from his military heroic days in Korea. He was under medical care. Even the psychiatric help from the old veterans' hospital left his life desolate and lonely from the rest of the family. He had always grown close to Julian. Even as a youngster, Julian would remember his war stories as they would all sit around the ranch house during gatherings and Christmas debuts. Now, his financial training and background were worthless, and he wasn't making ends meet in comparison to this day's bourgeoisie population—only in the financial sense of the work, of course.

All in all, he and Julian became the peacemakers of the family's black sheep specialists. Trying to live up to a dead man's image or even bringing him back to life seemed almost an impossible task at the time, but for a couple of domestic Californians as these two, this was surely the fantasy to conquer. And they constantly remember that when the man from Mexico died, so did the family. And when Julian would drive back to the country from the city, he would feel remorse, quietude, a release of pressure from this entire memory of a home, which was a home, a cause worth fighting for, only for the memory of a man.

Julian would look back and remember how the family disintegrated as time passed on after his father's death and how painful it was to look back at everything with solemn pride, the same pride that defeated him while in the army. But as painful as it all seemed, the truth was plain to view that the family was no longer the family he had once known it to be. His brushes stopped moving this time.

Two years would pass by, as if suddenly, two years that would determine a certain fate of justice for Julian or his possible ruin. Through all this time, Julian had reached his peak, a peak that had thrown him to one side intellectually. He stopped going to school intermittently, dropping out of classes every time as he had always been an intellectual dropout, which was most obvious as far as the way he played the game: an honest fool. The summer of 1977 appeared as if the summer of 1942 had lost its love for love. Damn hot!

"You can't have your cake and eat it too." But of course, we all know that the cliché has existed for years. Yet this feeling spread throughout the county hospital, which was now being threatened by the state of being shut down. "Never!" answered the personnel who had been working there for years. Certainly this fifty-year-old tombstone of a building was an everlasting relic. Besides, the institution of the clinic helped to pay Julian's rent and the cost of the ground school over at the airport. He was getting closer to soloing the airplane as six months at the school had gone by.

"It's your life. You do whatever the hell you want with it," shrugged off Kathleen, turning her back to Julian and packing her tapestry in the bedroom of her trailer house.

The roles and images of billionaire Howard Hughes and Pappy Boyington, World War TI Ace, was surely diminishing at the airport. Julian and Luigi Peluso were busy maneuvering low over the corn and cotton fields near Pixley while flying full stalls and emergency landings.

"This machine, this plane, will kill the 'you.' You will be killed!" yelled the instructor at Julian. And only the imagery of an arrangement of flowers hovered in the back of his mind. Flying an airplane wasn't a joke, and taking life seriously certainly wasn't a joke either.

And during those times in the air, there was another face. Padre Gonzales wasn't in reality a very hard man, just a bit stubborn, and even more so when the subject came to religion. And as always, Julian would go into St. Ritas, a Catholic church nearby the northeast corner of the county hospital, to pray at night. And as always, Father Gonzales would walk in and sit next to him on the altar and say, "I will have the front door open so that you can leave on the way out."

Several nights before the Fourth of July celebration, Julian encountered a plump-figured man whose name was Angel and told him that he was Father Gonzales's brother. The next moments passed, and the Father drove his Mercedes into the driveway with his bodyguard, a man from Farmersville, who was a farm laborer, a seasonal farm worker.

"How have you been, big boy?" yelled out the Father. "The church is locked tonight, but come in anyway. I'll show you the new house under construction." After viewing the structured skeleton of a building, they sat around a large table in the Father's living room and drank light beer to the brightness on the television set, and the *Johnny Carson Show* blazed on into the morning. Thirty minutes had gone by as did a six-pack of beer. Three figures could finally be seen standing next to the light that shone on the stack of white fir wood. The boards sat next to the foundation of the new building being built next to the church.

"This could be your house," spoke the priest to Julian. Julian stood to one side and flashed in his mind, remembering of his next-door neighbor who was a big, fat woman living next door to him. The method of how she knocked on his front door at three o'clock in the morning rocked his memory. He had only a towel wrapped around him.

"I only want you to kiss me good night," she said. There was silence.

"That's precisely the point I wanted to make out to you, young one," said Father Gonzales as if piercing through Julian's thoughts. "If you support prostitution, soon women will walk in with more ease and finesse, and each time your acts will seem to be more and more natural. That is definitely not right, for both of you will be living in sin."

Preposterous! thought Julian as he disagreed with him all the way as in most arguments. "And is your God so almighty that you need a gun for protection, and yet you sit there and ask me who is stealing your wood." Rambling on viciously through the morning hours while disagreeing on different issues constantly, the Father persuasively begged Julian to attend church on Sunday.

"Everything you produce is shit," stammered out the short man with an analytical endorsement. "Not until everyone comes to this church, Father, then and only then will I come to worship your way."

"Therefore, go home and go to bed, or the people at the hospital will think you're a drunk man. And stay away from those *Playboy* books." There were footsteps in the dark, and the door on the truck shut. Julian had walked away on a high note of intention, and the Padre was steaming away with his temper.

The following night at the hospital was not as busy on the first floor, where many of the patients were staying. Julian sat in the utility room, talking with the older crowd of a non-licensed personnel as he would always do. The room was worn down. The sinks and cupboards were aged and stained, and an old-fashioned steam toilet for dumping the bedpans sat in the corner opposite as forty-years-old air fan, which hung above the window from where Julian was sitting down with several of the licensed nurses. Typical to an early prewar dungeon of the 1930s, it's exactly what the facility resembled.

"You're a *menso* and a total fool," spoke a little vicious bitch, a nurse, plump and fat, who sat next to him in one corner.

"Why I would get all the people in this hospital and burn them up in burners, in piles?"

"You mean like the Jews?" fired back Julian, surprised and amazed at the words.

"Yes, definitely."

"I don't think I would do that," Julian spoke with more stern severity. "I would better get around to understanding and knowing myself…and realize my own weaknesses and take a look into why I dropped out of this damned society." She was finally silenced. "What's new?" And the footsteps became more sharp and alive. A tall figure wearing a white cape and holding a large-sized red medical journal walked into the room. The glasses that he wore dropped to the bridge of his nose. It was Dr. Wagner. He smiled at Julian and sat himself down without making any noise.

"Well, what's new?" he spoke as he crossed his legs in a praying position, and he touched together the tips of his fingers. He smiled like a scheming, hypocritical gay, yet curious enough to be serious, and yes, he spoke in his mumbling way—the intellectual beast that he was.

"Do you really enjoy flying, or are you building up your egotistical pocket book to leave to some redheaded dame."

"There you go again, Doctor, pretending to play God. Of course, you can't take any of this with you when you die. You live, and as you live, you die. That's right. Die!" Julian asserted himself. "And this beats leaving it all to some redheaded dame."

The doctor looked at Julian as if silently without spoken words that the orderly was yielding. The doctor chuckled and shrugged his shoulders as he viewed the others in the room. His laugh was sarcastic.

"Oh, he's probably just another draft deserter, just a demonstrator," stated the white-robed physician.

"Ah! Listen to this bullshit. You Germans are all alike," answered back Julian.

The room was quiet, and the doctor had left the area. The buzzard lights in the patients' rooms to the ward were beginning to flicker now. The patients were restless, and the smell of the sewer seeped through the windows. The rush of the gases produced by the oxygen-contained trucks outside of the hall could be heard as the large white oxygen tanks were being filled. There was a need to awaken the patients, and the morning care would soon begin. Dr. Wagner was back inside his quarters now, up the stairway to the end of the hallway, where the view of the fairgrounds was quite visible from the window of his room. Oh, such a desolate-looking fairgrounds it was. How sad! All this was happening while the entire world was steaming away, not taking notice of this starched grain of sand on the map, this sole catalyst for the seeds of truth to these Tulare flowers in the valley area.

The airplane began landing a bit more smoothly now, and Julian's butterflies would fly away to a place where they could be tended with more pride, honesty, and a place where darkness could sleep comfortably, complacent—away from a terrible war. He traveled to the city, south, Los Angeles. He drove his pickup truck.

The day was hot, and the air was stuffy. The streets lay placid, rigid, and shredded with garbage from the smell of car oil and smog. The corner of Washington Boulevard and Marmion Avenue was indeed the biggest shocking sight to Julian in months. The color of the two-story apartment had faded. There were cracks and chips, and the yard was drooling with a sad-looking appearance. Negro children played throughout the side street, and graffiti decorated the front walls of the warehouses and several of the markets. Julian parked his truck opposite the back door of the tenant house, felt exhausted after the long drive and began taking deep breaths between sighing. East Los Angeles, a backside hidden ghetto, was indeed a different jungle from his valley home. "This is the only— unica— neighborhood that we're respected in, Julian. The Mexicans are mean to us. They treat us bad," said one of his cousins, a descendant from Mexico.

I don't believe it, he thought.

"Yes, we all live here now, all but one aunt of yours who stayed in Guadalajara," spoke Julian's grandmother, Jesusalia. Her sisters, Anjelica and Christina, were present. That very night, they drove to the eastern, upper portion of the city where Anjelica lived to one side of the freeway that divided Los Angeles. And the lights appeared as if a jeweled menagerie had lit up the metropolitan area. And through each of these engagements, the feelings were all there. The cold feelings that this family was trying to also disturb the peacefulness of a dead man became very genuine.

They just never learn, he thought as they showed him a picture of a soldier dressed in field uniform and carrying a sword.

"This was my husband, your uncle," spoke the old woman, Anjelica. Her daughter, who never married, simply smiled at him. After an hour's time, they exited the front door of the house. Yes, Julian felt that austere feeling which clothed him, that same feeling which had clothed him conscious for many years. "These people are as abrasive as the family in the valley. When someone dies, they're dead, but they don't seem to believe it so. They just can't leave a dead man in peace, but instead, only resort to using and manipulating those last roots of his limbs like to that of a tired tree. This, they don't mind disturbing. This, they will disturb," said Julian. He returned to the valley. Katheleen was, in the end, living alone as was the way most had wanted, alone in her trailer house. However, she still cooked for her brother and his so-called quasi-Nazi friends. To the other extreme was Julian alone in his small cabin and continuing his pilot training, which carried him throughout and over the valley. He had also returned to school and decided that physiology and anatomy were his next steps. Two birds in a cage: each one stalling the other out, as if both hated living to the extent that they might as well have drowned each other out while jumping into a bottomless pit of water. For Julian, it had become that same bottomless pit. Only this time, it wasn't filled with water. Julian had built around him a well-formed shell fortified with thoughts of realistic boredom, seclusion, isolation, and pain, totally blocking out people from all corners. A twenty-five-year-old monster is what he'd become definitely, a far cry from Katheleen. Could this be what love was all about? Heaven's not! A hellish type of love Yes, definitely. Surely, no woman is an island, and life just continues on. Only a *Felis domesticus* can explain pain much better than any human being trying to demonstrate such an exposition in human behavior. Again, no one ever knew. Yet Elvis Presley had recently died of a heart failure or the usual overdose of this particular type of love. It was best to send the patient to room 108 toward the end of the hallway on the medical floor. There's nothing in the world wrong with him. Guilty all the way!

Julian's flight was becoming longer, higher, and further away, while Wanda, the woman prostitute, had gone to New York on official business— big dinero. And so what! Maria was working in Winetown, where her office was located next to the overpass on Highway 99, burying herself with her schoolwork. Rafael was working up north in the mountains as a carpenter, carrying with him his family, and Anna lived in a rumored whorehouse next to the San Joaquin River beach, which was close to Kings River College. And the cemetery was quiet, no flowers.

They valley was ever so beautiful next to the fall's sunset. Winter was on her way, and a traffic ticket had to be paid. A Santa Fe train did lose a race made by the white '57 Ford. Oh! And what a run to Winetown it was. El Camino Real was now a legend and no longer a myth.

During this time, Julian began an oil portrait of his mother to deliver to her new home in Winetown and subsequently wrote a poem. Strange, though, that it was exactly during this same time that the world seemed somewhat different, as if also questioning to herself the same thought. The leaders in the Mideast—the Israelis, that is—received a visit from President Sadat of Egypt, which proved to be a relief of tension. Here in America, President Carter and his wife paid tribute to the movie *Gone with the Wind*, which had received the world's greatest motion picture nomination award in Hollywood. "A thing of beauty is a joy forever," said the main speaker. "The original cast of characters are now all dead."

Another traffic ticket issued, and Julian was reported by the FAA for using the N1115X Cherokee as a crop duster. This, of course, was against flying rules. "The military used to fly very low over the water during World War TI to keep the enemy fooled and the radar jinxed," scolded his ground school instructor, Luigi. Titles were hard to choose:

Where I would have to go if I had to die alone.

Where I would have to go if I had to die alone. To my father's grave? No, that would be too forgiving, too childish, too easy…yes, to ornery…but true. It would be at a place where even the courageous and brave would be afraid to go and even in their fantasies about the world around me would they be afraid to conquer, like as simple as their friend and my foe. I would be afraid to go.

Where life was "gone with the wind," as the greatest of vanities were put on trial. Where almost nothing was copied in fear and the soul was new, original, a virgin, and at war. Alone to my father's grave.

And if my own arrogance had overwhelmed me in spite of those of others, if I were sure I had accepted it, I would then let it take me to a place where I would be accepted. Still too childish, too tempting, but I would still die alone. And if I had my way, I would go to a lonely countryside, to a deserted ranch. I would walk quietly, then I would hear voices. There was a crowd of people, and children were running about, and an old man was sitting on a wooden box next to a tractor and some pomegranate trees. The cotton grew wild and I would feel alive. Then I would die alone, along with a final breeze of the wind.

The date was November 1977, sometime after Thanksgiving, and the outside world was gi-ving tributes to a hell of a lot of people: celebrities, politicians, and mostly to the two generations that came before Julian's time. It was as if a curtain were going up for the last time. Surely, his interest and love for this revered culture of entertainment drew him toward a curiosity. The world was certainly cruel in this way, and he began reaching the end of the rope. His mother wanted him to move back to her house because of family difficulties and few problems with his older brother's son. The sheep on the ranch wandered about carefree. The ranch house lay adjacent to the highway. Again, he would look back at his poem. The fog from the early winter coming was settling, and General Hospital had now been painted a dark golden color on the outside. The cockroaches were coming back into room 7 of the motel house…then coldness and fog.

Julian once again dropped out of the science courses, ever seemingly realizing himself in his own folly. That same week, the first week of December, on a cold, misty fog-shrouded day, he flew N1115X over the valley and back to his hometown to where his father was buried next to the mountain that resembled the lying woman. Twenty-five miles was his legal limit from the airport. Twenty-five miles in the fog, he traveled to his father's grave. On his return leg, he landed on a small airstrip called the Sequoia Airport where B-17s of the older models were being repaired and painted a red and gray color. White, the sky was superbly white. Yes, two thousand feet was a good level to fly. One could see the land below. He followed Highway 99 back home to his cabin.

Julian passed up the Christmas party given by the airport. *I just felt out of place*, he thought. He had recently bought most presents needed for the year's conventional. Thank God! The prior day, he had spoken with an old friend of his over a few beers. It was a talk about an old wedding renewed. It really took to Julian about these so-called private people of this valley. People were afraid to leave their homes, and almost everybody had their cars for sale. No money. The bars seemed the place to go to, at times, possibly because of fear of getting involved, even getting rich! In complete, it was a timely test of putting off things to be done. What a way to grow up! Yet it was as if one were trying to live what was really in a culture that tried to portray its realness by novels, movies, music, television, and humanity's own reclamation of truth. Julian's thoughts built stockpiles of mental fits. *I'm confused about my own humanity*, he thought. *My sanity and, oh, am I tired!* He peered to the ceiling of his cabin. *One of my next-door neighbors died the other day, one of the oldest of the gentlemen and ladies who lived next to me. He left the trailer home to the state.* The yellowish-brown leaves were falling to the ground, and the valley turned into a brown-crimson color. Katheleen had moved out of town to Las Vegas, and with her went one of Julian's passionate flames. The following month, great, hard winds and a storm swept through the southern part of the valley, which forced Julian to remain grounded, and he was unable to fly long trips in the airplane. It was as if all the challenge for living had dwindled to practically nothing. Yes, there was nothing left to conquer in this valley of leftover sewage, except for the harsh yet very close memories of looking back on early years—as a matter of fact, very wonderful years, years of excluding and leaving out the business part of insurance matters. And "the hell with insurance" was a built-in attitude unable to rid itself of Julian's conscience for many early years—perhaps unfortunate, even deadly. Anne, Julian's sister, after spending several semesters at Julian's old college alma mater, was now working at a large shopping center in Winetown. In Julian's eyes, she had changed immensely, more in attractiveness. She stood at five feet and six inches, filled out, long dark-brown hair, large brown eyes, somewhat fickle. She was a fast girl, and her father's affection had indeed spoiled her ingenuity. Her boyfriend was of an Italian descent and also from Julian's hometown.

Back at the Fair Court Motel, the Santa Fe train was rumbling by, going south, where only fifty miles away a great dust storm with one-hundred-mile-an-hour winds and a torrent rain blew through Bakersfield and Southern California: a very unfortunate flight for Julian indeed. The winds were quiet, and at the court, there was calmness.

Al's memory of his wife, the imprint of her feet on the back porch of the landowner's house, had filled up with the rainwater. The managers of the motel had moved up to San Jose. Julian was alone again. The motel house office was empty, and there was no refrigerator present. The three thousand dollars that had been left to him by his father was not down to an amount of nine hundred dollars…hanging on!

The foggy day reluctantly cleared itself up by the high noon, and the weather looked good for flying at first glance. And out of nowhere, Wanda, who had been gone for the past six months was waiting for Julian at the front door of his cabin. He began walking back from the phone booth, which sat in front of the fairgrounds.

He visualized the periods of his efforts to fly, pushed the airplane away from the gas tanks, and a final check was performed by Julian. He jumped in and started up the engine, taxing the contraption out to the runway.

Wanda began walking Julian back through the front door with a large smile on her face. He could see the airplane again as it sped off and headed toward the direction of the mountains, and the clouds could be seen in the horizon.

"Did you miss me, honey?" she asked. "Like I miss jacking off." She pulled him over to the bed. Yes, this time, Julian was flying sky high as he crossed the mountains, nervous and edgy. His altitude was approximately nine thousand five hundred feet. He crossed Tehachapi. The sky was clear with only several clouds sparingly visible. The valley could no longer be seen as a low fog sank deep beneath the scattered whiteness and into her bosom.

"I'm living up in Raisintown now," she spoke in a gentle tone to him.

"Same routine?" he asked.

She nodded. "Yup!" she said in her Southern-burnt accent. And as time rolled on, off course, once again, did he go. He lost another twenty dollars with Wanda, and the airplane went speeding off toward the eastern side of the Mojave Desert. After playing around with near-military VORTACs, the plane landed in Landcaster one hour later. His next flight would be much more successful. A rainy season had drenched the valley, and the coast would be his destination. Fifty-two hours of flight time had gone by in his logbook, and Santa Maria was as dismal as some of his dreams. The valley was much flooded that day, and flying over mountains would be enough for him to stomach for a long time. But as this time continued, so did his flying hours increase. His skills took on a more sharp, trenchant character.

Indeed, the motel and the long driveway protected him from the crest of the outside world, a variety of outsiders and the people who could have been his enemies. The license plate on the pickup that belonged to the new managers read: "Illinois, the Land of Lincoln."

The sunsets toward the west became redder as the spring died away, and back at the mountain that shed the cemetery east of town, a large wooden house was being built upon her breast. The road to the crest read: "No trespassing." The orchards were as green as ever. In the distance, the noise of the plane's engine could be heard as its shadow flashed over the grounds of the cemetery. Tombstone silence and one-hundred-degree temperatures ripped the oncoming days.

And as costly as fools fall in love, so was living expensive. Unto whatever stood in the way, the hallways seemed endless, and the doors remained unlocked at the hospital. Yes, the iron fire doors gave the interior design a character of a military fort. She still stood; the buildings of modern complex style surrounded her grounds, including that of a welfare department. She withstood all those limmerant rains, all the havoc of crummy weather mixed with regimented politics as the political elections related to the tax revolt in the state. There was always business that availed with these limmerant rains of leftover welfare derelicts and the mendaciousness of a few running, scared conspirators. The economic revolt ended up in job loss and several schools closing. The value of the dollar shrunk a healthy fifteen cents and most of Julian's money was spent on long cross countries to Los Angeles county, a furiously big city. The air machine showed much wear and tear.

There he sat in his motel room, writing, cooking, painting, waiting, and doing a great deal of planning as the carnivals, jam sessions, religious revivals, bike races, and an entire growing up of a generation began to pass on. Oh, the pain of learning to walk! Everything amassed from experienced beforehand. He kept what was useful and discarded what was worthless. There in the room, he lived alone, and the world hated him for it. And he knew it, and people knew it, but he didn't give a damn.

And how he remembers on Father's Day, during that June of '78, he drove to his stepfather's ranch to spend the afternoon with the family. Juanita was there. So was Anna, his only sister. Joaquin's mother sat next to Juanita's mother. Terron sat next to his future wife, Sandra. Julian walked in through the large wooden front door, taking a bottle of champagne over to the kitchen. There they sat around a small table under the patio roof which was located in the back of the house. The afternoon was hot, and everyone wore light-clad clothing. He was late as usual and ate alone. The smell of the hamburger meat drenched over the grill of the barbecue burner. He quickly sat himself down into a chair at first, and they all treated him with undue respect as always. Rafael was not present with his family, for having to leave to the mountains, east, to begin another long period of work. Everybody was quiet at the greeting, and all eyes were on Sandra. The northeast breeze was cool. Terron sat unrequitedly, wearing his insurance hat, a golfer's derby. Julian noticed he was wearing glasses.

"Working hard," spoke out Joaquin. "Have a glass of beer. You'll relax."

"There's rumors they'll be closing down the hospital. Many people will be losing their jobs."

"Why not join the service!" exclaimed Joaquin's mother.

"Who pulled your cord today?" answered back Julian in a surprised, defensive voice. "I happen to be reject material, or have you forgotten already. There's a slim chance that the government will shut the hospital down. The poor people need a door to go to. But…perhaps…" Silence. Next, everyone chuckled a parcel.

Terron stared at him, while Sandra as always was busy entertaining Joaquin. The portrait of his mother, a painting he had completed after the final Easter had passed, was hanging in the large parlor all by itself, above the fireplace, and almost unnoticed as the talking outside continued.

Sandra was indeed an attractive Anglo girl, slim and with the image of a debutante; she carried about herself a secret gaiety of an easy-going nature. Terron had planned on marrying her, only he couldn't decide exactly when he should commit himself to her. Somehow throughout this gala, Julian carried with him a defense of false trust with her, a feeling that fluctuated with each time they met. It all took stage at his mother's house while sitting across from each other on the large wooden dining room table. Terron, with his hands resting and clutched behind his head, reclined on the large beige sofa. He was smiling with a confident gait as he had always done at family gatherings. "Orson Wells, the great scientist, met his wife over a dinner table and divorced her over a dinner table," he stated. And when the next Thanksgiving arrived, more criticism was thrown upon the painting. The lips on his mother were just a bit too red. Julian gave the portrait the name of *Hot Lips*. Winter fell, as so did the leaves, and the earth was brown again. The coming Christmas would be foggy and cold. The large tree that stood in front of the driveway of Julian's porch was never so beautifully decorated with lights and ornaments of gleaming colors. The tree was actually decorated.

School had finished, and Julian had finally passed the physiology and anatomy course. One year's struggle, finished. After running into the strangest blonde he'd ever met in class who pricked his attention, he thought simultaneously that he was falling in love with a thirty-nine-year-old woman whom he would sit next to during class, a brunette with big eyes as large as steely marbles. Life probably does begin at forty! One day, she bought a jar of horse testes to the anatomy class and showed Julian exactly what she thought of him. She was from back East, and it came to be that she owned a few horses. He had become infatuated with her. He tried to match his inexperienced emotions with hers. The year came to an end, and he never saw her again. The month passed. The airplane N75108 showed nearly ninety-six hours, flying time, and the winter weather came pouring in, dominated with fog. On many days, the most gracious formation of gathering, moving clouds the human eyes could imagine against the virulent, fiery sunsets could be seen. When New Year's Day passed; the first day of 1979 seemed as ordinary as any other day. The trees stood barren, showing off their trenchant skeleton against the white background of the winter's sky.

A Russian flu had beckoned to the location of the valley, and many people were caught in the eye of its hurricane. Julian was also taken prisoner, as were others at the hospital who soon fell prey to the bug. With this occurrence and tension at the hospital building itself up, Julian decided to leave town on morning time. He had three nonworking days to himself, and Los Angeles was only two hundred miles away. The truck sped off one hour before sunrise; some slight fog remained on the road. Julian was only thinking of how his dead father's relatives would react to seeing him and questioning who might some of these people be. He wondered. Trenched out in the back of his mind, he felt only a slight relief of freedom from leaving the valley, as lethal as a breath of fresh air. The side route at Castaic, a central mountain tourist turnout, was covered with snow. The sun was shining brightly, and the smell of ocean breeze saturated the wind as the engine of the pickup truck stalled to a suffocated forty-five miles per hour going up the grade. Up the grade and downtown again, the truck continued. The San Joaquin Valley disappeared from view, and the smog was all one could see.

Julian never truly had a disdain for his dead father's family and relatives, only an admiration toppled over by a revengeful grievance due to the mystery that engulfed him in his earlier boyhood years. As much as he didn't know well enough yet wanting to get back at them by dwelling into their past lives that were encircled by the memories of his father's roots, he plummeted and absorbed their hospitality.

Jesusalia was uniquely the one elderly woman who totally estranged Julian from as far back from the time she had lived with his father, her only son. But only a charlatan could possibly have given her such a name as that. Indeed! It did fit her image and personality quite well. "Jesusalia!" Yes, probably an old-fashioned Mexican priest gave her the name to fit. He could have named her Rosario. He most likely was the kind of man who couldn't fit in any other type of clothes himself.

She lived inside a small room behind a convalescent apartment in a lower-middle-class neighborhood on an avenue called Norton located in South Hollywood. Again, as always, a Catholic church rested on the corner and only walking distance from her apartment. There was a young black man washing down the front yard with a water hose blast while sitting in his pickup. It was a warm yet mellow afternoon in downtown Los Angeles, within the neighborhood. And as before, on many occasions, she greeted him with great surprise and without hesitation. He sat down, and she served him a cup of tea with lemon and some whiskey added. The conversation carried over, and as always, she showed him a family album with ancient photos of his father, the Man from Mexico. She hadn't changed much: wearing the rimmed glasses, gray haired, a woman of small stature and always wearing a large rosary around her neck. Her voice would suddenly remind you of a self-conscious, self-pity-stricken individual who spoke with a quaint lack of confidence. Conversations with her were a joy that lasted for only about one minute and finished as if a confession had taken place. "Ave Maria!" You could suddenly hear the church bells ringing and organs playing their sinful melodies. Yes, even though she was going somewhat blind, her eyesight managed to retain its sharp, trenchant, dangerous quality: a definite devilish vision. God, save the queen.

They both sipped on the whiskey for a couple of hours, and the chat became a personal trilogy which lasted through the afternoon. And as always, Julian had become the messenger pigeon for the family, the California Voice of Privacy or better yet the Wells Fargo Stool Pigeon. God had pity on this poor boy's soul after learning that Jesusalia had been robbed of her money one day while on the way back from the supermarket. She would walk. Three Mexican youth had pointed a gun to her chest. Julian could not believe it. He became enraged. Yet a trace of comedy remained after the time had passed. Who else could have believed that it would ever happen to this sweet little ol' woman! After two hours, she walked Julian out toward the front of the driveway; consequently, he noticed a nun draped in black, sitting down next to the large side windows of the dining room.

"I'll most likely be back tomorrow in the morning sometime," he told her. He kissed her on the forehead. A small hug followed. He climbed into his pickup, turned north, passed a school where children were playing in the schoolyard next to the church at the corner, and on his way toward North Hollywood.

The truck stopped near a gas station. The smell of clear ocean air was somehow strangled by the carbon monoxide exhaust from the noisy automobiles and buses passing through the main downtown boulevard. It certainly was a jungle of a site to see Los Angeles on a clear day in

January, but nevertheless, the occasion for Julian was a very different stage as compared to that of being in the valley.

He opened the truck's door and stood up, as if granted with authority by some unknowing, awesome power within the city. He began walking toward a telephone booth, as if his confidence guided him—a pretense to timidity. Her voice was recognizable at first, and she sounded protective.

"Hello! Oh, hello. Can I speak to your husband?" asked Julian.

"Why? Who is it? He's not home at the moment. Who is this?" her voice answered. Julian paused.

"Do you remember Terron Solbriozo? It's me, his brother, Julian. This is Viola, isn't it?"

"Uh-huh, Oh! Hello! Where are you calling from?"

"I'm downtown somewhere on the corners of Marks and Vine. Hey, how in the hell do I get out to your place?"

This was the entire content of their conversation. She told him, Franco, her husband, wouldn't be home from work until 4:30 p.m. and gave him directions to their apartment in Van Nuys. Surprised that Julian was in Los Angeles, she quickly spoke, "Come over…see you later." She hung the receiver.

Julian had not seen Franco since his ill-fated wedding, his first wedding. This was three years ago, a wedding in which Julian was made best man. Franco, who had been one of his oldest best friend had married a beautiful black girl from Farmersville.

The hospital was now indeed taking on a different appearance. The hallways were being painted of a different color, and the holes in the plaster were being covered up throughout the walls. And yes, a new stall of sheep was roving in, rushing out the old ones and the few traces of wood rot.

Before leaving Hollywood and on his way to Van Nuys, he remembered his gentlemanly hospitality. He stopped at his uncle's house, which was not very far from his grandmother's home. He was dressed neatly in clean form, Farah slacks, a dark Pendleton, and several people approached him, asking for money. Naturally. "Just like they used to in Tijuana," he remembered.

He approached his uncle's house. It was typical middle-class home that sat atop a small front yard, grassy hill surrounded with flowers and bushes.

One of his great aunts standing at the front door was waiting patiently, standing erect with one hand crossed over her chest. She greeted him.

The sign at the corner street read Arlington Avenue. His uncle entered about thirty minutes later with his oldest son. The door opened. His uncle walked over to a couch and shook Julian's hand cordially. The man shocked him a fling, as Julian retrieved him. As if shaking hands with his own father, he looked like him, spoke like him; even the gestures and the way he carried on reminded Julian of him. The atmosphere of his presence was like a frantic climax in a dream. But this man was not his father's half-brother who had lived in National City and died earlier. This man had a strange presence about him, as if he were hiding something. He also worked at a sawmill that was located about twenty-five miles away, south of the inner city, where he sold lumber products. Taking his cap from his head, he soon sat himself down and began drinking some tequila, straight…and so did Julian. A dish filled with sliced orange halves lay before them.

"Que hay de nuevo?" asked Julian.

"Naranjas," he answered. He spoke to Julian the way his father used to. Julian didn't expect an argument, being that he was not in his own home.

"How dare you to address your grandmother as Chayo. She's your grandmother, not your girlfriend. And just how many times do you ever visit your own mother…much less call her?"

Dumbfounded with the statement, Julian didn't know how to answer him. *What the hell was it to him?* he thought with a shy timidity. But that's the way his uncle was, and he didn't plan on making anything out of it. They both drank the entire bottle, stood up, and mentioned how long it's been, and as always, he said, "How nice of you to visit us." Sarcastically, of course.

"I'm on my way to see some friends of mine who live north of the city…okay?"

"And if you'll excuse me, I have to shower, eat, and get a haircut," said the short, chubby man. What a reunion! A last goodbyes, a door shut, and Julian disappeared.

Absolutely no English allowed within the house. Phooey! The nerve of the man, he thought as he drove away to begin his drive to visit Yolanda on the corner of Marmion and Washington. He arrived to find the door without bells and knocked on the wooden piece. Once again, as in the past, he peered through the stairway. A second door at the top opened, and the small figure of a girl peered curiously.

"Mama! Mama! There's a man here to see you. It's Julian."

Julian peered up the stairway, and Yolanda could be seen peeking out the second-story doorway with a younger child clinging to her side.

"Well, what's the problem? She's got more guts than the both of you. It's me, Julian. I came over last year, remember? Or had you already forgotten?"

"I don't open the door for anybody in this town!" she hammered out.

He slowly made his way up the stairs. "She does," he answered, pointing to the little girl.

Yolanda looked older in years, and her face and body was worn and appeared used. She was presently working as a full-time supervisor at a factory where clothes were made. He remembered very well the white cotton suit which she had made him a year ago. She combed her hair straight back just like a man does when he awakens in the morning, and a cigarette hung off her upper lip. Wearing pant-like paddle pushers, she looked like a professional street woman who was making a debut into the evening day.

They both began drinking tequila from an old bottle she had placed on top of her refrigerator, and lemon slices and salt was added to the tasting spree. The time was one-half hour before midnight, and Julian was tipping the glasses of tequila with straight alcohol now. Yolanda interrupted. "You see, Julian…That's right…I'm a bitch. I control all the men who work for me." Julian gave her a surprised stare. "I'm waiting for a rich man to come by and take me out of this dungeon." The conversation lasted until midnight. As Julian listened to her voice, he knew that she had been rejected by the immediate family who lived in Los Angeles. She was the perfect black sheep and a springboard connection to other relatives in Mexico. She was dangerous for the family, and the relatives in Los Angeles knew it too. Julian continued staring at her movement as she tipped her cup. She wasn't a bad-looking woman. Her blouse was partly open, revealing her breasts; the hungry passion that rushed through his mind made him refuse her invitation to spend that night on the couch.

"I really have to be going, so don't worry about me. I'll find someplace to stay before leaving in the morning," he told her. He shook hands with her and left her apartment through the living room's door. And he tapped his way down the stairway, taking with him all his sexual attitudes and perhaps leaving his last and only hope and futility to any undermining and connection to Mexican relatives. He had told her that if he did return in Easter, he would leave with her and the two girls to Jalisco. However, as cousins to cousins, his chances were very unlikely.

Feeling uneasy, cramped, and sexually aroused, Julian drove his truck down Vine and Hollywood and turned west on Santa Monica Boulevard. The time was about twelve thirty, and the street corners were crowded with a variety of people jamming themselves into the entrances to the discotheques and nightclubs. Sailors, marines, hippies, and traces of homosexuals could be seen beneath the flickering of traffic lights. A congested and dull atmosphere had settled into the area. Julian felt surprised; however, he was very disappointed to find out that Hollywood was no longer the great epitome of a popular hearsay back in the valley. Frankly, he felt the place appeared rather dead and stagnant. His eyes wandered to shut now. He knew that he had to find a motel room to spend the night rather than face the reality of spending the night with his grandmother or uncle. After rolling onto 77 Sunset Strip, he began hunting for a woman in his typical valley style. His erection began pushing and bulging to one side of his trousers. The strip was long enough for viewing; the nightclubs were too expensive to enter, and the time was becoming the early morning hours. Julian was physically dead and exhausted. The Chevrolet pickup truck began moving slower, and Julian had examined a dozen prostitutes. At first, he considered them fairly ugly, the majority being black gals from San Francisco.

He circled twice around the boulevard. His eyes were glued to a medium-size girl walking across the lines of the street where a large mansion-built convention center sat hidden behind a long row of tall palm trees. At the end of her walk, she sat herself down on a bench as if she were waiting for a taxi. Julian's truck pulled to one side of the roadway. Julian leaned over to the passenger side and rolled the window down. There were few cars on the street now.

"Say! How about a date?" asked Julian in a very casual in tone. "Okay, honey. I think you'd better park now," she replied. Next, she climbed into the truck and picked up the edges of her long light-pink dress in a very ladylike fashion.

She was a black gal. The high heels on her shoes matched the dark-brown stones of the earrings, and the long black hair curled down her back almost to her waist. A rose of bright colors was pinned to one side of her forehead. The definite features of her face complemented her large beautiful dark eyes. "Hello. My name's Rosemary. What's all yours, hun?" she quickly asked another question.

They both rode a mile before coming to a motel driveway. A neon sign overhead read: "Sunset Motel Drive."

"Sounds like a deal, babe, or would you rather make love here on the seat somewhere?"

"No. I need a place to stay for the night anyway. I'm just passing through town," he replied. Julian was less nervous now and somewhat calm. He parked inside the hotel drive and shut the ignition off. They both thought for a moment, because they had been followed earlier by someone in the area close by where a film shooting was taking place. She had conducted business prior to meeting Julian.

But what if he showed up now, here? he thought. What if he was her boss and she had been lying about her identity? He remembered the one time back in Raisintown when a gigolo approached him with a knife. "What's the matter buddy boy? Weren't you satisfied? Get the hell out of here now, Mexican boy. Weren't you satisfied? Weren't you satisfied?" the voice echoed louder through his right one, as if she knew when to read his mind. "Listen. Come on now. I've been waiting all day long for you, and you know it. Now, I'll tell ya, honey, you go pay her fura room up front while I sneak out this other way, meantime. These managers here don't like us street womens, ya understand? They'd call da police on us in no time—all these Arabs and Japanese dat run these here places, you know! Tell the manager a room for one."

And sure enough, when Julian approached the window of the office manager, a gentle-looking oriental man lay on the couch inside, watching the television.

"Say, I need a room for one," asked Julian.

"One sixteen dollars room for two. Twenty-two dollars. Room 12. Only room available." His Chinese accent carried on heavily. Julian hesitated.

"Okay. Okay, I'll take it. I'll take it! I'll be leaving in the morning."

He took hold of the keys and trotted upstairs where Rosemary was waiting for him. There was a cold chill in the air. She grasp the key from Julian, who was becoming very nervous by this time. The door to the room was jammed and hard at opening; however, with one huge push by Julian's arms, it flung open. The room was dark and cold. They both walked in, and at once, Julian turned on a small electric heater that stood against the wall. With one pull of the zipper, her dress fell off with ease, and her dark body was revealed. She asked for her payment of twenty dollars. "I'll stay with ya one hour, babe," she said.

Her body was fine, and she had enormous hips. There was no hesitation; Julian quickly handed her the twenty-dollar bill, took off his clothes, and jumped in bed where she lay flat and easy. He put his hands between her legs and grabbed her buttocks as he caressed and fondled with her large breasts, panting…sucking on her dark nipples. He plunged into her vagina, spewing juices all over the sheets. *Yes, a final exasperation, exaltation! How fortunate!* he thought to himself as he lay underneath the covers. A car outside had stopped alongside the boulevard outside the apartment's window. And all that could be seen were the high-rising neon lights of the nightclubs, restaurants, and the old buildings of what were left of Hollywood's backdoor, the remnants and ghosts of her past residing in her nightly sleep. "Good night, Julian. Good night!" whispered the wind.

Julian had never made this trip to Los Angeles very many times, and with each time he embarked, the closer the city would come toward the valley. Time was diminishing, shrinking smaller, smaller…and away went the tire treads to the Japanese-built truck, one hundred thousand miles, or four times around the world. What a haul it was. What a pile of unwanted garbage.

The spring of '79 rolled in, and the signs of summer began showing their curse. Julian's cabin appeared as an orbiting satellite spaceship. After five years of struggling with the idea of nuclear fission, he despairingly passed the chemistry course at the College of the Sequoias, which he so longed for. What a relief it was to have conquered a small portion of pastoral-minded intellectualism.

The old airfield, where the famed Rankin Military Academy during World War TI had operated, was located about four miles from where Katherine, the redheaded nurse, had lived. High above from what remained of the former hangars, Julian began his actual true flying days, performing flights and beginning aerobatics training. *This time he's really flipped his mind!* thought the nurses at the hospital. Julian knew only one thing certain; he had butterflies again. This occasion called for his orthodox behavior so much more now than ever. He acted like a flying bat coming out of hell and without radar. His aerobatics training was becoming intensive, and during this time, the hallways at the county hospital, which were being painted yellow, gleamed with new activity.

There was still no such thing or person who could be called a socialized doctor, at least not as people had known. But thank God for socialized medicine. Total rip-off funds resulted in about $180-per-day stay for a round of care during better times. A person couldn't afford to breathe too fast, or one would always end up paying between 96 cents to one dollar for a gallon of gas. Americans were spoiled, and so as their wet dreams came, so did Julian's. Even at this time, some of the orbiting satellites of the Americans were beginning to lose their symmetry, and more and more of them would soon be plummeting to earth during a "patient wait" by even more Americans. Yes, and in the hallways at night in the county hospital, the patients were waiting to die, and so were the workers waiting to die, waiting to die an unknown, forgotten death, like satellites losing their eminence, life, and the power to detect and observe. Certainly! This was exactly the way Americans acted. And why not? Their own lust for life had just left them; the great actor, John Wayne, had recently died. However, the walls erecting themselves outside of the county hospital seemed as ancient as the first day they were erected in 1922. Summertime was here!

Terron, Julian's older brother, had with him the patience to remain alone without being a married man. This wasn't saying much for marriage in those days during the past turbulent sixties. People just weren't getting married anymore. Living together and playing house was the most sufficient method to use.

The Church of the Sacred Heart was the same place in which their mother was married, and it was there that Terron married his second time. Julian was ironically on time in his arrival; he had driven over from Dairytown after waking up that morning.

The pews inside the church were vacated, and there were not many people using them. And the delicate sounds of music flowed from Rafael's guitar as he sang the songs that he had composed earlier as always. And the songs were very clergical and religious in nature, not so much folk as they were depressing.

Julian smiled—a quaint waving of his hand—as he walked down the aisle to the back of the church. He recognized the majority of the faces; many of them were Guillermo's old friends. His steps ended toward the entrance door, being that he had walked from the front of the church, the side entrance next to the altar. His uncle Samuel stood there at the entrance door as was Julian's sister, Anna. And his mother looked as glamorous and as beautiful as the day she had married Joaquin. Sandra, dressed in white, only stared at him. Whispering voices rang out, and the small conservatively dressed crowd waited pretentiously.

"Julian, Julian!" It was the voice of his mother coming from the waiting room. "What's wrong with you? Have you forgotten? Take both of your grandmothers by the hand, lead them down the aisle, and seat them. And when you return, take this other woman by the hand and seat her."

"Who is she?" he asked with a whisper.

"This is Sandra's mother, and this man is her father." Julian's jaw dropped as he looked twice. The woman was wearing a white veil and very attractive. Her hair was blond, and she carried with her a quaint quietness about her modest self.

"How do you do?" she spoke in a soft tone. There was a black man standing next to her; he was very light-complected and partly baldheaded, but the fact that he smiled and grinned so much detracted from his features. He quietly nodded in a casual greeting. Sandra was a black girl.

Surprised and after all forgetting everything that one does in a conventional wedding, religiously of course, his mother constantly reshaped him throughout the entire ceremony. Even after the bride and groom had walked out, she was there, telling him what to do next. A fumbling dumbbell is whom everyone knew, and Julian knew the same feeling within himself. He was the last and far from the purest of examples whom she had always hung on to in her mind, and Julian was always there evading from her hurt feelings. This was so much for keeping to the cherished memory of her dead husband and, for Julian, to the memory of his father.

The ceremony was not a long ceremony, less than one-half hour. Julian's nephew, the groom's son, sat next to him in the front-row pew. The fiery eyes of the priest fixated on Julian's actions until the time his sermon had finished. Julian would frequently turn around and notice how sad Sandra's mother appeared as she stood there in the opposite side of the main aisle.

Sandra was the only person who cried as she received kisses, hugs, and the usual congratulatory compliments received by most couples who became the newly-weds during this particular hour.

"All captains and janitors lined up with me in the rear of the line!" shouted Julian with a sarcastic tone. The next moment, he noticed Sandra's father walking out of the church with a short, fat-stomached woman, his second wife. The stream of activity was making some sense. And with conclusions, notwithstanding, it was to be Joaquin's second wedding. The visitors' cars departed the grounds of the church and dispersed in different directions to Maria's ranch, which lay twenty miles away northward for a final reception.

Dressed in his best white slacks, red shirt, dark tan tie, and light overcoat, Julian could have fooled anyone there that day, any strangers except members of his own family. So the world was indeed shrinking smaller in size, and its bigness was gone forever.

And in those puzzling and piercing sixty miles that separated him and his mother, Julian had led himself to believe his own feelings had covered sixty thousand miles around the world. Yet the vault that kept him locked up, the entombed passion that enslaved his own idea of freedom drove him to the cold, the cold that neither his brothers nor sister seemed to understand, they tried with all their hearts to avoid.

When Father's Day came around that year, he remembered driving to Smith Mountain to lay flowers at the cemetery, and afterward, having a watchman close the gate on him while executing an attempt to visit the lumber mill where his father used to work.

A quick flash struck his mind. The Avenue 12 road sign appeared to one side of the freeway and on his windshield. He knew that he was on his way to his mother's house, where everybody was waiting inside. A small, small world with large ego-inflated minds is what it was. And Julian was no exception.

It was a hot afternoon in Winetown, the same afternoon when Terron had married the second time; the sun was ablaze, setting toward the western skies and sinking to the horizon. As if the clear blue of the heavens had never noticed a wedding had taken place, neither had many people.

Julian's uncle, Samuel, had finished driving his Ford Mustang into Maria's driveway, as Julian himself arrived from the west side of the freeway. Both cars had one side door colored different from their original paint jobs. There were cars and vans parked everywhere. The crowd became more noisy toward the rear of the house where the reception was taking place next to Maria's twelve-foot-deep swimming pool. "I'll park here in the driveway just in case I have to make a quick getaway. You know?" chuckled Samuel with a sarcastic smile.

Julian grinned and carried with him a middle-sized brown paper bag that contained his cutoff pants and a few other small shaving pieces. "Mom! Long time no see!" he said jokingly as he met his mother. There was a mariachi orchestra playing away into the heat of the day, and a pit covered with palms had been dug to roast the meats. Guillermo and Rafael had spent much time obviously in preparation of the gathering. Many persons were not recognizable. Slowly, the faces began to fall into place.

Of course, it would remind you of a typical 1979 wedding reception, with only several guests fantasizing the days of the Old South—belles and gabachas. There weren't any fights, arguments, or threats until after the dark hours set in. Juanita's family was there, and Terron's friends were present. Julian, Samuel, and Joaquin were once again the only loners. The beer was plentiful, and soon a good number of the guests were in a drunken stupor.

A tall, slim blonde asked Julian to sit next to her side. She wore a large round hat covered with a pink bonnet. Louise was married to Alex, a long-time old friend to Terron who happened to be a little Terron's godfather and a manager for a chain market store near Sacramento. She kissed Julian on the cheek; he rather blushed.

"Those are my boys out there," she said while pointing to three young kids playing in the pool alongside with relatives and a crowd of others.

The honking of horns drowned out as a caravan of cars came plowing through the east-end driveway. A white 1956 Rolls-Royce, in which rode the bride, groom, best man, and Anna, Julian's sister, led the string of cars. Guillermo was wearing a large Spanish gangster bracero-type hat, a kind seen in early movies.

"We wanted everything to be white," he stated out. "I don't know about you, but I'm enjoying myself." It was Juanita who showed off her dancing talents, as she and Terron danced away for minutes to the tune of "La Bamba." For once, Julian stayed reserved. He had to because he hated to be the main center of attention, and many times he felt that he was at his own wedding.

Tagchi was not a physically tall person and stood at five feet, well below a six-footer. He was very muscular, dark-complected, and wore a mustache. His hair was so long that he was able to fit it all into a turbine on his head. He was from India and lived in Raisintown on his father's ranch. They had grapes as did many of the Indians who lived near this El Camino Real at the time. Julian remembered meeting this mysterious Indian. Tagchi had been discharged from the US Army. It was at that time in which Guillermo and Tagchi had become very close friends to one another. Tagchi's father was a millionaire, and so this millionaire's son carried much influence on these rural people wherever he would go to. He especially influenced Alex, a former Vietnam veteran who had always stated that his big desire in life was to join the mafia as a successful godfather.

David Segura was more of a freeloader profile and hard-going. Yet he was carefree enough to not give a damn hell about the more demanding things of society, being that he was also a casualty of the Vietnam War. Shot point-blank at the hip while in the jungle, he was shipped back to California.

"Why else would we meet here to talk about Chicanos and Cesar Chavez…about what you call *life*, David?" asked Julian.

"Because it's the best place to meet. Hell, it is too!" answered David. Louisa and several women sitting at the poolside pretended not to hear. Julian, as always, did one thing wrong once more; he became drunk and took everything too serious. Even the water of the pool became too cold as did an easterly breeze. The guest faded away into the night, and only those who were drunk enough to remain stayed sitting and drinking around the poolside.

The voices were becoming loud because of the beer. A few bodies gathered near the heating unit of the pool. Julian had a towel thrown over his back. The turbine of the Indian could be seen, and Joaquin's tall slim body came walking on the cement walk as he carried a bottle of tequila in one hand. The curtains began to fall all at the same time, as if a daydream had taken place in a God-given demented mind that could no longer hold back the epitome of any performance. The show was over. The stage lights were turned on like some do after concluding acts. The crowd began to disperse, and there were several applauses; however, there were more ears and mouths that remained shut. Suddenly, the splashing of the water came to a silence.

"Julian. Come on now! Your mother and I only did this…you know, the pool and everything…so that you, your brothers, and sister could use it," said Joaquin. "Can't you ever enjoy anything without having to criticize everything?" He could not have said it better.

Julian stared back at him; the adrenaline of this young man's stomach couldn't have turned to steam any faster. "Now just what the hell makes you think that I come to parties just to break them up, Joaquin. What makes you think, mister?" Julian's voice trembled, and his temper flared. "She never had to marry you. Besides, whoever said you needed to get married to her anyway?"

"As you're also against your brother getting married this time… right?" The voice interrupting was that of the Indian Tagchi. Julian paused and continued staring at Joaquin.

"Now, who is he supposed to be, your personal adviser?" Joaquin chuckled and looked toward Tagchi. "You know, Julian? Your brothers helped to set up all of this…preparations, plans…you know, the works," he said with persuasive eyes.

"If a man can't even use his hands because he doesn't want to, he shouldn't consider himself much of a man," said Tagchi.

The children remained standing and gathered closely together. Alex walked toward them, grabbed at them, and told them to leave the corner of the poolside. He himself also departed from the scene. Terron remained on the opposite side of the pool, uninvolved. And why should he get involved? After all, it was only a slight argument concerning interracial marriage, and Julian had the only talent for carrying it on without exploding into a fist free for all.

"Yeah! I know all about it. Never on earth are they my causes which my mother has ever supported. My causes have never meant anything. I never do get the break, do I, Joaquin? It's just like you with your own brothers and sisters and the similar problem you have with your own mother. Right, Joaquin?" shouted Julian.

Joaquin's face was blank, and he was unable to say another word; he walked away and mumbled to Tagchi that Julian was impossible. This was nothing new during these occasions. Tagchi stood there, picking his nose, and stared into the night sky, and Julian accompanied him and stood.

This Indian and Mexican stood awhile in an apologetic pose. Rafael and Terron were now singing songs with the few remaining guest, and the voices to these folk songs sounded melancholy and peaceful into a waning evening. Tagchi handed a large bowl of olives to Julian while many of the guest were leaving the house.

The corrals, which stood on the fairgrounds across from Julian's cabin in Dairytown, were old with spiderwebs. Being older than the hospital in age, this corral's paint, whose colors were red, white, and blue, faded into the dusty floor of the fairground's arena. And in these fairgrounds—a dismal, haunting place that it was—there bustled with activity and fervor during carnival days, with displayed farm equipment, conducted various amusement shows and rodeos. For Julian, it was a place to go to be alone. At times, during late nights, he would jump the fence and sit on the bleachers. Next, he would peer onto the track that was once used for racing quarter horses and was now used for racing motorcycles. She stood a frightening old place, but so did most other county fairgrounds. An old man could be seen from the road, working in the corrals, cleaning and dusting the floors, bailing hay and brushing and bathing the horses. A dozen horses would occupy those corrals; they ranged in colors from red to spotted black and white, from ponies to stallions. There was a particular mare that stood out in the sun with a glistening reddish-brown color. Julian didn't know anything about horses, and at this time, he could have cared less. Nor did he want to paint a picture of a horse either; however, he did one anyway.

During this time of any equestrian experience, there was a thirty-nine-year-old brunette woman he had met in college. Julian actually thought to himself that he was in love with this woman. She was married to a pathologist who lived in the better area of Almondtown. Their two-story-built stucco home was located near a golf course.

Julian wasn't sure why he ever associated with her. Perhaps an inner chauvinistic emptiness drove him to begin speaking to this attractive woman who reminded him of a famous movie star actress. She had four sons and was the owner of seven horses in Virginia. And through all of this, she had time to manage the affairs of her husband, who was a doctor at one of the hospitals in Almondtown. These city hospitals were the arch-rivals of the old county hospital, and the employees between this inter-county-city contest were always at war with one another. Julian wasn't certain whether he was being attracted to her or using her to manipulate the auspices and reputation of the medical society of the county area. There were not many persons Julian had become acquainted with because of manipulative tendencies. He never dared people in this manner.

Early that same summer, Julian would leave his work station at the hospital in the morning, cross the street, and sit inside the rodeo judge's box next to the arena corner that overlooked Saint Rita's Catholic Church. The mornings were hot, but Julian did not hesitate to begin sketching the mare inside the corral and in the arena where he met Melanie. Melanie made the horse behave in a way that he had never seen before in his life. She was from a nearby town. Her French last name matched her long dark-brown hair and eighteen-year-old appearance. He was awed by the way she turned the horse. She acted like horse trainers on the television and the youngest one he had ever seen in real life. She was a very quiet person, very reserved, and didn't speak much. When the sun had shown the high-noon shadow, it didn't speak much. When the sun had shown the high-noon shadow, it didn't make any difference how hot the weather became. Julian received a first close look at horses for the first time in his life.

"Can you make the horse spin?" said Julian as she rode by the judge's grandstand. "Would you allow me to ride her?"

"And just who are you?" she asked as she turned to his direction.

"My name is Julian. I work across the street at the county hospital."

"What do you do there anyway?" she asked with a puzzled expression.

He only smiled at her with searing eyes. "Oh, I just more or less mind my own business there," he answered and grinned. His pencil moved across the sketch pad between each pause of the conversation. The sketch of the horse began to visualize the action that she instilled in the animal.

"I'm from the northeastern side of Almondtown, and I've heard plenty about that hospital," she said. "I've heard that it's a very nice hospital." The statement struck the bells with Julian. Both of them spoke about their mothers who were teachers.

"I just don't know whether I've learned anything from my mother," said Julian. She kind of chuckled at the statement and stepped back with the horse. Not even the horse trusted Julian. "How about having a beer with me over at my place? My room is across the street from the grandstand."

"No thanks!" she answered. "You bring it here to me, and I'll drink it."

Julian soon learned that most of the other girls who'd bring their own horses were from the northeastern area of Almondtown. They all had one color in common, horses.

Horses were not the only disturbances and curiosities in Julian's mind. Every Sunday, Julian spent the afternoons shooting his .38-caliber revolver at a range between Almondtown and Dairytown. This day was the only time open to the civilian public. After leaving the range, a time before dinner, he began conducting visits to the golf course in Almondtown. He'd stop at the doctor's house, where he had been contracted to paint the picture of the horse.

"Who's he trying to impress this time?" asked the police officer who was acting as the chaperon at the range. He thought to himself, *He's one of the strangest ones out here!*

Fairmount Drive was a dead-end street. Butterflies rose inside Julian's stomach after driving into the street's oval terminal, and his anxiety increased each time he approached the front door of the doctor's house, the home to where he delivered the picture of the horse. This encounter resembled an old movie about the Deep South, and the doctor's wife would help along in staging and keeping the fantasy alive. The painting of the horse had taken the character of the '79 Christmas. The stallion was completed: velvet-colored black, wild, and untamed against the blue sky and white clouds of dust from the ground.

Final testing for the fall classes at the college in Almondtown was being completed. Julian played "Aura Lee" on the piano for a music grade, and how monotonous and boring was the soaring Cherokee airplane as it flew over Smith Mountain on those ill-fated weekend flights that Julian had made back to his hometown, Lumbertown. Julian's Christmas shopping spree had taken him to several department stores in Almondtown. When the doctor's wife had sold him a small yellow bird similar to a parakeet, which she had pulled from her patio's birdcage, Julian felt his duties were finished for the vacation. He took the bird to his mother's house that same week only to find that her white cat had different ideas of trying to keep the flying creature alive. A cat-and-bird game—a bird in a cage—is the way everybody criticized the occasion.

Several evenings before Christmas Day arrived, Julian sold the painting of the horse over a glass of Cutty Sark and a rather bizarre family gathering as the doctor's wife handed him a check for two hundred and fifty dollars. Julian could have stopped his story here; after all, there were countless deals made in the history of the world not necessarily over horse races but over love affairs that turned out to be less than disastrous. Moreover, fantasies that exist in people's minds can also result in a rather severe earthquake, equally disastrous.

The doctor's sons were there that night. Her youngest was in a wheelchair; he was paralyzed from an automobile accident, long haired and her favorite. The oldest was a salesman and a student in San Diego. The doctor looked on with sad eyes, sympathetic, and took sides with Julian at all times. Julian was reserved and stayed that way until the time he walked out the front door of the house. The Sunday before Christmas, the doctor's wife handed him a photograph of herself, which had been processed back in October. The photograph would be transformed into an oil painting as always. Julian was becoming a bohemian wholesaler, but this time, he was trying to sell his only snub-nose. Like a cheap detective, he conducted his business.

After the New Year's celebration was over, Julian was fired one night at the county hospital. Julian walked out of the stone building very sullen and deliberate; he carried a letter of termination, which had written on it that his services were not needed any longer. A fat nurse whose last name was Jewish sat at the nursing office desk and solemnly handed the note to him. He walked through the hallway with his head down and trotted his steps to the back door. After he boarded his truck in the parking lot, he started the engine and rode across town.

His mind couldn't believe it. He thought, *All I said was that there should be a better way to rear hospital children with all of this county education.*

What would he do now? Money? Should he move? Instead, he lay relaxed on his bed mattress. He stared at the holes in the ceiling and remembered the prior morning at the hospital as he expressed his views about children at the hospital on the medical floor. He was told to keep his mouth shut by the supervisor nurse whose last name was Jewish. A blessing in disguise was another word for insubordination. The hospital was a large old building at the corner now; she stood there more frightening than ever, impeccable, undeniable, memorable, and no longer Julian's place of work.

In the weeks that followed, the pursuit of his medical dream utopia was waning. After debating with a crowd of angry money-hungry scavengers, a group of eager Chicanos from Earlimart, he sold his old 1957 Ford Fairlane to an Okie from Almondtown. Julian received a modest sum of four hundred dollars for her. She was gone. At last, sold. Her weight was taken off his shoulders.

"I think I've killed her," he whispered to himself.

The spring had passed since that car sale, and Julian found himself flunking the chemistry course at the Almondtown College. A field trip sponsored by the school had taken him to Sequoia Lake located in the mountains above Almondtown. The day had been spent trying to find a hidden cabin used by several of the science instructors at the college. Once again, employment lay on his mind.

After school was finished, Julian went to work for a medical pool agency in Almondtown. Like a cheap-paid butler, he began working for a handful of anonymous millionaires. The spring had ended, and his earnings were very little.

The thought of becoming a police officer had never run through Julian's mind. His weakness about the fantasies in television cops and government espionage centered itself about his own image of an illusory detective fighting windmills and sawmills.

"He wasn't fit for law enforcement work" is what the deputy marshal, a retired police officer, had told him. Julian remembered the words. "We don't need your kind in our business. What I'm interested in is a security guard, not an overrated John Wayne bastard prototype. Understand, Julian?"

Julian resigned, handing the supervisor his badge and uniform. He had only stood guard at two dances, three Sundays at a county flea market, and a few nights at a supermarket that was losing a great deal of money because of the active shoplifters it harbored. He was never able to catch anybody red-handed, acting as an undercover guard. *It's plenty of trouble for just a small bag of stolen flower seeds*, thought Julian.

Indeed, for a simple bag of seeds, the trouble to find them was seen upon as a futile task. An R & N Supermarket was the grounds where he tried out his security undercover debut. Despite having a .38-caliber detective special, a two-inch snub-nosed revolver, he failed the qualifying exam for having the weapon state certified at the nearest police academy range located northeast of Almondtown. He began working at a convalescent hospital in Almondtown when he wasn't working for the medical pool agency. The convalescent hospital was a feces dungeon—long morning hours, adult school classes, and a county view of an old hospital revisited.

Julian was assigned to one particular millionaire, an old man who was a home call live-in partner. It was at this time that Julian met Shirley during a late evening of this June of 1980. The millionaire's apartment was located near the main highway that led to the mountains and was only a short walk across the traffic to a corner restaurant-bar lounge called the Flame. She was a fifty-two-year old woman, tall enough to meet the eyes: reddish hair, huge round eyes, plumpish stature, and smoked simultaneously as she tipped a glass on her lips. She sat there on the couch with a large pink bathrobe over her naked body.

"Come on in, man! Take off your boots and have a seat. Calm down!" she said. She mumbled a chuckle. At first hand, Julian thought she looked tipsy like a drunk woman. The old man with a brown oak pipe sat in a corner in front of a television set.

"How do you do? Sit down," she commanded after a soft and mild question. And with this call of voice, Julian would be paced in the months to come not only by this man but by others as well. And there were plenty of millionaires in Almondtown.

Julian began talking with her. She was from New York and was living in Florida before coming to California. Throughout the entire conversation, she hinted from time to time that they should go to bed together. She bent over him, showing as much cleavage as possible and puffing on her Tiparillos. As he tried to show his growing sexual intentions, Julian felt uneasy while he sat next to her on the couch; he would wonder about her big city accent and slick, fast character. Her breath smelled of vodka and burnt cigarette smoke. The same smell of her breath was always contiguous every night that Julian arrived to the apartment where the millionaire lived. The time of Julian's arrival was always at ten o'clock in the evening. She would tell him to use the empty bedroom, and she always slept on the couch in the living room. This situation was soon to become a live-in basis where he would stay the night over.

One night, she walked into the empty bedroom where Julian lay his body down and jumped into the bed with him.

"Make love to me," she told him. Julian froze in a reluctant pose.

The late show appeared on the television. *The best thing for me to do is to leave. Now!* he thought. An uneasy feeling overtook his intentions, and he never did more than kiss her on her lips a few times, once or twice. She lay there in bed, belly up and holding onto a cigarette in her left hand. Julian was sitting up into a semi-prone position and staring at her with his head turned down.

"Well! Now…just what the hell is so wrong? What are you anyway… some kind of a fag? Hell! You don't even act like a man." Shirley's voice began to rise above the tumult of the bed sheets. "Where did you learn how to touch or hold a woman? You know something? You're nothing but a filthy son of a bitch!" Julian passed any revenge with that remark, remaining silent as if reluctant to swallow his pride. She sat herself upright in the bed, slipped into her nightgown and walked into the living room.

"Go ahead and stay in bed," she consoled him. "Don't get up. Stay overnight. Good night!" Feelings of shame and guilt overcame Julian's conscience. And no sooner was he getting dressed that he walked out through the living room and toward the front door.

"Typical of him," she spoke to herself.

"Who in the damn hell are these people anyway?" he asked himself the question during the drive back to his apartment, the motel. "I'm supposed to be working as an assistant for the nursing agency and not acting like an imaginary insurance agent for the New York Playboy Club." Each time he would leave their apartment to return to his motel room, a familiar feeling of alienation overpowered him with guilt, hatred, and an estrangement long remembered and burrowed deep within him since his early childhood days.

The days passed on, and Julian spent several evenings with Shirley and the old man during assignments with the agency. After he and this woman ironed out each other's differences, they became compatible for the first time in this untimely acquaintance. A relationship was indeed taking on a moral heaviness with Julian.

It was the last time Julian saw Wanda, a local prostitute, in his motel room by the Santa Fe tracks. An early summer day afternoon, it was the day before he moved Shirley to a new apartment located next to the college in Almondtown. These were those evenings during the late blossoming months. Julian was in the midst of his motel's mattress of saying hellos and goodbyes from the cracks on the walls of his kitchen, to the stitchery of the roses formed on the curtains of his closet. The portrait of the doctor's wife stared at him with even greater surveillance as he lay against the head of the large bed. The fading fancy of his business deals were evident from the dried sticky character of his pillows.

The knocks were heard at the front door again as similar to in the past. Wanda stepped inside, slow and cautious. The museum-like feeling of isolation was quickly broken by her presence—the sound of the old cracked laced screen door shut while children played outside. The barking of dogs could be heard. As always, Julian lay on his left side; he faced the closet. The next moment, she crawled into bed with him and huddled herself close to his long slender back. The cooler noise was drowning the sounds coming from outside the cabin. He felt her warm body and her breast against his own figure.

"It's a beautiful picture," she whispered. "I like it. She's a very beautiful lady. Who is she?"

"She's married to a doctor in Almondtown."

"Oh yeah!" she replied as she crawled over him with her legs. "How much did you say she'll give you for it?" she asked, smiling and chuckling. She stared into him and continued questioning his position.

"Where's your wallet. Where's your money?" The sounds of the water dripping down the cooler's pads hissed within the quiet cabin. With every revolution from the pulley of the fan, the knot on the rope that substituted for a belt was the only noise being heard. *No belt, but plenty of attention, plenty of attention today*, he thought. The belt was absent, and in all forms of discipline, there was a local discovery. When a young man of twenty-seven finds out what a piece of life is all about, he not only finds out, but he then begins to tell everyone about it. When no one listens, he'll begin to paint a picture about it, trying to materialize what he's found, like a giant rat scratching the walls of a maze when looking for the piece of cheese at the end of those hallways, and to think of all those unlocked doors, its image and memory by friend and foe become remembered as it races through the catacombs of its mind. Moreover, the beast within seems to give its glance at every corner, like a giant black cat haunting everything within each and every step it takes. If Freud were alive today, he may have decided to have given up his practice. The belt was gone.

Driving through Almondtown in an economized dented truck and being seen with an older redhead woman of lived years didn't bother Julian. Nobody exactly knew who he was anyway. As for Shirley, she could be seen next to the college. With a small walk down the alley toward the light post on the corner, a Pizza Hut, a hairstyle boutique for women, and a small-claims office, her room was locked underneath a two-story complex with a medium-sized swimming pool on the corner. The depth of the pool was twelve feet.

"Why don't you move in with me, Julian, and move out of that shit shack by the tracks? You can't be that dumb now, can you?" Shirley asked him and pleaded with him. Those same feelings of mixed emotions raced through his mind: preponderance, guilt, and fear of revealing his identity to a strange woman from a big city. These feelings and her tempting approach handcuffed his awareness.

Who was she, really? he asked himself. His eyes suddenly turned into a squint, like a look of a detective when he finds a lead on a big score. She was certainly no prize for the senior citizen ring of common folks' valley dream, nor was she exactly a spring chicken neither. It wasn't her looks or appearance or even what she professed to be that he fell in love with. Her past is what he really fell in love with. This is what he clamored and thirsted for deep inside, like an ulcer disappearing with every movement of a hungry stomach. Julian felt that he was home again, and the small voice inside of him was speaking to him. "Oh, dear black sheep! You've gone astray once more. It's time to go to mass and hear confessions… confessions about your past."

How else could Julian have handled this affair? If you had departed from work where you smelled human feces and rotten decubitus for eight-plus hours, you decide that home is the best place. When you find a strange woman dressed in a black nightgown, sitting in a chair and telling you that she dated Nelson Rockefeller and had a social acquaintance with the late Marilyn Monroe, first you would wonder in amazement—a lying verdict—but in the end, you would listen. You would sit there and listen, because the older generation would always have something to talk about…more so if you just sat there and listened.

When you fall in love with the past, it's because you're afraid of facing the present or falling in love with what is presented to you. Another person perhaps? Next, one goes about dwelling into the person's past by changing those events that might have been avoidable regardless of how unavoidable they might have been. Racing through life, as in a fast-paced scene, trying to emulate another person unconsciously, acting out separate roles, we meet each other with our feelings. Do we, by chance, enjoy salutations with one another, or are these encounters serious duties of search and seizure, as in police and civic tasks, where a person's age and the time mean nothing at all? The only free cherishables are the emotions, wants, and desires. The appearances and looks show the past, perhaps too blindly! The voice inside of Julian rang out once more, "Dear Lord, I think I've caught me a criminal. I might as well become one myself."

"I just can't believe what you're telling me, Shirley!" exclaimed Julian. "I can't sit here and have you believing that I confide in what you say."

"Believe what you want," she answered back while puffing away on the cigarette. She stood herself upright and prepared him a drink, vodka with 7 Up. The hours were always spent watching late movies on the television set. They would lie around the living room and do nothing.

"You can use the empty room in there," she said, pointing to one of the bedrooms. "I'll sleep out here on the couch." As she had always offered hospitality in a demanding tone, Julian would always refuse anxiously by leaving through the back door of the kitchen, boarding his pickup truck, and then drive back to his apartment. As if being pressured by a great number of tantamount commitments, he returned to the shack by the tracks, the make-believe office in front of the fairgrounds.

There he was, looking at the ceiling. A jailhouse silence cloaked about his own timidity. Wanda never came around the cabin anymore. The portrait of the doctor's wife was no longer sitting on the chair in the kitchen, and the only image that haunted him was the older redheaded woman, Shirley. He definitely felt the age of years creep up on him, now whispering, "Old man, you're going too fast. Slow down! There's too much to be seen. You only think you're an old man, but you're only a fresh speck of dust afraid to be blown into the wind. All around you, the endless grains of sand, lost in those small bits of iron, remind you of fool's gold. You fool! You're really not worth that much at all."

Julian found himself staying with her at the apartment much more that he had realized. She was a home to him, so it seemed. She also let him know it too. He remembered how she would come on to him with a strong and aggressive personality, encumbering his own inexperience like a mother at times. She was a hard city woman and remained a friend…a mysterious friend.

The Fourth of July had arrived, and the Friday night was filled with local activity in Almondtown. Julian had been relieved from duty during the evening shift at the convalescent hospital. He headed for Shirley's apartment and entered through the kitchen's sliding door. The television set was turned on, as it always was when he arrived. Cigarette smoke filled the air as did the burning scent of Acapulco Gold. Cans of beer covered with burnt ashes blended in dark against the sharp shimmering glaze of the cocktail glasses. The figures of people sat around the living room with eyes staring onto Julian as he walked through the kitchen floor. The shadowy figures revealed themselves one by one, and strange faces appeared.

"How's it going, Julian? Come on in. Sit down and have a beer," demanded Shirley. Another voice echoed out, "Well, check it out! It looks like a doc. Hey, Doc! What do you know, buddy?"

"Hey, ese! What's happening, man?" said another voice. And the voices began coming on now, and more questions were being asked.

Julian sat down on the couch between a tall, fat Chicano who was twenty years old and a huge muscular-built long-haired Anglo also in his twenties. They offered Julian a joint of marijuana, and like always, he refused the urbane hospitality. Shirley looked toward him with receding eyes, as if telling him softly, "You'll never make it, kid…you chicken-shit tight-ass asshole."

"Give him a beer, and he'll be happy," commented Shirley. "Jesus Christ!" She was exasperated. The room became quiet.

It was obvious that Shirley loved to harbor strange guests, as Julian found out that most of these guys were former inmates from the sheriff's farm at the Sequoia Airfield. Shirley considered that these guys were the real-men prospects of the future. Hard-core dudes who wore no colors were exactly who they were. *Perhaps this was the method the crew of a nuclear submarine was reared by the US Navy. What depth! What a course! All torpedoes look strong, protruding, and stiff with weak minds. But when do you surface, and where and just how long does one show his face?* he thought. "How long does one perform in the face of the enemy—that is, of course, if you're interested in finding out who your culprit is: the supplier, the supporter, the merchant. Who in the damn hell is this sailor, anyway?"

"Do you love him?" the chubby one asked Shirley. With an abrupt movement and in an instant gesture, he turned to Julian. "Is she your mother?" Julian set his glass down, gulped, and held his breath all at once. He stared into the fat boy's eyes with untamed rage, not knowing what to say at first. Shirley leaned over with her hand on his neck and whispered into his ear that he shouldn't worry. Most of these guys lived next door or down the boulevard lane. They were shoddy characters with frizzy hairdos and deep ethnic faces which would frighten you at first glance. But underneath their pot-scented characters, they were plain scared and running away from the law.

The clock on the wall showed one thirty in the morning. The kitchen door was wide open, and people were walking in and out of the apartment, others unaware they were walking at all because of being so drunk through the night. Outside, the noise of cars filled with teenagers raced up and down the boulevard, wild, while the sounds of Harley Davidsons drowned out the mufflers and brakes on the street.

The alley was dark, and a liquor store separated the parking lot from the streetlights. The group of partygoers walked to the rear of the parking lot, where they took to leaning up against the bed of Julian's pickup truck with beer and whiskey in some hands and marijuana reefers in the other hands. Julian, not pretending to be drunk, stood there next to them and pretended to listen. Shirley had her arms around him. She began kissing him on his cheek very slowly. He completely resisted her when two bike riders drove to where they were standing. The bikers had roared into the alley with their girlfriends clinging to their backs. They were Anglos, wore dark glasses, black jackets, and dark sunglasses. All these riders on their machines had large smiles on their faces.

"Hey, man, what gives?" a tall, bulky one spoke out.

"Not much," Julian blurted out with a sarcastic note of a laugh. "I'm just passing through and shacking up with this rich old lady. You know?"

"Yeah! I know what you mean," answered the bulky one who was more brave than the others. "We used to belong to a Hell's Angels group in Sacramento. You know!" He continued speaking with a reserved tone. Next, he turned to Shirley, who always became enraged if someone mentioned her age.

"And you know? You ought to buy him a big two-story house with a swimming pool so you can invite my girlfriend over and give her lessons on how to make love. You know?" By this time, Julian didn't know how to act or what to say. They all laughed. The bikes left the area. Shirley dragged Julian into the apartment. She locked the kitchen door once she and Julian were inside the building.

Summer nights will always be summer nights: a cliché you'll always hear from people who look forward to an underrated time of the year, only because they work their asses off the remainder of the year. Teachers perhaps? Yes. It was during these same summer nights while working at the convalescent home, Julian began taking in offers too many, for he never refused to go swimming in the nude with her at twelve o'clock in the morning the many times he spent overnight at her apartment.

Strange enough, he never made any strong sexual advances toward her. She'd turn off the television set and strip herself down naked. Acting like a fifteen-year-old girl who didn't know any better, she viciously began stripping off his clothes from his body. Pulling on the clothing, she grabbed him everywhere she could think of. Julian was nude now, alone with this fifty-two-year-old woman. After lining up a few pillows on the rug, she offered another drink "Why don't we just go to the bedroom. Wouldn't it be easier?" spoke Julian with a soft tone in his voice.

"Are you kidding, baby? It's too stuffy in the bedroom. Come on…I want you to screw the hell out of me!" she yelled some.

If this is what the crazy woman wants, he thought, *I'll do it.*

He was uneasy at first. *Distasteful* and *gross* were not the only adjectives going through his pia mater. She was there, available, willing, and forceful. *If someone walked in unexpectedly and noticed a twenty-seven-year-old man screwing the hell out of a fifty-two-year-old woman on the floor,* Julian thought, *he wouldn't bother to turn and look. The caller would think to himself, shrug his shoulders, and say, "Oh well, summer nights will always be summer nights," and close the doors with a hopeful sigh.* He crawled on top of her, and her stomach jutted outward toward the ceiling with a benign gracefulness.

"You can have all you want, baby," she whispered into his left ear. "It's all yours."

The morning came. The sunlight shone through her living room window, and the rooms smelled of cigarette smoke. Empty bottles of beer cans and empty cocktail glasses decorated the tables. Shirley lay nude on the couch and was wrapped up in a huge white sheet. Julian stretched, yawned, and found himself on the large king-sized bed in her bedroom. Putting on his underwear and other small bits of clothing, he walked through the kitchen stealthily and out the back door without waking her up. He walked to the door of his pickup truck and unlocked it. His legs turned waterlike, and his feet became heavy with a tingling sensation. He noticed the silver toolbox on the inside corner of the pickup's bed was gone. After opening the door to the passenger's side, he lifted the back side of the seat. Moreover, he realized that his .38 special was also missing. In self-regret, he slammed the door shut and followed it with a kick to the side of the truck. By this time, the situation was tantamount to what the little truck needed. With a few more dents here and there, the truck began to take the appearance of a prized possession that only the owner of the local junkyard would relish when driving out through the heaps of car skeletons. Desperately, the owner will look for parts and paraphernalia.

The noise had awaken Shirley. "What's going on? Why are you up so early?" she said, yawning and parting her red hair with both hands and tumbling her body against the walls of the apartment, inside and outside of the back door. She walked through the carport in a daze, and she tripped herself now and then with the floor-length red gown that she wore. Yet through all this lack of stamina, she questioned Julian's anxious mood. She couldn't believe that he would be so ignorant as to be keeping his pistol in an unlocked pickup truck. *He deserved it*, she thought to herself.

It had only been a few weeks earlier that Julian's parents had come by her apartment to haul the truck back to Winetown because of a damaged clutch that needed repairing. It was only a short time after the clutch incident that Julian had to ride the bike of the next-door neighbor's young girl to nursing orientation classes at the convalescent home. It was a four-mile bike ride. He remembered how people made fun of him, especially all the girls at the adult school. *How else does a security guard, acting out the role of an orderly, get through life on hot summer nights?* he thought.

The summer August heat was belching forth her toll over the ground, and the early autumn began making her rendezvous for another season. Once in a while, Julian would drive back to the Fair Court

Motel, where a certain national familiarity seemed to overpower the commonplace appearance of the shack. Somehow, the idea that he was paying one hundred sixty-five dollars on rent for an empty room didn't strike the match in him anymore.

One morning, during a Sunday, the day after when Julian graduated from the nurse's aide class, Shirley surprised him once more. His spirit was lifted, but he continued make-believing he was some kind of a big-time detective, important and intelligent.

"I have a surprise for you," she plummeted with a sly, prudish gesture. She walked with a stately gait to the lampstand and turned herself around as if she were about to audition for a local talent show.

"Just yesterday, I was at the garbage dumpster. You know, the one at Almond Street. A couple of the neighbors' kids and myself was sifting in the garbage, and look at what I came up with!" She bent over, reaching underneath the table stand, and pulled out the .38 special. It was inside the pouch of the holster strap and looked as if it were in good shape.

"My gun! I don't believe it. How can I ever thank you!" He questioned her in his most sarcastic way. He hadn't meant what he had said in hiding the fact that he was disgusted and unhappy in seeing the gun again. "Just think, Julian! If it wouldn't had been for me, all your work across the boards would have been for nothing. Right?" she asked with a widened smile on her face. He hesitated. There was more silence, and he was at a loss for words. Sitting himself down on a chair, he allowed the butterflies to build up to the point of pretending not to be there. He was a cold character in more ways than one, and this one instance was nothing new nor different from other times earlier. However, New York Woman, a nickname he later gave to her, continued to make him feel comfortable in every way she possibly knew how!

The summer had ended, but that unquenchable flame had not died out. Julian really believed he was in love with this woman, at least he thought so. Julian thought too much; it was his main problem. It was similar to thinking about home; he could never get away from it. As he neared closer and closer to this woman, he forced himself to become careful about keeping his distance when going to bed with her. Not only does she have the energy of a fifteen-year-old girl in bed, but she also bred a flare for suddenly turning into an ever younger naive girl at times.

This is exactly what Julian explored. This is what he fell in love with. He wasn't in love with a fifty-two-year-old woman; it was her past which he fell in love with.

"But you can't have the past, Julian. It's not yours to keep," whispered the voice from inside his conscience. "You can't have it, because it doesn't belong to you."

She lay on her couch one evening and was wearing a black nightgown. Her face took the appearance of an exotic Bettie Davis with large droopy eyes and hands holding a Tiparillo in a sophisticated manner.

"I told you before, Julian. I spent a little over a year in the New York State Wakefield reformatory prison for women. My roommate was Ethel Rosenberg—you know, the woman who was accused of being an avowed communist—along with her husband," she said. She turned into a strange woman with a sudden barrage of ideas she spoke of. Julian listened tentatively with his hands supporting his chin and his eyes wider than ever.

How can I sit here and believe this woman? he thought to himself. *Why in the hell do I keep coming back to her? Why in the shit do I keep knocking on her backdoor? She's an old woman not attractive, fat around the stomach, long thin legs, and has wrinkled hands that you'd notice with each time she touched you. Man. Brother! Are you crazy or what? You should be hanging out with a real young broad somewhere.*

"Silence, silence!" whispered the voice inside of him again.

"Hell! What do you know, Julian? You're just a young catcher in the rye. I told you that there were two detectives in New York who were working for the mafia at the time. I was handed a bad rap for not supporting evidence when it came to testifying in court," she spoke. At this time, they were in a room, in a class all by itself, alone, curtains pulled, windows shut inside a cell, enclosed and separated from the present world. He felt alone with her now, and his questions were ever more personal and becoming more serious every minute.

"What evidence are you hiding, Shirley?" Julian asked, intruding like an exclusive defense attorney. "I wouldn't doubt that you probably killed somebody. A man perhaps? That's why you fled to Florida, and then from Florida you proceeded on to California?"

"Don't be silly, Julian. How could you say such a thing? Jesus Christ!" The capillaries on her face flushed to a crimson red. "What do you take me for, anyway?" She paused. "I already told you. While I was in New York, I was seeing a cop who turned out to be a stool pigeon. He was working for the mafia. This mafia threatened to kill me, if I talked in court."

"Who threatened to kill you?" He broke the conversation with a direct question.

"I told you…some men from the mafia. I was trying to protect the police officer. I went to prison, because I wouldn't talk in court!" There were knocks at her front door, and she stopped talking. Julian held his breath. Shirley answered the door, and there stood two figures both of darker complexion. Both the older woman and the young one had dark eyes and hair.

"I want you to meet some friends of mine, Julian," said Shirley. At this point, Shirley gave up the fact that she thought she was doing him a favor. Simultaneously, he thought he was doing her a favor.

It was only but a few days that had passed, and Shirley walked through the front door of his motel room. The younger of the Jamaican women followed her inside. Traces of the evening, a sunset gazed in through the kitchen window. Julian, lying in bed, covered himself with a blanket and acted too surprised to see that Shirley had brought with her a Jamaican girl whose name was Clara. Clara was the same figure who had visited Shirley the very same night Julian had paid her a visit.

Clara spoke an almost perfect Spanish. She was also a student over at the college next door to where Shirley lived. At a first appearance, she would remind someone of a Tahitian goddess: roses in her hair, large graphic eyes, rosy lips, and a blend of a dark complexion—a quiet disposition. To kiss her once was a haphazard experience. If you kissed her the second time, she would remind you of a typical Chicana from the valley—a not-so-typical female.

Both women removed their clothing and jumped into the bed with Julian—Clara to one side and Shirley to the other. He felt too uncomfortable in his self-honesty with what Shirley had done this time. He simply lay there with his mouth shut, and this kept the conversation from dying out.

So this is the woman who said she could get me anything I wanted to have. I guess this is her way of showing and keeping her word intact.

She figures that she'll grab me, use me, form, and brainwash my small-town country-boy mystique. She has the act for it. His thoughts raced through his mind. Julian gingerly crossed his arms together, clasping his armpits with a discouraged feeling of being ashamed. His body froze. He listened.

"I need a light, Clara. Pass me the cigarette lighter," said Shirley as she yelled into the dark and reached over Julian's body with her left arm, rubbing her chubby body over his nude, thin frame.

"Boy, what a turkey!" exclaimed Shirley, chiding Julian with a sarcastic style of verbal expression. Clara giggled with a series of seducing smiles. They both began puffing away into Julian's face, casually and then deliberately. The conversation took to a circus ring of female talk— girl talk.

"This is the only way you'll ever get this guy to go out with a girl, Clara. He's ridiculous!" hammered Shirley with a sharp-pitched voice, coughing incessantly as if she couldn't breathe at times. "I don't know about him. I just don't know about anything. I don't know!" She began to mutter now, and soon her crying silenced Julian and Clara and altered their conversation. Julian pretended not to hear her, chuckled, and laughed. He thought this would cheer her.

Clara spoke out softly, as if trying to console her. "Don't worry, Shirley. Don't worry. You'll get what you want someday. You will. It takes time, and you're not going to get it overnight."

Julian waited until they had both fallen asleep. Clara was no longer puffing on her cigarette, nor was Shirley sniveling away her last tears. Crawling out feet-first to the foot of the bed, he silently walked over to the toilet and sat down. Tired and drained of his delusions, he reconciled himself that he hadn't had a wink of sleep all night. The music from his mother's clock radio was playing very low in tone. A Mexican radio station could be heard coming from the restroom, and the next moment, Julian was looking up toward Shirley. He stared her in the face. She stood there, nude, and puffed on her cigarette.

"Hurry up and get off that thing. I have to use it," she whispered with one loud rancorous heave from her lungs. Clara had awakened by this time.

"Well, Julian? Don't just sit there. Go and get into bed with Clara and enjoy yourself. Hell! What are you waiting for, you turkey?" Shirley began peering through the windows with wild glances. She secured the curtains, keeping a watchful eye for onlookers. Simultaneously, she dressed herself stealthily, grabbing her clothes with her free hand. She reminded Julian of a desperate auctioneer who had only recently showed her bad luck at the local fairground's auction sale.

"I'll tell you what! I'll get busy and fix my hair while you guys have fun. Okay?"

Clara answered, "Okay."

Julian just lay there, looking into Clara's eyes. Her smile was very noticeable as if a result of some kind of a hypnotizing trance had been cast out by Shirley.

This was the tempo that Julian established between himself and Shirley in the weeks that followed. Here, age didn't matter if a person remained without a rose garden. Age had nothing to do with being a twenty-seven-year-old man from the valley. Perhaps it has much to do with society's opinion of where the drowned sorrows of immigrants go for filial acceptance of intimacy. Yet it may have nothing to do with self-love and celibacy. Yes, perhaps human experience draws from the hallways of hours walled in miles where the shaping and identification of an artist figure begin to form.

The tempo ended one night with a sudden, jarred moment of domesticity. Julian might have been too good an actor, or he misconstrued the calculation about his own judgment of women. He could hear his mother yelling at him with her fingers painted in disarray and her mind in slight fever. *What the hell! What did I have to lose?* he thought. His teeth perhaps?

"Remember what I told you about hanging around with strange people," her voice could be heard in his mind. Instantly, he saw himself slouched over Clara, mangled on her body like Jell-O. Shirley looked on like that strange keeper from the museum.

There he was, several nights later, sitting in Shirley's kitchen. He was reading a book about organic chemistry. Confused and misunderstanding why she would do such a thing after the first tomato hit his writing hand, he quickly turned toward her direction. He sat in the chair next to the kitchen table and received a lettuce directly square in the face. The bread followed as did the entire bag of groceries. All that was needed was for

Julian to walk over to a Chinese market that was located at the end of the alley to get himself a refill of food. He decided on another option. Taking on the image of a married couple, Julian became like an "old man in the sea" alongside Shirley.

It was time to leave back to my motel room, he thought. Staying reserved and intact with his temper, he began picking up the groceries by placing them back into the bag. He felt like a store counter clerk who had been fired by the store manager for minding his own business.

"That's right! Pick it all up and get the hell out of here, you son of a bitch!" said Shirley with a composure very foreign: untired, harsh, real, and like an inmate who has been locked up for several years. That's right! She had all the keys now; she'd become the warden, standing tall on her territory, defining the boundaries to her turf. And now, she was telling him to get out.

"You don't care about me, Julian! You never did. You're nothing but an empty creature. You know that?" she yelled.

"We're only friends, Shirley. Remember?" Julian reassured himself in a low tone of voice. He quietly moved himself outside the backdoor of the dining room. She followed him with a fiery, stern look in her eyes. As she moved her way out the kitchen, she picked up the coffeepot. Julian moved toward the front end of his pickup. Shirley stopped at the gate of the backside patio of the carport, hesitated, and stared at him. Both figures looked to each other with a fixed and regretful stare. Shirley held onto a cigarette in her right hand as she hid the coffeepot with her left hand. The pot did not move an inch, and Julian held onto the grocery bag.

"We can do so good together, you and I, Julian. But no…you want to keep acting like a stupid, stubborn Chicano," said Shirley. The alley was dark, but you could still see faces because of the lights at the end of its roadway. The traffic on the boulevard had quieted, except for a few brave and lonely motorists.

"But you're too old for me, Shirley," said Julian as he turned toward her. Spontaneously, the ringing noise of the coffeepot clamored like a bell without its chime. The pot fell from the pickup truck onto the pavement. It rolled a fling. She'd flung the pot as hard as she could right square onto Julian's face, cutting open his lips. The blood fell to the pavement, a spurt.

"Too old for you? Shit!" she blurted out with a revengeful tone in a low-pitched voice that sounded like a man's. Closing shut the gate to the patio, she walked back into her kitchen and shut the glass frame and the curtains to the kitchen window, as Julian held his hand over his mouth, keeping some of the blood from dripping. He stood there for a minute before he bent over and reached for the pot. He couldn't believe himself. He lunged the pot onto the bed of the pickup and drove off into the night with his radio playing loud.

"It just doesn't sound like the thing for you to do, Julian. She's bad news for you, all the way," said the voice in the apartment. A large masculine hand offered Julian a beer that was poured from a large keg in the corner of the room. The voice was that of Clark Stevenson.

Clark Stevenson was a blond-haired middle-aged man. He wasn't another scapegoat figure of a sad sack who, upon recently having graduated from a military school of gourmet cooking, was good at telling stories about having taken a tour of Vietnam during the late sixties. No. God forbid! He wasn't exactly a gay-liberated person as claimed by members of opposite peer groups—peer groups that had black belts in Karate—and the international students located near the University in Raisintown. He was a good ten years older than Julian's age and had more experience with guns, Karate, and cooking. Being of an Irish-bred stock and coming from Oregon in his early years, he spent the remainder of his time in California.

"I mean, you know what I mean," said Clark as he tried speaking in a fatherly tone in a consoling manner. "There you are, driving off to a motel room after leaving some dizzy dame from New York—and some old bag of fifty plus, at that—who had finished cutting your lip open. Only twenty years older than you, Julian? You should be proud, boy! Julian, be proud, soldier. Stand tall. Walk straight and be proud of everything you've done! What's the matter with you anyway, mister?" Clark's voice continued, "Here, have another beer. Hell. Let's drink to the day. Salute!"

"Salute," replied Julian as if he had only finished listening to a ghost from the grave. They tipped their beers and lifted their jaws in solemn gestures. Julian had never known anyone in his time who could drink spirits like a fish that swims in water. There they sat and drank as much as they could, surrounded by radios, televisions, stereos, and both old and new electronic equipment. Various junk and tools, electrical in nature, lay everywhere, and a large picture poster of W. C. Fields covered the wall of the front room. The apartment belonged to a friend of Clark's and appeared to be an appropriate place to talk at times.

"Fifty-five percent Mexican-American or Latino," he recalled the interviewing sergeant tell him. "Five percent black, and the rest are all Anglos." The statistics didn't move Julian a shot. The jail's condition would indeed grasp the focus of anyone's attention. Julian continued trusting his curiosity and followed the deputy chaperon to the first-floor cell block. The quickened scent of an open, cold atmosphere dampened the walk and the floors; the feeling had encumbered his curiosity. He felt as if he were back in the military. They approached the elevator door as if an emancipated feeling of precaution were reaping at their eyesight.

"Did you say you wanted to talk with Leonard Escheverria?" the deputy guard asked with a benign virulence.

"Yes! That's the name. Which cell block—I mean *floor*—is he in?" asked Julian. "He's on the third floor. That's the floor where we keep the third-degree scammers. You know, the sex offenders, robbery cases, and all the felony committals…the big boys! That's where we have your friend, this…Leonard Escheverria." The guard was billowing the phrase out with a quick and sudden movement as he lit a cigarette. They were in the elevator now; the doors closed, and they began moving upwards.

"Hey! What did you say your name was anyhow?"

"Julian." A pause. "Julian Solbriozo."

"You looked familiar at first, but…no. I'm from the bay area. You know? Hayward. I guess I wouldn't know you," he said.

Julian pushed himself against the wall railing. He grabbed on and held his breath. "No…I suppose not," he answered.

The movement of the elevator stopped. The doors opened, and the bright lights from the ceilings cast out upon their faces.

"Is this the third floor? Can I go see him now?" Julian was asking in a serene, nonchalant manner.

"No. Not now. This is only the second floor. This place is for first-time offenders: public disturbance, drunk driving. You know." They walked down the hallway that circumvented the perimeter of the cages and cell blocks. All that separated them from the human mass of stench and stagnant masturbated flesh were the steel bars and iron gates. Their footsteps had taken them halfway around the cell block when suddenly in one echo the sound of a flurry from falling cans, pillows, and blankets could be heard. A hurricane of articles was being thrown by the inmates against the outer walls to the hallways with one large blast. The chaperon grabbed onto Julian's arm and held him back at that moment.

"Hey, copper! Hey, you, cop. Come on over so we could see ya!" the voices yelled out, and the screams grew louder and louder from inside the cells. The guard pulled Julian over to behind a corner wall and took a small round mirror from his pant pocket.

"Stay in the back of me," said the deputy, who was stretching out his right arm. With one twisting movement of his wrists, he focused his eye on the picture in the mirror. Julian desperately tried focusing his vision also. "This happens all the time. They do it every time we make our rounds at night."

"Can't anybody do anything about it?" asked Julian while remaining timid throughout the noise.

"You want to try? Go ahead," repeated the guard. The voices kept ringing out loud. There were bits of debris flying past them now.

"C'mon, copper! C'mon, you son of a bitch!" went the voices. The flippant hands and peering faces could be seen in the small mirror while some remaining articles were being thrown against the walls.

"These motherfuckers don't deserve a damn thing as far as I'm concerned," said the guard. "Let's go! I'll take you up to the third floor. Then I'll have to take you back downstairs."

"Okay, let's go," said Julian with both hands in his pockets and a shoveled disposition centered on the expression of his face. A second deputy approached them both as they entered the elevator.

"Well, well, well, Simmons," rolled out a voice. "And just what do you have here?"

"Who's this?" said the second jailer whose bald head dominated his appearance.

"This is Julian Solbriozo. He's from the police academy across the freeway. He claims he's doing a research project for Sergeant Taylor," said the chaperon. "You don't say! Well, I'll tell ya, buddy. Anyone who's looking for a job in the jail has got to be out of their mind." He stared at Julian for a moment as he puffed on a cigarette. Julian stared back at him with an offensive gesture. Yet a defensive gleam of resignation shot through his feelings about being there. He moved back against the wall of the elevator, somewhat repealed with caution and a tidy carefulness.

"How do you do?" said Julian at first glance. He sighed, and a strange vengeance submerged. "How's it going?"

"Pretty good! A person gets use to this place, you know," said the half-bald-headed, blondish deputy.

"They must keep you going at that academy, don't they?"

"Yeah! Sort of," replied Julian.

"So you're trying to get a job as a cop?" he asked again as his voice rose up to a stronger monotone.

"Yup!" answered Julian with a calm, collective expression of determination. His eyes hit the floor with a flit of glances.

"Well, in here, buddy, there ain't any ifs, buts, or any of that kind of shit. You either are or you aren't," stated the deputy. "You can't feel sorry for anybody in here, mister. You hang it up if you do." Julian resented the perplexed yet demented advice of the officer. He blinked his eyes and stuttered for brave words of any kind. Instead, he swallowed and took one deep breath. For several moments, he stood quiet and reserved.

"Okay! Julian, let's go this way. This is where we have Leonard Escheverria. This is the floor."

"Let's go!" Julian raised his voice with an exuberant warning, trying to evade the soliloquy and esoteric tone of the other deputy who stood by the elevator. "See ya."

"See ya later," replied the cigarette-smoking officer. Their shadows disappeared from the floor beneath their feet. The lights above lit the hallway with even composure. The chaperon opened the iron door's lock to the entrance of cell block D, third floor. He continued pushing it open, and Julian followed. Once inside, Julian felt a feeling of an open despair with anxious butterflies and vivid nerves of a forlorn bravery that he hadn't sensed in years. They both walked slow and with tandem footsteps down the hallway.

The air was damp, and a quiet resolute atmosphere seemed to quench their desires for speaking too soon. Julian held his breath; his footsteps would echo with uneven taps. They both moved alongside the dark metallic sundry of the cages. Radios could be heard as an intertwined and betwixt medley of melody and acid rock clamored the imprisoned eardrums of the human touch. There were several bodies on the beds who were draped in half overalls. Many of these inmates lay there half nude and comfortable in their iron castles, which shaded their starved, masturbated fantasies and demeanors of recluse character. The cells themselves would remind you of the cubbyholes of pack rats or gophers, if you were of the more rugged, pastoral outdoor personality. Blankets were strewn about the floors, and some came draping down the walls, including the bars that formed the wall separating the hallway and their sleeping space. Mirrors covered with pictures of nude women blanketed the walls in the background. The remaining walls were cluttered with family photographs and small artifacts and miscellaneous curios. These so-called hard-time offenders were indeed living like kings in a maze of wrought-iron jungle with amassed terror of inescapable frolic. The smell of sweat, breath, and feet were traceable and quite sharp to the taste buds and nostrils.

These are the hard-core offenders who have existed almost next door to me…all my life? Julian questioned himself with self-inflicting thoughts of a recurring nature. *They all act like tamed kitties in a tiger's showcase. It makes me feel like a comic—a clown of the kind who presents himself in the middle of a three-ring circus and before a crowd of hungry aspirants. The anxious and impatient eyes are looking at me, questioning me with their thoughts, asking me how it feels to be locked in a cage. Then they wonder in amazement why is it that suddenly I've forgotten my material, my lines, the one act that I'm supposed to follow. I've almost forgotten who my real identity is now. I've become a comic. I can make them laugh, all these hungry faces who are tired of the outside world.* Julian's mind was now enmeshed and synchronized.

"Say, Joe! How's it going?" said the chaperon. "Are you hanging in there, today?"

"Sure thing, bud!" replied the tall, slim inmate whose voice reflected the verbose sounds of a Mexican-American male. He was only one of the several who appeared to be Mexican American. The movement in the cells began to reemerge and add life to the rancid atmosphere of the quietude. Julian murmured to himself in his meekest of poses. He was thinking of the words he would say to Leonard upon meeting him. Another voice rang out.

"Hey you, what's happening, brother?"

"How's it going?" spoke Julian as he nodded in a friendly gesture and cunning character. Next, his hand would lift from his side hip as if to insinuate complete surrender of a fast-breed humility.

"We're almost there, Solbriozo. He's right here, somewhere to the next cell," said the deputy chaperon. His steps became shorter and grew softer with every breath. The steps came to a solemn halt, and the shadows stopped moving. Julian stayed alongside the wall and clung onto the cold cement with a novical insecurity, which he recalled when he had last seen Leonard somewhere in their hometown years ago.

"Someone here to see ya, Lenny. He says he's an old friend," repeated the deputy chaperon.

"I don't have any old friends," said the tall dark-brown, ruddy hulk. Julian had his back to the wall with both hands pressed against the cold concrete. He looked like a man who was resigning to some kind of guilt he had secured in the past and unwilling to unleash it to let it go forever. Leonard turned around inadvertently and without any careful measure worth keeping a secret. He was pulling on the tail of his dark-purple T-shirt with both fist clenched in rolling fashion. His large dark-brown eyes opened wide in a fervor of amazement.

"Who in the hell is it this time?" His voice faded. "Hi, Lenny. How's it going?" asked Julian. He interrupted with a sharp tone of voice as if a solace guillotine had just fallen down to meet its target. The chaperon turned to look at Julian with a quaint smile of resolution. "I'll be back after a while. I need to finish making my rounds."

"See ya later!" said Julian. The guard walked away, passive and nonchalant. "Julian! Julian Solbriozo! I don't believe it," exclaimed Leonard as he moved forward in his cell. He approached the bars and took a hold of them with a finite grasp. An unwillingness to bring his arm forward for a casual shake of hands stifled Julian's presence. Julian moved from the wall in front of the cell and neared the bars. He put out his left arm slowly. Leonard took it with his right hand.

"I don't believe this. I can't even remember the last time I even spoke to you."

"It's been a long time, Leonard…something like thirteen years! I saw you riding in a car downtown with someone. I forgot when. You were sort of low-riding through main street. I could barely see your head," stated Julian.

"It's good to see you. And how are things going with you?"

"Oh! Not so bad! After thirteen years of coming in and out of these places, I'm used to it. It gets old after a while. I don't even think of it anymore," replied Leonard as he tried to rationalize his explanations.

"So I've heard," said Julian. "I've heard plenty of stories about you. You know…the kind which floats around the neighborhoods and streets, the kind which change over the years. You know? Hell! There is even talk about you at the police academy."

"Well! That's nothing new, Julian," said Leonard. "I have a reputation all over the state, all the way from Tehachapi to San Quentin. It doesn't bother me any. I'm used to it."

"You should be!" cried Julian.

"Hey, listen, guy. I think I'm managing," stated Leonard with an abrupt change of posture. He tried desperately to avert the subject matter in vain effort and drew back on an old question renewed. "You never answered my question!"

"What's that, Lenny?" asked Julian with a fluid, tangible question.

"How's your mother?" asked Leonard.

"Oh…my mom is doing fine. Just fine," replied Julian, brushing his boots against each other, with both his heels on toes and hands dug deep into his pockets.

"Is she still teaching?" asked Leonard with still more questionable looks.

"Oh yeah! She still teaches," said Julian.

"That's good," said Leonard while a smile from nowhere lit up his face.

"And you, Lenny? How's your mother?" asked Julian.

"Umm. Oh! The last I heard from her, she's doing fine," replied Leonard.

"That's good," replied Julian.

"Yeah! Everybody's doing okay, I guess," murmured Leonard. "My younger brother. You remember him, don't you?"

"Yeah!" said Julian.

"Well, he's going to law school. He joined the navy. He does pretty good. You know?"

"Yeah!" repeated Julian.

"Me! Well, I've become part of a jailhouse lawyer. You know?" said Leonard as his eyes lit up. Next, he would resign into a remote shyness.

"Hell! You ought to be the cop, Lenny," said Julian.

"I know a few things, Julian."

"Yeah," said Julian. "This last time I was put in here on charges of a one-eighty-seven and a two-eleven," said Leonard with his serious, resolute statement.

"I heard about it," Julian murmured in a quieter tone. There seemed to be a shining gleam in Leonard's irises as he dropped his head forward and lifted it a few times with a rocking motion. A few seconds of silence passed as Julian appeared as too faint with remorse.

"So how does it look? Can you get out?" asked Julian. "What I mean is…is there any way you can get out of it?" There was a mellow croak in his throat. Leonard stood there, sure of himself and unmoved by any other statement.

"No…nah! They have a good hold on me now, these people. Everybody! Hell! I don't know, Julian." Leonard was flabbergasted with a revered look of pure disgust as he brought his hands together in a same plane of effrontery. The claps resonated with a loud chain-reaction sound. Leonard's jaw fell below the level of normal communication, and a familiar exhaustion began probing his airspace.

"After all the shit was over, I was taken from the county and placed in San Quentin. You know Quentin? It's the big time…where the big boys go." Leonard's chest began to rise, and a new expression plummeted from his dark ruddy face. A new proudness stood high and mighty. Yet the novical flavor of an amateur criminal permeated the environment; it began to reveal itself.

"But it's all right, Julian! Everything is cool…and I'm going to make it," said Leonard. "You see…I'm tough. I can take it. I know these halls and prisons. I've lived here for over one-third of my life, guy. I've been with the big boys. I've been there, Julian." Leonard became self-righteous and demanded an immediate command presence, the kind one would expect at a police academy. Julian himself coerced his self-made image to provide a feasible explanation for his presence. He was shocked to hear Leonard's voice to know with one lasting request that Leonard's intentions were set aside. The important and Narcissistic attitude projected could only be shown because of what Leonard was proud of.

Julian could only recall the memories of their fathers brought back to him with Leonard's presence. In keeping his visitation in cognate form with the police academy assignment, he realized his time became a precious commodity, and Leonard's permission for surveillance was becoming more fruitful like a ripe-seasoned apple tree. This time, the subject was of a depleted nature, a rough nature, covered with the fuzz and powdered fertilizer snow dealt in blows through the hot, airy fields of peaches. The shade was the only space to hide, and the ladders stood high into the sky, with the fruit buckets. The deadly stench of peach fuzz lay about the muddy field of jimsonweed. The insects were all waiting to be extricated from their positions: the gnats, mosquitoes, and bees. Julian remembered. And in that fluid moment of his mind, the steps coming from the hallway clattered and grew louder, as in thumps, like the buckets of peaches that filled themselves with flaccid entry. The hollowness was no longer there. It was the deputy chaperon, Simmons, as Julian recalled his name. Simmons was walking by each cell, making certain his rounds were of a complete and fulfilled duty.

"I'll be back in a few minutes, Solbriozo!" said the deputy. "We'll have to be leaving soon. We're only allowed so many minutes, you know."

"Hey! Don't push the man!" shouted Leonard. "Can't you see we're talking?"

The deputy smiled with a befuddled look on his face. "Sure… you're talking," he said as he continued along his way and greeted other prisoners. He turned the corner and was soon out of sight.

"That's right, Julian," Leonard spoke up. "I'm proud of who I am, and there's no way I can go back and change the clock just to make things different. Just like you, Julian. You can't change anything, no matter how damn hard you try." His voice grew musty and grizzly. "You're on that side of the bars, and I'm on this side of the bars, guy."

"Yeah! That's right," resigned Julian into a stupor of apology. His face was turned downward toward the floor once again. "So be proud of who you are, Julian," echoed back Leonard with a command. "If you're going to be a cop, then do it. Don't turn back. Don't look back. Just be proud of who you are. Don't regret what you do or what you have to do. Just do it, buddy."

Julian took a deep sigh and tried relaxing a moment's folding. Leonard was becoming an ambivalent, incognito touch of fate. His lecture, by this time, definitely drew the inmate, inquisitive attack brought upon by Julian. Julian remained perplexed and confused. His expectation had looked forward to a much more ill-natured Leonard Escheverria. But only the most frenzy of similar thoughts could be going through Leonard's mind as well. The bars guarded and protected their most precious secrets and frayed aggressions, and God bless that such iron and metal showed no signs of any rivaled weakness, wear and tear, or emotion of whatever kind was possible. The music in the background was still playing the "soul on ice" music. "Oldies but goodies" were what they used to be called. "So they remind me of you," and so the song would go on and on. Breathless seconds and a motionless urge gripped at Julian's intonations and tired heart. He sighed a little.

"And, Julian! You remember that emblem you drew for the boys club that one year back in town…don't you?" cried out Leonard with a surviving gleam in his eyes. Julian thought for a moment as he drew up his left hand—fingers with palm cupped—and reached for his chin and lower lip.

"That's right. Sure! I remember now. Yeah." Exasperated, the tall, slim-framed individual whose figure cloaked in khaki uniform leaned against the iron bars. Patches from the county school were quite visible on Leonard's jet-black jacket.

"I remember now. It was a picture of an athletic man running, and he was carrying a torch," said Julian in a dialectic tone gulp of spoken words.

"Yeah! That's it, Julian! That's it!" Leonard intervened. "But there was another picture you did. Remember?"

"You mean a picture of a power symbol…a fist!" replied Julian.

"That's it. That's right," Leonard exclaimed. "A fist. It was a picture of a fist."

Suddenly and almost instantaneously, the tap on Julian's right shoulder could not escape the conversation, but he felt it. It was the deputy guard; he had come out of nowhere.

"It's time to go, Julian. Time is up!" went the officer's voice. Julian's eyes turned toward the deputy. Leonard grabbed his nose with his left thumb and index finger and pulled down on the bridge while shaking his head. "I'll wait for you at the forward gate," said the deputy. There were two gates where one had to pass through before entering the elevator. This was the jail's means of double security.

"I'll be at the gate, Julian," spoke out the deputy. "Okay! I'll be with you in few moments," replied Julian. The deputy walked away, and all the domestic memories of the past began occluding the demented atmosphere of the cell block.

"I'll remember that very well, Solbriozo. That picture I remember very well," said Leonard.

"Yeah! I remember now," repeated Julian. By this time, Julian's eyes were penetrating the solace and solitary grace emanating from the man, Leonard. He stared deeply into the large dark-brown pupils of the huge figure. Leonard stared back, and that familiar gleam in his eyes began showing a trenchant sign of weakness. A tear began gutting the manly vision of this human being whom he had known so well at one time.

"Well," said Julian with an exasperation, "I've got to go now. I'll be back to visit sometime during the next few weeks. I'll get a chance. I know I will." But by all misfortune handed to anyone, little did Julian know that he would soon need a mandate of permission from one of the judges in order to make any more visits in the near future. And securing a mandate of permission from a judge was not an easy task. Julian would not get another chance, and this fate of his rendezvous with Leonard is what he did not know.

"Hey, guy! It was great for you to come over and talk with me," said Leonard. "You know, there aren't too many people who will take the time to do that, Julian. The world is changing, people are changing, but I still stay in here, and they stay out there." Leonard was holding his head up high as he examined the bars and walls that surrounded him. He knew that his hunches and quixotic guesses were telling him that he would never see Julian again, perhaps for a long period of time, so he resigned himself to an avowed serenity.

"I'll bet you, Leonard," spoke Julian. Leonard turned around and looked toward the back wall, and Julian walked away with a brisk and confident pace.

"Take care of yourself, Julian." Leonard's voice could still be heard coming from the one cell. The voice faded. The bars to the cell block shut tight and exploded with a deafening punch—unmelodic it was. Julian and Simmons, the guard, were inside the elevator. Several inmate voices could be heard. Then silence. They did not waste time in walking through the jail's entrance, Julian and the guard. Their casualness and anonymity gathered the attention of the other guards and jailers as their footsteps left the tank. The jail officer's eyes gathered their focus with bold stares. They had expected to see a big fight between both of these Mexicans. It would have been the highlight of the day. These redneck cops were thirsting for it. The guard opened the release doors for Julian. He found his way into the unloading garage. Here again, the electricity was demagnetized, and Julian pushed open the door. He adjusted his black cap and shut the door behind him.

"Okay! All shut!" went the voice over the intercom system. "All shut!" yelled Julian with a forceful blast of enunciation. He buttoned his black jacket and, next, toted his valise to one side of his left shoulder. He never looked back as he walked upon the rear driveway of the jail structure. A low-lying fog could be seen high above the building's lights. There were white buses parked alongside the walkway to the top of the driveway's hill where the second floor was even surfaced with the ground level. And so went the serene dark figure of skinny frame, with cap and gloves worn, up the sideways aisle and onto the outside parking lot. There was no one else on the street that night, except for a few anxious visitors waiting beside their cars. They appeared to be from Mexico. The following morning, Julian drove his bicycle to class. The weather became occluded with a deep winter offering touch of cold and icy dew point. Here was this skinny-framed figure, with his cap and glove, strolling through the street on his bike. He became a sore thumb of a cavalier who stood up from apart of pedestrians and shifty low-riders with youth at the wheel. His Achilles' heel protruded as he walked up the stairway to the academy room on the second floor. The cadets pretended to glance at him with revered stares. He walked cautiously into the instruction room and carried his brown bags with gym clothes and gray briefcase, sitting himself down with a placated character far removed from the austere look given to him by Becky Frowling.

"Good morning," he spoke so that Becky would be assured of giving him an answer. "Oh, him! Hi!" And that was all she said in her most remote look of feminine expression.

She's just another young female who's working her way into the police ranks, thought Julian as he tried arranging the torn brown grocery bags in a fashion that would appear less conspicuous to the jeering eyes in the room. He fixed, with an adjustment, the blue name tag that sat on the table in front of his posture.

"Well, ready for another weekend…uh, Becky?" said Julian. "I suppose so, Julian," she answered. Her disposition became less radical as she sank into a more relaxed, fluid feeling of being at peace. She immediately began talking to the cadet who was sitting to the other side of her. Julian did not hesitate to ignore her. He was, after all, just another small-town police cadet attending a small-town community police academy with various folks from the rural area.

The man speaking in front of the class was one of the firearms instructors who threw in lectures as if the message he were giving was one of a last and final resolution. He made a person feel as if there was only one day left to decide whether or not one should learn when and where to pull a trigger. Of course, this meant a question of life and death. Next, he would discuss about a time when he remembered so well, a time in which some member from one of the classes had loaded one of his demonstration guns. Upon beginning his demonstration, a live round had fired into the ceiling. Thank God it was only the ceiling.

"Each and every one of you will have to kill someone someday. The only important question is…when will you do it?" said the man who claimed to be from Oregon. His voice would go on and on. Familiarity began filling the void and impersonality of the academy.

It was also during that last and final week that various officers from the surrounding cities began lecturing to the few cadets. There was this one officer from Almondtown who stated he had been on the investigation team for the assassination of Senator Robert Kennedy in 1967. And there were others who had important experiences of certain events and sequences of tantamount dates to share. The chain of events that week had drenched this particular familiarity of a local newsroom that established itself so close to home. These people were coming out of the woodwork. Despite this newly inaugurated menagerie of a resplendent kind—reclusive, paramilitary, and notary—Julian's debut once again was coming to an end.

That last and embittered Friday had found her way through Julian's schedule of acrimonious events. However, he did get his chance to listen to more experiences from these individuals who exploited a modern Don Quixote image they themselves knew so well. Their knowledge of the penal popular few did not enhance the fears and insecurities brought upon by Julian himself. He had nothing to hide from anybody, except his true identity. Even now, the law enforcement community had been given their share of information, which concerned the persona of extraordinary individuals.

Julian did get his chance to have made a claim on shooting his weapon. It was not until they were called upon to learn and demonstrate the basic techniques of self-defense and interrogation stance that Julian was called into the office by the director of the academy. A smoking gun issue.

His criminal law grade was showing a depleted weakness. The knowledge he had of criminal law was not that strong. He knew why the director was calling him into his office, and he already had a good explanation at hand—a good, reasonable story he would tell the director. A warning had been issued to him concerning his criminal law grades. He had been asked about his study habits. But once again, Julian had tried, and nothing became of his own demanding inquiry created from his enthralled and perplexed dilemma. He was that much of an evasive person who had made an evasive decision to attend a police academy.

Julian wanted it bad, and no one else told him so in the police academy. He left the second-floor hallway that morning after exiting the door to the director's office. Upon securing the books and several bags from the hallway locker, he walked downstairs and headed toward the gym to the room where the self-defense class was being taught. The class was in session, and he would peek through the door with a shy, timid launch of suspicion. He handed the pair of handcuff keys to one of the cadets, who had asked for a loan earlier, prior to being called into the office. The cadet looked on with a cold and sanguine shock after Julian told him about the news of the termination from the academy. Others turned to look and listen during this period of wrestling and mocking each other with take-downs and throws. Rebecca Frowling looked on. She knew already of Julian's fate; she neither smiled nor frowned. Julian told that one cadet goodbye with a friendly adios and an "olla podrida" look. Telling the cadet that he would see him in a few weeks to pick up the keys, Julian backed away from the door and began walking toward the pickup truck. With a small sigh, a few relaxing thoughts trickled through his mind. His conscience told him so; he felt content walking away from the building as he crossed the baseball diamond. His figure was now seen walking slowly passed the campus with gray sweats, a cap, and a pair of tennis shoes he still wore on his thin feet. Throwing the jet-black jacket over his right shoulder, he appeared normal and unmoved.

He drove his truck to the boulevard and headed in a southerly direction until he came to that once familiar corner he had known so well and stopped his vehicle behind Shirley's apartment. After knocking on the window, it appeared she might be home. There was a pause and some silence. The curtain moved and drew with a sudden flash, opening the view with one wide pull. Shirley showed her round face, and her bright eyes didn't hesitate to cover the resilience of her authoritarian motives.

"Oh, it's you again, Officer Solbriozo…So what do ya know?" She hesitated. "Come on in," she said.

Julian shrugged his shoulders and blew off a little steam with a cynical chuckle. Next, he stuck both of his hands into his pockets, as usual, and walked into the apartment with a staunch look of retreat and respite. The old cry of secret passion was well retained by this rifled character of well-disciplined feelings.

"I was just cleaning up around here…you know?" she flustered with her early-morning novical chaste words. "I have an appointment at the cleaners this morning—I mean, the hairdresser," she rambled on like a parakeet over a hot stove. "The television repairman is coming over this morning to take a look at the television."

Julian sat himself down in the large chair, unnoticed and unresponsive to her statements. People already knew of the news because movements moved like a fire in this city. He knew. She knew. Everybody knew. The only curious happenstance that remained to be seen was how curious people went about hiding the truth of all and everything they knew. It was a coquettish little community. It had always been that way.

"Really?" exclaimed Julian. "So you must be busy today?"

"Oh, boy, buddy! You know I am," said the elderly woman in her fifties as she entered the restroom, adjusting her necklace and outfit in a petite frenzy of motion. "So what gives? What brings you around here, anyway? I thought you're supposed to be in class?" She would glance over to view Julian as he sat in the armchair.

"I was in class," he answered her, and he stared at the television. "I had to leave school…I'm out…out of the academy!"

"You mean you quit?" she asked.

"No. I had to leave. The director dropped me from the course," he said.

She feigned in hearing his statement and pretended to shy from the intimacy of his downtrodden, defeated attitude. In trying to cheer up a spineless caricature of self-pity epic, she walked away from the restroom and quickly began adding fish food to an aquarium that stood to one side of the living room and to near the wall. She was oblivious and casual.

"Gee, that's too bad. So what are you going to do now?" Her statements and questions scattered any signs of vitality and change for survival, the sentences of excuses and reprimands conjectured in Julian's mind.

"Heck! I'm packing up my things and heading back up to Winetown," exclaimed Julian with a finicky look of an unsullied frown.

"Winetown?" exclaimed Shirley. "What the hell are you going to do in Winetown…live with your mommy and stepfather? Ah! I don't know about you, Julian." There were some quick knocks at the door in the instant. She placed the cover top over the aquarium. "Uh! Maybe you're better off going back home and staying with your mother, boy! You're a mess!"

She staggered into a frenetic and anonymous appearance as she opened the door. A voice rang into the room. "Hello there! Good morning…Are you the lady with the broken television set?" The television repairman stood in front of them. He was early on his arrival.

"You bet your booties, sweetie! Come on in," gleamed Shirley's voice. "The sooner the better, you know. It's right here." She pointed to the set in the corner. The short, chubby figure of a man walked in, carrying a medium-sized toolbox with him.

He rescinded into a quick salutation before Julian could get in a word. "Good morning," he said, and his eyes quickly recognized the familiar uniform displayed by Julian. This green-hand cadet had slipped a pair of beige khakis onto his body earlier at a corner standard gas station. His sweats still hugged his legs underneath.

"Good morning." Julian grinned with a stymied look of hand-knit absolution. The television repairman glanced over to Julian a second time and fired on with a slight chuckle of an emotional smudge.

"So you're not working today…keeping busy?" said the man as he began opening his toolbox.

"Yeah! Yeah! As a matter of fact, I am," answered Julian, and he took on the aggressive look of an astute military figure. Julian stood straight up and stretched his arms upward as he tried to reach the ceiling.

"Well…I guess I'll be shoving off, Shirley," he said in a yawn, which drew back the syllables. Shirley's eyes lit up with encouraging intonations and a relieved disposition.

"Oh! All right!" she said. "Maybe you'll drop in again sometime?" Julian shook his head with short, quick rocking movements.

"Okay! Sure! One of these days, I'll drop on by again," he said.

Julian began taking his steps further toward the back entrance of the dining room with a diminutive gracefulness. The television repairman had torn apart the machinated equipment, and by this time, he began revealing his voyeurish eyes to one corner of the entertainment set. Shirley walked Julian over to the door in a hurried fashion and in an even-paced tempo.

"So I'll be seeing ya around," she said. "Take care of yourself now! Gee! That's too bad about you having to leave that police school. I hope your luck changes. Take care!"

"You too!" said Julian as he opened the wooden gate, which revealed the parking lot and the back alley. *So what of it?* His thoughts began raining visions of humility and wanderlust as he drove back to his cabin. *I'll probably never see her again for a good long while. Just like Wanda and all the rest of them. Oh, oh well! I'll try to forget. I gave it my best shot. I tried. At least I tried.*

He wasted no time in gathering all his items and loading each and every artifact onto the bed of the pickup truck. He had more junk than he could imagine, and he always carried it with him wherever he would go. He hurried and, in the maelstrom of activity, left behind a carton of homogenized milk in the refrigerator. He paid Joe and Eve the remainder of the month's rent, acting as if the payment were an alimony quote that had to be met by demand from solicitors from the Internal Revenue Service Agency. He hurried.

"Here's the remainder of the month's rent, Joe!" exclaimed Julian as he rushed into their home next door. "If I were to come back and rent from you again, would you give me the same room?"

"I don't know. I can't say right this minute," said Joe's son, owner of a nearby convalescent hospital located in the adjacent neighborhood.

"Sometimes that room is empty, then again, somebody's always using it. I just can't tell you when or what time. Sorry!" Portuguese people were always bohemia and showed much hospitality. Julian cut the conversation short and drove out of the driveway in a rush uncommonly heard.

The hour was getting close to lunchtime as the truck sped out to the direction of the main highway. Within the movement of the local traffic, Julian could feel an uneasiness about him: a tepid domestic churning in his gut that was reminding him about ditching school before the lunch break. An academician sense of rebuttal told him that he was missing something important. He glanced over the area of Green Acres.

His thought diminished. When the truck arrived in Winetown, his sense of platitudinous character had also diminished. He was trying to forget about Almondtown, about the police academy, about his vain effort in edifying his own reassurance of self-stubbornness, about trying to create a reality that needed more room in expanding and breathing, about all the glory and vicissitudes he had about his own adulthood life.

He succumbed to a point of realizing his own eccentricity and folly, his jousted appeal to become a deadweight local vagabond artist shifting his weight around from town to town, back and forth, and with a flippant reaction of instability. Afraid to return to his mother's house, he became fearful of his own thoughts—a residue of dura mater he had left behind in Almondtown.

The truck crossed an overpass that overlooked the southern terrain of this foreign community. And in the bombastic view of this new overseer, he could barely construct the precipice of his mother's home. The view sat a mile and a half in the distance to the north and somewhat covered by the edifice of a motel along the highway. There were many foregrounds that obscured this domicile haven next to the freeway. Grape vineyards covered each side of the freeway, and a few ranch homes scattered the rhythm of the countryside that set south of the city. The trucks slowed down in speed as its weight crossed the freeway overpass. Julian turned right and headed toward the direction of the motel. He passed by very slow, and the huge neon sign glittered in the sunlight with its archaic stained look; it read, "Casa Grande Hotel."

The truck arrived at the house, and he was almost afraid to drive into the driveway. He held his breath at the last minute. There was a brown and white sheriff's car from the county. Julian hesitated upon seeing the sight, but pastoral providence told him to drive into the roadway. He expected a sublimated oblique salutation from his stepfather. It was too early for that. Instead, he opened the kitchen door from inside the garage and could see his mother sitting on the big green chair. She was talking to a deputy sheriff. They were both aware of Julian's presence. They said not a word.

"It's just me, Mom," said Julian as he walked to meet the both of them.

"Who's there?" She turned around to see Julian.

"Oh! It's you! Did they let you out early today?" Julian did not answer. He walked over to where the deputy sheriff sat, on the sofa, and cordially introduced himself.

"Well, I want you to meet Deputy Santo Ramos. He's from the sheriff's department downtown. He's taking one of my Spanish classes." They both stood up and shook each other's hands with an astute formal edge of cultured unanimity. The deputy was a large, husky-framed man with the posture of a power lifter's physique. Julian could not equal the composure of his own uniform's appearance: a tall, lanky, thin cadet's uniform. The deputy had mentioned the fact that he pleasures from looking at several of Julian's paintings. In a quiet exhaustion, Julian sat down, and his face turned red with an almost enhanced embarrassment.

"Well, I'm home!" he told his mother.

"Are you finished for the week?" she asked.

"No, I had to come home. I'm finished for good," replied Julian.

"You mean the director finally let you go?" she asked a second time. The second question made Julian swallow, and his eyes filled with flush activity of shy, reluctant tears. He was a glutton for showing self-restraint; nevertheless, he tried to be his most humble when in the presence of certain company and the requisition of his own mother. She understood Julian too much. She always tried polishing him up in front of such company's type. He was home again.

* * *

The spring of '82 showed no shyness about revealing its plunder and mixed mysteries. Its arms leaped out with a roar of thunder and wind…a grace of fever. Julian was a new man in the household. He was always one of Maria's sons; however, he remained an occluded character in the presence of his stepfather, Joaquin. He remembered well the first night the tall dark-skinned man came home to find out that yours truly was another victim of not being able to cut the ice at the Almondtown Police Academy. He did mention the fact about this vain attempt at defeat in rendezvousing with the living dead in Almondtown County. Joaquin pretended as if he had never known what had happened, as if a strange grasp of forward humility had embraced his own conscience. He remained quiet about it, and so did Julian. And so this umbrella of a personal anonymity became the homely setting that cut the atmosphere on the ranch house where his folks lived: the mechanic and the college professor.

No sooner than later was Julian back at the hospital and tearing at the commonplace memories of the duties of his usual job. Establishing a place in his room again, anonymous, iconoclastic, reclusive, and unwilling to bet down any comforts of his parents' home, he secluded himself, creating a world to fit his own conscience between the terrain that covered the area from the room and the hospital located down the road from the corner on California State Boulevard. The distance was becoming the only privacy he had come to know. This short walk down the freeway was the road that connected the hospital to his folks' home. He reached further for any signs of ghost or ghastly remnants of his past, his parents' past and the past of a few individuals.

The people at the clinic hadn't paid much attention to him: the patients and nursing personnel who worked there. Here, he came to work on the floors of the hallways, imagining that he himself was a cross of hope and fate all at once in the eyes of the health professionals, good or bad. So went this self-made forensic specialist and good personage undermining the lives and minds of these so innocent few.

"I think it's just a question of having to study more," said the chubby blonde clerk who sat and did her work on the medical-surgical nursing station of the second floor. She was inquisitive. As for Julian, he began subliming any kind of inquisitiveness he carried within a tumult of work and eagerness. His charts were beginning to show signs of impatience and frustration, regardless of his own disposition. The other nurses and clerks were all too fast and oblivious to patronize his soliloquies and dastardly habits. They eyed him, one by one, at each and every corner of patients' rooms: downstairs, in the cafeteria, in the labs, as well as upstairs in the intensive care unit. They tattered and tattled with him, played in between breaks with him, all working in a way that appealed to a demurring heart of perfection and self-poise.

"Patient in room 242 needs some water," said the clerk as she viewed the monitor that would keep abreast of any foreign cardiac movements coming from the few rooms where heart patients lay. The doctors rushed the corners. Laboratory people, with nurses, crowded the cross-shaped hallway that spade through the upper level of the hospital. Julian stood there, dressed in white clothing, and shielded himself with the sole presence of his stethoscope that dangled from the base of his neck.

"I'll get it," replied Julian. "We're still working on that one admit which we received not so long ago."

"Um!" went the clerk's voice. She smiled with a look of disdain and querulous thought. Julian recalled her telling everyone about her brother being shot to death in a nearby town where he had been on duty as a police officer. She would always bring the topic to make known and give warning to the younger crowd of nursing personnel about the haphazard and co-hazards of the system's unfair play on justice of the downtrodden and punishment for those sulky individuals who had the audacious talent for escaping the throes of the criminal justice system.

Julian had heard her message very loud and clear. He polished her frankness to some of the other directives that competed in requisitioning her own talent for remaining an incognito. He walked down the stairway to his own room. The thought of getting to know one another deeply and intimately was too close for comfort. In a hospital where the seemingly minority were Americans, people from the valley and where a new song of a familiarity to what was stereotyped as being foreign—as in foreigners—became the oblique focal point to the majority of individuals of this complex and demanded profession.

Julian abased himself with the clinic work. He was becoming a glutton for overbearing senile and invigorating dedication. He surmounted and passed his limits with eccentric and intrinsic fashion. Throughout the convocation of umbilical rapture, there was one particular nurse who fared well at achieving the downplay severance of cutting such a cord. Her name was Margaret Farrington. At first, Julian conceded at achieving a close distinction in comparing her to a well-celebrated national ex-matriarch of the model Cheryl Tiegs. He fantasized the colloquial as well as her clinical image at every corner of the hospital where he found himself working. She did have that attractive American appeal to her, embracing each and every fact that shaded her true appearance. There were times in which she would even go as far as to remove the front two incisors of her upper palate just to prove to Julian that she was not only a good nurse but an ugly girl as well. Julian confided in her and stood next to her side at each and every one of these corners. They would test each other like two raving maniacs competing for sole dominion and control of the floor, authority-wise, experience-wise, and female-wise. He would argue in a demented yet discreet way, barricading words and expressions of deep-seated caution. This blend of linguistic melody became a guilt array of clinical showmanship, which could be penetrated by any nurse for miles and miles. They both fought each other and actually hated each other in times of reserving an unwanted will to get along at showing compassion and familiarity on these wanton halls of blood and clinical arabesque. How could a young man be so jealous of this nurse whose medical experience was far above his. This was one nurse he conceivably enjoyed fighting.

"Hi there, Margaret!" stymied Julian, swallowing as he exited the dinner line and encroached the approachable mess tables where Miss Farrington met during the dinner break.

"Hello there!" she answered in a sullen crocheted statement of luring panoply. Julian would sit directly in front of her and tried in a desperate earnestness to display an untainted mirror image of experienced tremor and forwardness. He failed miserably.

"So…when are you going to come over to my folk's house to look at the art work which I was telling you about that one time?" He paused. "Do you remember?" he asked her in a genteel, reserved move that only a devout city man would say in an abominable time as this, and in a time when such a man would be reconciling with his parents in the most earnestness of ways.

"Oh! Don't worry! When I get the chance, I'll be over there. I will… make it!" she stated with an enduring tone of respite. She was only one nurse in the dozens who worked there by the freeway's edge. Regardless, Julian tantalized her with an utmost insecurity, and he would feign and shy away from the others in his daring effort to remain, at best, a stranger by the wayside. At one point, he asked the nurse if she wanted to go see a movie with him. This was a bold, new move for him—outlandish. She refused, and he was no more surprised than hurt by her answer. Most of the women of the hospital backed her rebuttal, and most of the men backed up his own severed cord of demeaning character. And in all of this, he can't recall that he had dated any of the nurses.

Julian was indeed a loose screw that had drifted from over the other side of the rainbow, from that mirror image and fresh imagery of rich delights and discovered dreams. He hadn't been come to be known as the only "hot potato" in the hospital. As a pure matter of fact, he was in his cool-down stage now. Like a defeated bacteria whose decline had surpassed its exponential stage, he had transformed. There was still a strange, haunted image that left its harangue and immobilized indentation on Julian's conscience. Something or someone from the past was telling him a few messages and words of candor. They were far from being threats or trite remarks of another sort. That ghostly image began to haunt him again and again and again. He lived in his room like a butterfly in its cocoon, waiting patiently and forthright, forthright for the right moment's notice of freedom and free flight for tomorrow.

The weeks would pass without notice and hardly a wink of an eye; a tour de force of spoken words were mentioned by Joaquin, his stepfather. The potpourri of a confluent nature under the clinical guidance and supervision of Margaret Farrington did not cease. The upheaval approach of his patient mother filled his life with a satiated thrust, yet subordinate character, withdrawn and elite in nature. And with all these sequential order of amalgamated personalities veering themselves wildly around his open window, he remained at staying alone by himself most of the time.

There was no doubt about it. Hoards of people met at the hospital with subjects to discuss. But all of this, however, did not appeal to Julian's fervid ways of abiding within the auspices and boundaries of his stepfather's and mother's home. And it was incredulously planned during these hours of being alone—whether he was painting, studying books, masturbating, or watching the glorious colors of the television set, which posted itself near the fireplace—that he began calling up Natasha's mother. And when nobody answered the phone, he would dash out the side door to the garage with his long worn-out tennis shoes and wearing a pair of cut-off jeans. Next, he began a remote, silent jog next to the freeway. His destination was always La Casa Grande Motel. The leg-strengthening exercise was a two-mile run. Again, he would even go as far as to make the second phone call from the motel.

He was dastardly pretentious and stubborn. And it was precisely before this summer had ended that he spitefully enrolled in an abnormal psychology course at the University in Raisintown. This class had been recommended to him earlier by one of the police instructors at the Almondtown Academy. The face of Miss Farrington was disappearing and becoming more and more oblique, and the vivid face of Natasha was beginning to appear on one of his blank canvasses. He recently finished a picture of a red sunset and was also sketching faces from some old photographs of his dead father.

"Hello," said the voice of the older woman. "Who is this?"

"Hello! This is Julian Solbriozo," said Julian. "Could I speak with your daughter?"

"Oh! It's you! Hello," went the woman's voice, which appealed with a luring itch of cosmopolitan flare and high-class Anglo profile. Her voice was not pleasant; however, it was sharp and would truncate a vindictive approach.

"I just called to ask you if I could speak to your daughter," said Julian as the butterflies and jitters ran rampant through his spine.

"Which one?" she said.

"Natasha. Who else?" replied Julian.

"Well, I'm afraid she's not home. She's somewhere out. I don't know exactly where. She just goes, and she never tells anyone," said the woman.

"Oh! I see," said Julian with a resplendent cause for procrastinating an end to the conversation. The woman shot back at him with a foreign tone.

"Julian…I think you'd better stop calling over here. Why don't you get interested in some other woman? Natasha is just not the girl for you," she said.

There was a pause for silence and rapport as a huge thump engorged an empty spot in Julian's throat. He swallowed and waited to gather up the courage for a barraged embarrassment of words.

"Oh, well. I just wanted to talk with her, you know, as friends!" mumbled Julian.

"She's been real upset lately, Julian. I don't know." And her voice mellowed out to a much calmer tone. "But I will tell her you called."

"Okay! Could you do that for me?"

"Sure! But like I said, one can never predict exactly how she's going to act next. As for me, I don't pay attention what goes on there at her trailer house. Her affairs are her affairs," she said.

"You don't really mean that now, do you?" asked Julian with an ever more nervous, comical giggle in his throat.

"Oh, yes I do," she exclaimed with one lasting defense of her own pastoral providence. "If you decide to come over, you'd better watch out.

You might even be sorry." Her voice was protruding the only way a true native from back east could hammer down any kind of loose nails with fever and rage. She was a Missourian.

Julian expanded on his breath. Her words had given him more exactitude and reason for going over to her house to visit her.

"You mean she'll get mad?" asked Julian with an impatient enthusiasm. "Worse than that, boy!" she answered.

"Okay!" And the word sounded like *okie*. "I'll see ya later," replied Julian. He hung up the receiver, dashed out from the kitchen door, and ran to the motel and back. The dogs cheered him on wildly. Exhausted, depleted, and without any strength left, he showered, shaved, and dressed in some of his best slacks and sports shirt. Here, he stood all alone by himself in this big country home with only the stereo's music to keep him company. He stared into the latrine's mirror. Away in his pickup truck, in a brash movement, he departed before the time that his parents arrived. The tattered and tattooed truck enhanced his looks ever more so. He crossed the overpass and was soon out of sight.

He would always play the "musica" loud and sang delightfully to himself. The truck clattered down the road to Natasha's house. He turned the one corner and could see the front hedge of mulberry bush that hid the front yard to the mother's house. His innate butterflies would roll over and over in his stomach. He held his breath to a tumultuous height of raw edge and nervousness. He pondered the thoughts of the hospital, and his epiglottis moved. While making the turn into the driveway, he tried acting casual and non-oblivious to the open door of the mother's house. Yes, he did everything he couldn't think of, but he always kept his eyes straight and direct to the curvature of the pebble and rocky-laden driveway. The mother peered on with eagle eyes of her own. She spoke no words, and then she withdrew into her living room. Julian would always open the driver's side of the pickup and stand directly in back of the old junker as if he tried in vain to portray the image of a long-demanding aggression and a genteel sharpness. Then he would wait a few seconds before deciding to shut the door to the old clunker. When he'd walk up to Natasha's doorstep, he'd always posthumously keep his hands in his pockets while observing the imagery of a funeral procession. The image of a mausoleum lined with well-trimmed hedge and neatly cut grass was fresh in his mind. The dog and horse feed were always stacked and covered in a mottled yet orderly fashion. Without walking up the small iron stairway, Julian leaned over the iron railing and managed to knock on the screen door.

"Who is it?" her voice yelled out with a leveled and dished-out shout of enthusiasm.

"It's me...Julian Solbriozo," he said in a loud voice. "Do you remember me?"

"Oh, it's you!" he answered back. "I thought I told you to stay away and not come around here anymore, especially without permission." She came to her front door and unlocked it. She was wearing a loose blouse that was cut off at the armpits. And she had worn a pair of Levi's jeans to full recognition. Her thongs on her left foot revealed the majority of her dark, tanned skin. She walked out and quickly began spraying the lawn with the one sole water hose. In trying to ignore him, she accidentally wet him with a splurge of water spray.

"Hey! Cut it out! You didn't have to do that," cried out Julian.

She laughed a fuss.

"So what is it this time?" she asked him without even turning around to stare him in the eyes face-to-face.

"I know! You want to take me out so you can hug and kiss me, and then take me to bed. Why don't you go away and leave me alone? I told you last time that I didn't want to see you anymore. You're just like all the rest of them."

"Don't say that!" exasperated Julian answered with a chill of a croak in his throat as he peered on with a receding hairline. His right hand fell atop his mid-cranium and forehead, and he leaned himself up against the old wood of the wretched fence with one boot crested along the base of the red wooden structure.

"It's true!" she screamed "What in the hell do you want with me anyway besides take me to bed?"

Julian moaned and held himself to a stolid restraint. "There's a play that's being shown at the Rock House Theater in Raisintown next Sunday," he spoke gently and with a mellow acquittal.

"Oh! Really?" she said with a sarcastic tone.

"That's right!" he said.

"And…?"

"And…so I came over to ask you if you'd like to go with me to watch it. It is a play which was written by Neil Simon called *Chapter Two*. I'm enrolled in an abnormal psychology class at the University. I need to go watch it. It's part of a homework project." Julian's voice was pleading with her.

"Oh…really? So you're taking some classes at the university?" she asked with new enthusiasm.

"Sure! Why not?" asked Julian with a detective attitude.

"So I suppose that now you'll start talking like a psychologist using big fancy words?"

"Not really," replied Julian. "Our professor teaching us how not to be like that."

"Like what?" she asked again.

"How to act normal and without the worry and boredom of impressing people." He became more relaxed, and with a change of attitude, his intellectual predominance began lighting up a few lights in Natasha's mind. "So who's your professor—a young beautiful blonde?" She almost stole the words from Julian's mouth and continued watching the grass and the grounds in a nonchalant fashion. Julian smiled.

"As a matter of fact, she is a blonde. She's a psychologist from Quebec, Canada," stated Julian.

"Really now!" she said.

"Yeah! She's supposed to be appearing in the play next Sunday night as one of the characters. He paused a moment. So would you like to go with me or not?"

"Well…I really don't know. I mean…what I mean is…is…that I can't tell you until later."

"How late is later?" asked Julian.

"Listen. Don't worry about it…okay," she mauled with an absolute satisfaction and resignation. "I'll let you know in good time."

"All right!" said Julian. He blew out an expiration of air, and he felt more relaxed now, but what I really came over for tonight was to ask you.

"Ask me what?" her voice took a nosedive with one edged and rigid forcefulness.

"I was just going to ask you if you wanted to come with me over to my folks' house so you can meet them."

"Me? Tonight?" she exclaimed.

"Sure! Why not?" answered the stud with a question. Natasha grabbed for her neck and melted down to a forgiving expression.

"Well! I don't know. I'll need to go over to my mother's house to find something to put on something decent to wear."

"Okay! All right. I'll go with you if this is what it takes to prove to you that you should stop seeing me," she stated flatly and finished her final sentence, dropped the water hose, and walked across the lawn near the garage to shut off the faucet. Julian retained a smile on his face and listlessly stood there next to the fence.

"Go ahead and wait inside my trailer house. I'll be at my mother's house. I won't be long."

Julian was happy and contently satisfied because of her acceptance toward his offer. He opened the old screen door and walked inside the room where he sat down on the floor pillow chair with a complete sureness and recompense to the warm security he now felt with Natasha. Noticing the medium-sized framed photographs of Natasha's daughter and friends, he began thinking about her past, his own mother, brothers and sister, friends and enemies. All his thoughts plagued him. He began to feel as if he were married to this middle-aged woman Natasha, glancing twice at the picture of the daughter, pretending to be the father, and whispering to himself of all the things curious and clear conscience he had about his own uneasy state of affairs.

She seemed to be taking an unusual amount of time in making herself look pretty, he thought. He departed the trailer house and drove the pickup to the front of her mother's house. There he waited for her. Her mother, Natalia, would every so often peer out the front door. She was a self-guarded elderly woman. Julian could hear their voices coming from the kitchen. The truck by this time was parked directly in front of the mulberry hedge. The house lights were shown in the background. Her figure was made visible on the front lawn. She appeared on the avenue dressed up in a loosely hung dress and hair styled. Her elegance stymied Julian for a moment. Next, he would open the car door for her entrance as he extended his arm to the side to push open the beige metal piece.

The tall, thin cosmopolitan figure of a female appeared at the window and brushed her dress and her fancy hairdo against the green thicket of branch and berries.

"I'm sorry, Natasha. I didn't mean to park the truck so close to the edge."

"Oh my god! That is all right," she said as she sat herself down, going through her hair with her fingers slightly; she tried removing some dried leaves. Relaxing to a smooth exhaled breath, she imparted herself from the scenery.

"Okay! All right! Let's go," she dared Julian with a slavish tone.

"Like I said, don't worry about it!" exclaimed Julian, who had become extremely excited to a point of frivolous haste. "We'll only stay till one hour or so. Okay? I just want you to meet with them, that's all!"

She turned her head slightly with a smile on her face. "Well? Let's go."

There went the battered and tattered pickup truck rolling down the avenue. Julian turned the radio on as the vehicle did a left turn toward the freeway overpass. The time was in the evening now, and the sun was setting down into the Sierra Madre Range.

Smartly and with a gauntlet poise of touch, Natasha brushed her fingers through his hair, almost imparting the waves with her red fingernails.

"This doesn't mean that you have to get excited now," she said. "I'm just admiring your hair. That's all."

"I didn't say a word. All I know is that you're running your fingers through my hair," said Julian.

Natasha braced herself on the armrest. She sighed heavily and took a deep breath. And when the truck stopped in front of the house, she began turning into a neurotic, nervous frenzy; her body, rigid. She froze.

"Relax, Natasha!" cried out Julian as he turned the ignition key to the "off" position. A stillness gripped the air. "Hell! My folks don't care how you dress. Don't worry about it! They're probably wearing old ragged clothes. They don't mind!"

"It's not that. It's just that I become all perturbed and high energy whenever I meet people I've never known before."

"Okay!" Julian sighed. He opened the door, but she managed to open her side before he could even get around to looking genteel, courteous, and masquerading ineptitude of a smooth courtship. The dogs met them both at the gate and whined and gnarled with deep sensuous barks of untamed fury.

Natasha pretended to be scared, and she coaxed her urbane-looking purse upon her flat and cloth-decorated chest.

"Do they bite?" she queried.

"Nah! They won't bite," said Julian. "You just stay close to me. We'll go in through the front door." They both walked across the sidewalk that led to the front alcove. Julian hit the door a few knocks with his fist before pushing it open.

"Well! Hello there," said his mother. The stepfather, Joaquin, was sitting in the parlor on one of the large chairs. He had his back turned.

"Hello, Mom," said Julian. "I'd like you to meet Natasha. Natasha, Danate." It was a fast, unrehearsed, casual introduction. A pastoral scene in the background mixed in with Julian's adamant desires to show a city, urbane flavor of having a delegated personality.

"Oh! Well, hello there. How are you?" asked Juanita.

"Hello! I'm fine. How do you do?" Natasha greeted with a bucolic shyness.

"Won't you come on in?" explained Juanita.

"Thank you!" said Natasha. Joaquin stood up from the love seat and quickly offered his welcome.

"Hello! Hello! How are you? Please come in and have a seat," commanded Joaquin as he stood up straight to an astute, rigorous posture. He leaned forward and took Natasha's hand with a lightness of touch and a friendly embrace.

"Hello!" said the tall dark-skinned man.

"Hello!" said Natasha.

"Here! You can sit here in this chair," blurted out Juanita. Afterward, she opened her palms in an offering for the second love seat, which sat in the middle of the room. With her fingers pointing to the large green-covered embroidery of nylon that resembled silk, she wasted no time.

"Thank you very much," stated Natasha as she brushed her skirt in an Ivy League fashion and ladylike montage. Joaquin eloquently shut the television off.

"Would you care for a glass of wine or champagne…something to drink?" asked Maria. "How about some tacos? We just sat down for some tacos not too long ago before you came over."

"No thanks," stated Natasha. "A little wine would be fine."

"How about you, Julian?" And Maria continued offering dinner, this time to Julian. Julian stuttered before agreeing to have a bite to eat.

"That's right, Julian. You go ahead and eat. You need to eat. You're a little thin, besides," said the long, slender dyed redhead as she crossed her legs in a serrated fashion and tipped the glass of champagne with every adjustment of her dress and stockings. The very next moment, she and Joaquin began talking, and with spurious speed, she had nearly finished the glass of wine. Bursting forward with giggles and off the wall remarks, her voice would transpire into a statesmanlike and approachable appeal of a diplomatic nature. By this time, Juanita had sat down to Joaquin's left side, and Julian was chomping on the tacos next to Natasha's right side. Natasha asked the demeaning question.

"And so what do you do?" she interrogated Joaquin at the first instant for arriving at the batting mound. Joaquin answered her. The question was again paraded; this time she directed her voice toward Maria.

Maria quizzically stood up and paroled the area and picked up the empty glassware like an impatient waitress in an everyday quixotic bar. She shaded Natasha's question.

"Here! Let me serve you another drink," said Juanita.

"I'll help you," said Julian. Julian became nervous in the kitchen and spilled the wine from one of the glasses. Instead, he served Natasha a glass of 7 Up soda juice by mistake. "I'm sorry," said Julian. "I'll get you another glass." Julian walked back into the kitchen and prepared another glass of champagne. This time, he stealthily carried it over to the large green chair where Natasha sat, and with a tedious movement of his body, he handed over the light-yellow drink.

"Thank you. Thank you very much!" said Natasha with a commanding urgency and sequence of impatience in her voice. Maria, at this instant, began telling her what details of her own profession. Natasha flustered and spoke abruptly.

"Well, you see! I happen to know a certain professor at the state university in Raisintown." She mentioned a certain name. "Do you happen to know him?" she asked.

"He's a fantastic person and great to be around with." Julian's eyes opened wide. Joaquin listened intently, and Maria became sundered with a flush gaze of mediocre delight.

"Oh! Really?" exclaimed Maria.

"Yeah!" blurted out Natasha. "He's great. He knows all kinds of languages and is great at parties!" Julian hadn't even sighed to the fact that he as well as the others droned over the subject of education. A few solemn minutes fleeted past them. Natasha turned toward Julian.

"I think I have to be going now," she trimmed her voice down to an austere refection of a prestigious lady pressed for time and attention.

"Sure! If you have to go, I can take you home this very moment," said Julian.

"It was a pleasure meeting the both of you. I really have to be going now. I have a lot of things to do." And her sentences followed each other in rhythmic tone as she stood up in the parlor. Julian led her out the front door as if she were his wife. Both Joaquin and Maria had said how much of a pleasure it had been to have met her. There were no other words spoken as this unlikely couple walked away from the front of the house in a solemnly, cold fashion display of esoteric pride. They left. Julian took her to her mother's property. She instantly told him that he should leave as quickly as possible—a serene good night, goodbye, and a last note that they would be seeing each other next Sunday.

The next Sunday had come around sooner than they would think, and Julian began dressing for the play. He was lucky. Maria and Joaquin had both agreed on loaning Julian the car, gave him the keys, and a telephone number where he could reach a certain insurance number if necessary. They both refused to go to the play with Julian after his invitation. Julian climbed aboard the olive-green Mercedes-Benz and sped off toward the front gate. The melodic gaiety of the classical music spilled tunes from the fine-tuned FM radio, which was built into the front dash of the car. Joaquin gave one cautious wave of his right hand, and Julian pounced about the driveway's entrance. He pushed open the wrought iron fence with both his arms.

Whereupon, the green car came to the other driveway. The front door of the house of Natasha's mother was open as always. Once again, Julian came upon the grassy edge of the oval driveway. He stopped the vehicle and parked it in an etiquette of showcase fashion with the front tires slightly turned to one side. He walked up to the iron stairway of the dusty white trailer house and saw the daughter stretched out on the floor lounge sofa, watching television. His knocks on the door's entranceway brought a fidgety ring of life and fullness to the air.

"Who is it?" asked Natasha. Julian could see from the corner of his eye that the draw curtain was closed shut, and in a separate dressing room, Natasha was preparing herself with makeup and brush.

"It's me, Julian!" he shouted with a loud commanding voice. "I'll be with you in a minute," she clamored back.

"Hurry! The program starts in about one hour," he said.

"Okay, okay, Julian. Now you tell me. For heaven's sake!" she chided him with a backward expression of a twilight-enforced regret. The young girl lay on the couch with her eyes fixed upon the television screen. The mother passed by her, and carrying a small finely knit purse, she explained to her one last time about their going on a date to see a play in Raisintown.

"Goodbye! And don't forget to have fun," said the young fourteen-year-old in a mellow, soft tone.

"Goodbye," repeated the tall, thin-looking couple. They both walked over to the car. Julian opened the trailer's door in a manner that a gentleman would to a lady. Natasha wore dark-purple jumpers that adjusted with a twine wrapped above her naval. Her shirt was loosely drawn about her waist, and long-sleeved ruffles cuffed her wrist—buttons shooting up toward her neck. Her collar had ruffles. Her hair was short and styled to a matted fashion that curled about her skull. An exotic slim model of gypsy wizardry that imbibed about herself and her body is how she appeared. Long earrings drenched from her earlobes in an eloquent shine. Her lipstick was light pink, and her eyelash and eyeshadow had overcome Julian's reserved shyness and timidity. She was a whole grain of rich wheat in a large patch of weeds, thought Julian. And he felt more so relaxed now that he had ever felt in a long time as he sat next to the queen of old canary now. The wake of olives could be tasted and remembered.

Julian decided on taking the long way into Raisintown through the countryside. He slouched back in the driver's seat and turned up the volume on the radio. Natasha continued rolling more lipstick on her lips, imbibing both upper and lower lips to spread evenly the pink-rose bullet-shaped stick of lady delight.

"You could have told me that you were coming over earlier. At least, we wouldn't be in such a great hurry to get there."

"Oh! Don't worry! We'll get there," hindered Julian.

"You mean, you'll get there, you hope? Boy! Aren't you lucky tonight! You get to use the family car. And now you're talking about… what kind of insurance phone number did you say you were carrying in your wallet?" she asked.

Julian told her the name of the insurance group in a wasp of a pompous and adverbial description. She feigned a revealing gesture and geared her head over slightly. Face-to-face, her full-front profile confronted his. And without any kind of tainted warning or awareness, she flickered her eyes in a way which revealed a full crescent of green and blue mascara. The countryside blew past Julian's line of vision as his glassy-covered face matched hers with consuming idolatry. The flash of a *Glamour* magazine appeared across his fast-track mind as he gazed into her deep blue eyes, which entombed a jeweled cosmopolitan look.

The car was racing down the avenue at a tremendous rate of speed, faster than a runaway city taxi. Julian glanced with the quickness of an exalted race driver and noticed the background to the countryside. A not-so-old sawmill stood along the railroad tracks, and its main buildings were made plain and visible under the lavender silky sky.

"Years ago, my father worked over there," he stated.

"Really?" she answered him with a question. "Julian! Do you have to drive so fast?"

"But we'll be late," he answered.

"And for heaven's sake! Why don't you change the music channel to the radio? You know something? My first husband listened to nothing but hard classical composition, and I enjoy listening to the contemporary top forties my daughter listens to!"

Julian changed the station on the receiver's knob, and from that point onward, an acid rock played continuously into Raisintown. This younger driver remained tantamount until the car reached the end of Olive Avenue to where the Tower District nestled itself into a pall-mall of assured hospitality for theatrical and fanatical show-goers of the valley so sweet.

The car was parked opposite the entrance to the theater. A light arcade of pearl bulbs that resembled a Christmas season glittered back and forth. A parking lot that sat next to the long rectangular white building housed a vast array of limousines and frightful-colored Cadillacs. They both climbed from the vehicle. Natasha helped herself to her own saturated effort of not answering Julian's so-called gentleman's manners. She hurried out of the Mercedes-Benz.

"Wait…not so fast!" exclaimed Julian. He trotted over to the side of her door and locked it. Next, he returned to the driver's side and spent a difficult time locking his own door. She stood next to his side as he fondled with the key.

"So…are we late?" she asked the question in a low-keyed monotone, holding up her posture to one side of Julian's bent-over figure.

"Not hardly. Maybe. Just a few minutes," he answered back. They both crossed the street and hurried their steps. Suddenly, Julian dashed to the entrance of the playhouse like an impatient child veering for attention. As if happiness could show itself with many years of hidden, concealed puppy love, Julian portrayed himself.

"Not so fast!" she yelled out as he left her to cross the street alone. He waited for her at the entrance.

"Okay! Are you ready?" he asked with a blatant energy of unmeditated power.

"Of course, silly," she replied.

Julian tried to calm himself down as he narrowed his vision because of the excitement. His nervous energy was telling him so. Trying in vain to bring forth an unhidden masculinity and astuteness of a gentleman's etiquette, he felt clumsy, chastening himself to open the door. She slid past him with a quaint, petite smile of tactfulness. Her purse pressed up against her chest, and her hands both coveted and supported the material to her belongings.

She's been here before, probably many times at that, Julian thought to himself, and they both paraded up and down the red-carpet-covered floor.

There was a small line of persons standing in front of the box office, and music could be heard coming from behind the large red-carpeted wall. One could see the expression of the chaperon's face as she stood near the staircase and waited to collect tickets. Soon, it was Julian's turn at paying for the tickets. He neared the window and suddenly became aware. A profusion of embarrassment soon masked his awareness of the playhouse. Natasha shoved him aside somewhat as she grabbed to open her purse.

"That's okay, Julian. I'll buy my own, thank you." She came down with such resolute forcefulness that was strong enough to win anybody's heart. He fretfully began examining the artificial leather to see the amount of money he had left for the night.

"What's your name, ma'am?" asked the teller. Julian thought he had heard it twice. The word, the name she had given him, was her former married name. Julian remained calm and dared not to ask her any kind of personal question or deal in any kind of threat. He paid for his own ticket.

"Will you both be sitting at the same table?" Once again, the teller asked a second question. "Sure, we're supposed to have reserved seats with the psychology class, which came in earlier," answered Julian in a confident tone.

"No! That's quite alright. I'll sit at a table by myself," Natasha interrupted. "That will be fine."

"No!" cried out Julian. "You can come over to join the class."

"The lady at the door should be able to sit the both of you on a separate table," spoke up the teller, who continued tending the line. Without any hesitation, Julian led Natasha to the top edge of the staircase, which consisted of a few steps. A dim gloomy lit room bore a bar in the foreground. The lady chaperon, who had stood near the bottom of the staircase, waited for them to approach her. There were decorative tables arranged in random fashion, and soon afterward, the chaperon sat them both down at one table. The large floor room still had a shade of darkness that cloaked the few lights visible backstage. Julian began pointing a finger to the direction of the psychology class.

"See, Natasha! Over there in the corner. That's the class I'm talking to you about, the psychology class."

"Oh! Really!" she said, "Well, if you're really that hard up, Julian, go ahead! Go ahead and sit with them. I can stay here!" She was forcing the pitch of her voice. The lights began dimming, and the voices in the room began to silence. The show was about to start. Julian grabbed his lapel and then searched for a notebook he had packed earlier in his shirt pocket.

"Okay, Natasha, I'll be with you later. I'm going to go sit with the class now," Julian stated with a diligent tone of confidence.

"Oh! Okay, goodbye," she replied with an insincerity of an arrogance and slyness of attitude. She hadn't even bothered to move her face. Not even a glance did she give Julian as he stood up from the table to adjust his overcoat. He himself had not moved away from the table. Instead, he stared at the forlorn faces who looked on the foreground—pews and bar. He walked away in a sullen mood and eager pace as he neared the other side of the floor.

When Julian sat himself down, the mood of the crowd was on edge of the commencement of the play. He sat to one corner of the table next to a woman and her daughter. Several of the classmates welcomed him as he pulled out his notebook and pen from his shirt pocket. There was a large-sized black woman who sat in a seat in front of him.

"Were we supposed to take notes?" she asked him.

"I do it all the time," said Julian. He began writing down dates and headings.

"*Chapter Two*, a play by Neil Simon." The words flashed across the white sheet of paper. Julian kept peering over to his right side, trying to bring Natasha into view. The play wasn't to begin until another fifteen minutes. To begin with, everyone listened to one of the local community groups—large vocal choir of church kids singing to the tune of an old Dixieland flavor. A vast array of lights and special effects flashing across the ceiling and floors of the playhouse. There was a small intermission between the dance team and the opening act of the play.

A woman sitting next to him began showing her public features and revelations. She scooted her chair a few inches closer to Julian. Once again, Julian smooched over to one side to notice Natasha refusing a waiter's offer to buy a drink for the opening act. He frayed his body back and forth, swayed forward, and took on the profile of a comical character in front of his classmates and people from the public.

There were people packed in the upper balcony to an overflow capacity. Most of the figures were from the upper class of Raisintown. They were reamed with makeup, garmented with bright lit jewelry, and clothed in suite and tuxedos with evening gowns. For a spur of a moment, he felt out of place, and he would hide his garments in a way that both of his boots would move flush with each other. As long as the boots came closer to each other, they would appear not to look like boots.

In all the abominable time, however, the woman who sat next to him could not detest from asking what his name was. She appeared calm and eloquent. Not only her style of dress but also her face revealed the northern Raisintown cosmopolitan reflection. She was a sight of rare beauty to look at, as was her daughter. Both females wore their hair up in flips with the earlier colonial flavor of the Southern belle. Next to them sat other socialites from a proper attire of the city's super rich. Julian would only nod in a somewhat friendly salutation to these upper bourgeois faces. At last, a moment of shell-broken silence covered the table, but Julian was still looking for the face of Natasha. It seemed clear that the other side of the floor was beginning to fill itself to a capacity crowd.

"Were you looking for someone?" Julian turned around to the voice that sounded crisp and trenchant to his eardrum. The woman spoke in a fervid tone, aggressive and spontaneous at first. "Oh, yeah…sort of," he replied. "A friend of mine…she's sitting on the opposite side, over there somewhere." He moved his hand to show the direction.

"So! Is that what brought you over here tonight?" she asked. "Actually, I'm with a psychology class from the university. Most of them are sitting here at this table. Our professor, who is one of the main actresses, helped the studio in presenting the play. She gave us an assignment to write a report about the acts. We're studying abnormal behavior—a psychoanalytic ring," he said.

"Oh, really? That's interesting," she said with a parlance of a puzzled look. "Are you a criminology major?" Julian shook his head with a sharp retrieval of expression, and he placed both palms of his hands on the crest of his supported knees. He tried sitting with his legs crossed in a way that a sophisticated gentleman would reflect a higher echelon of this so-called playhouse society.

"I'm actually a chemistry major at the university," he said. The woman's face became even more confused and bored with listening to his answers. "I was recommended by a retired police officer who teaches at a police academy to take this course no matter what the cost."

"Oh! Really?" she blurted the refrain with the face of a usurped, arrogant termagant. She mentioned that her daughter was studying to become a model. Those were the least words she spoke to anyone at the table.

Model? he thought, and the word reminded him of Natasha. The stage was a pitch-black arena of darkness. Suddenly, the lights were turned on, and a roar of commotion became the crowd. The opening act was quite an entrance of two actors who would work with the psychology professor. Unlike any other play he had ever witnessed during the years which had taken its toll, he recollected a *Hello, Dolly* play presented in high school. The actors were fully developed stage people, including his teacher, the blonde professor. The play itself was taken from a series of short stories in a potpourri style of this famous American playwright Neil Simon. Julian frivolously began taking notes in a manner that made him forget everything around him, and this of course meant Natasha as well. She did not totally slip his mind because of his own fast lane of forgetfulness.

There was a great many number of conversations to take hold of the play. The only real thing Julian seemed to be concerned with at the time was watching and keeping a close eye on the professor, as she came trouncing on stage, wearing only a thin jet-black negligee. She was appalling yet appealing in every sense of the word. According to Julian, she was now a completely different person on stage than she was off stage.

"Natasha! Oh no! No. She's reminding me of Natasha again, her looks—tall, blonde, thin, and very striking. Hell! She'll be all right. I told her I'd be sitting over here with the class. But she prefers to be all alone. She's Italian…that's why! No…wait a minute. She's really sort of just another white girl. An Okie," and Julian's thoughts began collecting on his notepad. And Natasha was over there sitting by herself, all alone somewhere among all those strange elite-ridden faces. Act I was quickly coming to an end, and all the characterization created by the actors was becoming to enliven the drooling mood of the crowd. The applause was lengthy. Once again, the lights dimmed.

Julian lifted himself from the seat and stretched to a casual position to the meticulous, arrogant character of the crowd. People knew by this time that his drive anxiously sitting next to Natasha had now become a demanding test for endurance and stamina. He neither dared turning his head to one side to notice her presence nor bothered even looking for her throughout the local environment. Now he casually, and in a less perverted character, walked across the floor to the direction of the restrooms, which were located in the back of the stage. A few minutes passed. He walked out to the opening performance of Act II. There was more yelling and crying because of the emotionalism displayed by the two brothers in the story, as well as a sister-in-law and several girlfriends. Once again, in genteel, nonchalant fashion and with reputable character, this Julian Solbriozo became the tangible evidence of the envious and pervious detective whom he had once acclaimed himself to be. He glanced over to get a good-sized view of Natasha as he leaned his body forward to focus his eyes.

"Boy! He is weird!" several whispers cried out with a sullen mockery of summated criticism. "This is embarrassing," said another voice. But the voices on stage were getting louder now, more than anyone, as was the conflict. Natasha was not sitting there! He looked again, and this time he knew what he was viewing.

She's gone! The thought struck him in a terrible way, which made his thin frame shake and heart rumble. *Where is she? Where could she have gone? No. Nothing's happened really! I know. She's gone to the restrooms. She'll be back again. I know she will. She'll come back!*

His blood was beginning to boil for some uncanny reason he himself could not decide. He thought a while more and decided he should sit himself down. There were people sitting around him. Most of the long drawn-out giggles were coming from behind him. These people were beginning to take their seats, and it seemed so that the opening scene of Act TI was beginning to assemble itself onstage. The crowd breathed and shuffled somewhat as the lights began to show a trace of life. She quieted. Everyone but Julian rose up from his chair and bellowed to a front-faced standing position like an odd twig that had been broken from a frame of an oak tree. His face appeared somewhat flush and vain; a seriousness and fervor struck the stars from his eyes. He looked over to the direction once again. Natasha was not there. She had gone.

Nevertheless, the show must go on. Guilty feelings began to quickly drain away in the hot steam of attitude and disposition. New discoveries in character and the beast of an abominable playwright should never die in the self-created passions of self-indulged criticism and dedicated audience. And the show did go on. And so did Julian, without Natasha and all of the supportive feelings that she herself had tried to create abound the quismical security of a date. Homeliness and a forsaken locality.

It was at the terminal end of the first act when Julian had concluded that Natasha was one older woman who had ever made him feel at home in a long time. And with a saluted tandem of the current theater, the second act roared on, as did the third act. Julian, unlike most members of the crowd, frivolously took notes to complete his university assignment. The only side he had were the characters on stage and the soft yet violent deliverance of the creative epic produced through the transit resoluteness of the playwright, Neil Simon. Julian did not heed to rush the characters or the rhythm of the last and final act. But one thing was indeed certain in his mind, and that was the question of where Natasha was. Why had she avoided the second, last, and final act of the play? These only thoughts, so dismal and charred, are from the cold facts that she as an older woman carried with her certain relished etiquette adorned to a higher character. These thoughts existed apart from Julian's naive idea of overprotecting her.

"She's probably gone home. Perhaps a taxi?" rang out his fading thoughts. He brooded heavily over her disappearance. When the last and final act came to an end, Julian's enthusiasm reeled itself to a play-acted pretense. He pretended to ignore the celebrant and celebrated faces who sat around him. Everybody clapped, and so did Julian with a disdain nature, a disgusted look of illness and a mooted attitude for communicating. The lights lifted, and the actors came from behind the stage and bowed one final time. The crowd also lifted from their seats and benches, and in one gigantic roar of applause, the noise made Julian feel lowly and embarrassed. He rejected his own company with a resilient display of self-esteem, downtrodden and disappointment. Figures were walking all about the floor now, and Julian himself decided to gallop over to the men's restroom, a final trip before leaving for home. And once in the poorly lit hallway of the backstage dressing rooms, he ran into the tall, slim, blonde professor. She walked out to greet the class on the floor.

"Well, did you enjoy it?" she said, brushing up her long blonde hair in a pastoral and consoled fashion. And her eyes penetrated the imbibed once defeated, analytic personality of Julian's profile.

"It was great…and you were great!" replied Julian. "I've never seen anything like that before in my life," he gasped once again.

"I never have either!" said the professor. She had a large smile on her face. And in the several minutes which followed, Julian covered the floors and area like a philandering detective who recently lost little covered evidence. After covering the inside corners and leaving through the exit of the theater, he policed the outer premises and the street and mall. He made a second trip inside the playhouse. What few people remained there, they only chided and sullenly criticized his behavior. Standing on the outside entrance near the street, they waited until the theater emptied. Most of the elderly people were the last to leave the playhouse. Soon a tall, large-built figure of a man walked out to say good night to several of the quest with blunt statements and off-the-wall greetings. It was the owner and manager of the playhouse. He was making a few remarks about talent—an enthusiastic drive to go to New York for some reason. However, to Julian's inquisitive ears, the conversation contained an airy fringe of fakeness to it. Julian pretended not to hear and turned his back to all of them. Next, he dug the ignition key from out of his pocket and crossed the street. The first stop he made was at a telephone booth. He called Natasha's mother. There was no answer. He drove the Mercedes-Benz north on the main avenue to a very busy commercial avenue located in northern Raisintown. The nervous and worried character had had enough play acting for the night. The country road awaited his arrival.

Julian thought about Natasha all the way to her mother's house. He even cried just thinking about her disappearance, her anonymity, and her insolence. Above all matters and regardless of how older of a woman she was or who she claimed to be, he definitely had to go see her. And that was that. His blood curled, and his disposition aged ten years as the car approached her mother's driveway.

He could not believe he was back at her house, and the night had matured. The Mercedes was laid to rest in the back of the house. It faced the trailer house. He walked up the stairway as always. There was no answer. Next, he stepped his way toward one side of the house, around the planters. Once on the front porch, he waited several seconds before making the knocks. The lights in the house, except for a very dim red light coming from the parlor, were turned off. Natasha could hear his footsteps as he approached the front door. She waited directly behind the door, covetously anticipating his presence. Julian's knocks were loud and solid and without refrain. As she opened the door with a soft pull of tediousness, Julian was grinding his teeth to a halt.

"Who is it?" murmured Natasha's voice as she cracked the door open enough to allow a fine slit of red light to penetrate through the opening. She peered through the entrance with a timidity uncalled for yet in a way her own mother would many times. Julian looked on with scorching eyes.

"What in the hell happened to you anyway!" spoke out Julian with a high tone of voice and much forcefulness in his character and became demanding. Natasha flustered to a familiar tone in his voice, and her eyes jumped back and forth like she had nystagmus.

"What do you mean what in the hell happened to me?" she pounced back at him with a sharp revenge. "Listen to me! Nobody even stands me up that way."

"What way?" asked Julian. "This is the first time ever in my life that anyone has ever stood me up!" went her voice. She never dared stepping out from behind the door. She wore a dark-red nightgown. She had already been in bed earlier. The crossed look on her face dominated the traces of outside moonlight cast on her body.

"But we had agreed earlier, remember?" cried out Julian.

"How dare you leave me sitting there all by myself? No one has ever done that to me before. No one!" she continued with a flurry of accusations.

"What did I do? I told you that we would be sitting on different tables. I went over with where the class was sitting," said Julian.

"I thought someone had mugged you…or something terrible had happened to you! Why did you leave? You could have at least told me that you wanted to go or that you were leaving." Natasha listened intently. "You could have hit me on the shoulder or slapped me on the face. Anything!" Julian's voice was beginning to lose its ground with a shaky character, loud and truncated. "You could have said something, Natasha," he said one last time.

"Listen. Why don't you go away and leave me alone?" She stood her pace and held her personal territory behind the door.

Julian persisted. "How did you get back over here anyway?"

"A friend of mine brought me back over here," she answered. "Just a friend."

"Really now!" And soon his interrogative voice rose above the nocturnal silence of the country atmosphere. "You must have waited somewhere."

"I did!" she stammered out. "And now, go away!"

"Wait!" he interrupted. "Give me your hand, Natasha."

"What for?"

"Just give me your hand!"

Natasha hesitated at first. She held her left arm up to her flat chest, pressed tightly, invigoratingly. Next, she gently moved her arm, fully extended with her left palm pronated and faced upward. Julian unloosened the grip from his own fist.

"Here! Take it. It's yours," he said as he grabbed for her arm, placing the crimson container of lipstick onto her left palm.

"You forgot it!"

The movement appeared to bring a slow, morose, sponge-like tear near her eyes. She remained startled and somewhat shocked for the moment. Julian grabbed both of his lapels, adjusted them, and walked away, nonchalant, unfeigned, notorious, and vain. This time, he neither dared look back. Natasha peered out the door a few inches noticeable.

"Julian, don't get mad. Please don't get angry!" she pleaded.

"Good night!" And that was the only word that could be heard in the distance. Julian gathered his wits, boarded the Mercedes-Benz, rang up the ignition, and gunned the innocence of the machine. Dust! The car left behind a huge cloud of yellow dust against the moonlight. The muggy screen, nettled of white color, settled over the front yard and over all of Natasha's shortcomings. Julian kept his memories quiet, gathered, and colloquial to his own résumé of fast-hand dating and pseudo courtship. Natasha is everything he would think about. He thought of this while grinding out in afternoon sprees of jogging and make-shift running debuts along the freeway and near the neighborhood area, which outlined Natasha's trailer house and mother's home. He was well on his way in believing that he had actually fallen in love with her as well as being infatuated with her mother. His jogging and his track took him well past beyond the Casa Grande Hotel, which sat alongside that freeway called the Ole El Camino Real. Yes, his pace took him as far as the old sawmill, a wooden producer that operated on a part-time basis throughout the year. The mill was almost five miles from his stepfather's home. He remembered Natasha fluttering her eyelids and her wide open stare.

The next several weeks were spent working his usual evening shift at the hospital next door. There were those lowly afternoons when he had made an attempt of calling up Natasha's mother. They'd talk over the phone about common subject matters, no more, no less. Julian concluded that his brash moves for the summer could only have been for summer's sake. This was true, and not because he was pawning for another excuse for settling differences of total satisfaction between him and his parents, who dearly took their hands at trying to reshape and develop him. He was, as he would recall, behind the brim of the supporting crib. It was also those weeks that he paid his first dues with a local karate club studio. He had never known about self-defense the way he had learned about it that summer. This not only excited the overprotected ways of Natasha but stimulated the elderly, cosmopolitan, and experienced appeal of her mother.

And so it was one evening that Julian had gone over to visit them on his yellow ten-speed bike that he could say now that everything was for precisely summer's sake. He pondered greatly on his debut and involvement with this semi-Italian and mid-Western family. Within the usual flavor of the evening, Natasha wasn't home. And once again, he did not hesitate to knock at the front door to her mother's home. With a demented determination of a sales-type person instead of an everyday house caller, he calmly withdrew from an angle of attack. Natasha's mother opened the front door. He stared at her for a moment's time.

"Yes…who is it?" her voice faded. She also blanked her vision in a fresh stare. "Well! Hello. What brings you over here, Julian?" Before Julian could get a word over, she interrupted.

"No…hold on! If you think you came over to see Natasha tonight, you're out of luck, I'm afraid." Now her voice revealed itself with a more positive sternness. She neared the screen and brought forth her figure. She was wearing a deep-red, sleeveless outfit that blanketed her bareness with a low-back and low-front chest line. Over the top of her shoulders hung a white shawl piece which affixed loosely about her neck and opened in the front, revealing her light-pink breast line. Julian looked downward for a few seconds to view the black high-heeled shoes and dark shady leg stockings she wore.

"I had hoped she would be home this week," said Julian with a timid croak of excitement in his throat. He appeared to be shocked at her elegance and coquettish appearance.

"Well, she's not here this week. She's gone to the coast, and she's taken her daughter with her. She needs a rest, Julian. And she's going to have some fun for the week. She's been working hard at the plant and deserves a break."

Julian was merely looking for an answer and not a potpourri of sequential excuses.

"I see!" he replied in the most sound of detective voices one could experience. She paused a moment and soon reached for her neck with both hands to button the small see-through shawl. Leaning over slightly, she exposed her cleavage without any hesitation.

Goodness! thought Julian. *She's a reserved woman, and there's nothing to be worried about. We're all alone, and we're out in the country. There are no other people around, so it seems.*

She asked him to come over earlier when there was spare time on their hands. The subject of eschatology was in the air, and she was one of a few handful of local teachers who lived in the valley. Julian was neither enthralled nor enthused about learning the art of scientology or its own shortcomings. However, it was the one way that she had explained it earlier that led his interest into their household. She was indeed an exceedingly beautiful woman for her age, and her daughters were always enticing to look at. If he kept her interest, he would keep Natasha's interest. So he precluded.

"Well, would it be okay if I came in to talk through a session with you about eschatology?" asked Julian.

"Well! I don't know. What I mean is I don't think I'm prepared for it tonight," she said with a note of hesitation and reluctance. She glanced to the area beneath Julian's feet and scoured her rigid decision. Lastly, she bought her face back up to Julian's eye level and began adjusting her hairdo with her hands, touching her forehead and earrings with a soft movement. She blurted out and flung the door wide open with a warm hospitable smile and a friendliness that he had never seen her display.

"Oh! All right, come on in. Come on in and have a seat," her voice simmered to a natural halt.

And so it seemed that she was indeed the only one left in the house that night. Natasha's sister wasn't there, nor were any of her older brothers, a group of close-knit Italian honchos who had neither cared for Julian nor had ever welcomed him there. He remembered that last time Natasha's sister had met him. She eyed him the entire night with a sharp burning stare of a martial vindictiveness as she told him that he would have to pay some money for studying eschatology with their mother. Julian walked inside and recovered his composure as he took the large parlor chair that sat near the entrance. He sat down. Thereafter, Natasha's mother also sat herself down in a chair across the rug from him and next to the perpendicular wall that travailed into the back part of the house, the inside patio. She gingerly crossed her legs and established an astute erectness of a paper posture more commonly seen among high-class bourgeois models. Julian focused on her image.

"Go ahead and make yourself comfortable," she said in a collective and calm voice. She did not look toward him as she talked but would view the parlor directly in front of her. "Would you care for anything to drink while you're here?"

"No. No thanks," said Julian. "That's okay!" Now, Julian himself could feel his blood circulation, and he adjusted his posture on the armchair.

"Very well! So…exactly what have you been doing with yourself?" she asked him. Julian knew how to answer her. However, he was more so interested in getting to the meat of the conversation. After all, she did seem to have something to present, and he, among most people, was willing to listen. At first and in a not-so-midway-foreign house, Julian could not decipher her gypsy-look presence. Gregariously and undauntedly, he sat there, waiting for her first question.

"So! What religious background do you come from anyway?" she asked in a psychoanalytic approach of a revered clinician.

"I'm Catholic. I come from a Catholic background," answered Julian. "I don't really consider myself a dedicated churchgoer, whom most people tend to envision."

"Well, if you decide to want to come to study eschatology, you have to keep in mind the fact that it is not a religion which supports any one sect or church denomination."

"Not even Catholic?" he asked.

"Not even Catholic," she replied.

Julian erected his posture to a more forward position in the chair.

"It sounds like to me that society of scientology would only sell itself the tracts it has to offer people who are willing to buy!"

"No…no, Julian. You have the wrong idea about this teaching," she defended her position. Next, she turned her head to look at Julian.

"This teaching itself has nothing to do with taking sides with anyone or any one denomination. You have to be serious about this now. You have to put your mind in gear in determining certain factors about life and truth!"

Life and truth? he thought silently to himself. "Truth?" he said out loud.

"This is what you're looking for? Isn't it, Julian?" she repeated, and with a more defunct look of solemn audaciousness, she winked her right eye at him without warning.

"It would help. You know?" he replied.

She was adjusting her dress line on her knee, and it draped over her legs in an easy fashion, which showed no trace of strain nor struggle.

"Julian…listen! You have to take this seriously if you want to learn it. I don't want you causing any kind of trouble or stress on yourself," she said.

"What do you mean trouble?" he asked.

"Now, you know what I mean!" she blurted. "If you want to learn, you are to come over here to see me and not to see my daughter, Natasha. Now if you want to keep raising the issue, you will not be able to flow into the first steps of the learning process." She paused a few seconds. "I've told you once already that you are to stay away from Natasha. When she says that she doesn't want to see someone, she means that she doesn't want to see that person."

"I know," he blurted out with a frigid tone of animosity in his voice. His guilt was trying to repress itself about his concocted brashness and insolence.

"I sure hope you know, Julian," she stated back with an assured smile on her face. She was making herself more comfortable now.

Julian listened intently. The next several minutes she reverberated with a flurry of tandem explanations about the science of eschatology itself and how Christ was returning for one final act of delivering judgment upon the masses and the world incarnate. She must have used the word Jesus Christ at least two dozen times. How could she have been so eccentrically enmeshed within her own idyllic view of altruism? How could Julian have been so vulnerable to have succumb to her invitation? Indeed, he was in love with Natasha to a point of rendezvous and time. He was determined to impinge on his own demanding rights to bury himself within the boundaries of having half of a foot in his grave, as his mother would concede. This, he felt, would envelop a relationship of modern-day matricide. Julian wasn't confused about love this time, but he was becoming vindictive about the theme itself. His conscience drew him to listening intently as before.

"And so…how are you making out these days, Julian? Are you still living with your folks?" she asked.

"Yes!" he answered.

"How do you feed yourself? Are you still working at the hospital?" The woman was becoming inquisitive in her so-called interview. Julian continued answering.

"Yes! I'm sort of an on-call person at the hospital," he said.

"You mean you don't work full-time?"

"No! I'm sort of an on-call person at the hospital," he said.

"You mean you don't work full time?"

"Yes!"

"What do you do with all of your time anyway?"

"I'm preparing myself to enter a police academy," he answered.

"A police academy?" she exasperated. "Well! By all means, Julian. You shouldn't have any problems practicing eschatology in learning to become a police officer." She was becoming glutted with joy. "By all means, take advantage of the situation."

Now Julian was beginning to relax. "Come to think of it now, I also received an application the other day from the Department of the Navy. They said that there is a chance that I may qualify for a submarine school. You know! The letter sounded something like an invitation for cruising the seven seas in an American-built nuclear submarine."

"Hell! It doesn't matter, Julian. Why, you could even take your eschatological studies with you on your submarine," she stated.

That was the bottom line, Julian thought, *Now the woman is trying to rid me of her presence. Perhaps I shouldn't have come over to see her. Is this all too foreboding, too forbearing? If I left now, I could forget about all of this. I could forget about eschatology and all of this jumping-into-conclusion frenzy, all these misgivings. Natasha? She's over at the beach. She's having fun, and here I am sitting in front of her mother. I'm trying to be an eccentric about who I am, what I know, and what I'm doing here. I've chalked up a good image about her mother, and she's very enthused about it. Why, she's crazy about it. In fact, I think she's infatuated with me. Oh! She's such a devilish, sexy, horny old woman. She'd just as soon take me to bed and hold me close. Never! It's all in my mind. Nevertheless, here I am talking about her, and she's all glammed up like a woman would be in a red-light district. Perhaps everything has become to forbearing that I should conjecture a seemingly paradoxical conclusion about my relationship with people, preferably women.* The next moment, she began handing Julian a spoonful of notebooks and typewritten papers.

"Before you go, I could go ahead and give you these workbooks, which explain the basis for learning eschatology. Some formats, outlines, and introductions are included. You can start with these for now. I also want to give you a book that will give you the clear story over the teaching itself. You'll enjoy it, I'm sure." She pulled the book from out of the wall case that covered the back room of the parlor. She handed it to him.

"We'll get together again, you and I," she said. "I'll be busy next week, but you and I could find some time to get together in the future."

"I'll give you a call sometime. I'll keep in touch with you," said Julian as he felt a repugnance and disillusioned character remit his reasoning. He felt that she was pushing him out of the house—a feeling, no doubt, existing with her mother as well. He walked out of the front door and was soon out of sight from the mother's view. She stood next to the small narrow porch, and traces of noise were coming from the bike as the tall, thin character sped off down the rustic, country-laden avenue.

That very same night, Julian continued into town on his bike with a relief of content and fresh new adventure in his heart. His legs pedaled him over to an old shanty place called C Street, which ran from a north to a south direction. It was a relic of taboo and condemned homestead, one of the older streets in Winetown. The street had its history of having its haves and have-nots, for its reputation was too liberal for a saintly few of the town. After hearing many stories about the street, the sensation came clear to his mind that this particular street was only a carbon-copy replay of the many sore-thumb relics that stood apart from many small towns of the valley. And who else but the Mexican, those majority of huddled few who amassed themselves about the habitat, would live there? Julian had no problems finding what he wanted as he flowed into the crowd of shoddy, hard faces that lined the streets' sidewalks and walkways of the tavern. He pedaled his bike to the center of activity, a barroom called La Primavera Clubo. Stopping the bike in an instant, he began recollecting his thoughts in an adamant and reoccurring nature about his sweet, delicate memories of Natasha.

"So she's having fun, says her mother!" His mind marooned to a low gaunt and alembic stature. He tried to avoid bracing the idea with a gracious, inept courage, not to worry with all his built-in stress and insecure tendencies. After all, she was an older woman. Parking the bike over the dark foreboding drain of the sewer peephole, he locked a chain around the bike frame with a combination lock. Securing it to the drain, he fastened his brown leather belt, which coaxed his waist and gave a friendly yet stern greeting to some of the older gentlemen who stood on the outside of the bar's entrance. Within the boundaries of the sidewalk, they meddled in clusters and wore shady clothes, working clothes, the apparel field workers wore to pick grapes. Some with shoddy hats and riveted boots, they seemed to add to the pastoral flavor of this discreet agricultural arena, Winetown. Julian pushed open the single-hinged swinging door. The door was an old woodened cracked piece coated with a pale-pink color of a quality that was in contrast to the green and blue walls. And those stolid, hard faces lined the corners and pool tables, and several more characters controlled the seats at the bar. They turned to look at this newly initiated stranger. The stares only lasted several seconds. Julian broke loose from the mood. Walking away from the door, he leaned over his thin posture and sat down next to some dark figures positioned along the bar. There were a few women sitting there, and more so, the workers in the back of the bar were also women, pregnant women. Wide-edged mirrors placated the background, reflecting the rounded, semi-spherical figures of the female bartenders. Their Spanish-speaking tongues alluded the heaviness of the smoke-filled room, and smiling, homely faces endeared the customers' presence. Julian tried expressing himself in Spanish words; he placed both his arms on top of the counter and precluded with a cynical attitude. At first, some of the figures pretended not to see him, oblivious yet surprised to see him in the bar. Rumors traveled farther than the cynical attitude in this abode of agricultural amenity and embossed character. "Could I have a beer? One Coors, please," said Julian.

"He's just another stud, another flirt," said one of the women behind the bar.

"She would know," mumbled another. Julian delighted himself in their witty humor.

"Thank you," he said. He took the beer in his hand and nursed it with the genuine balance and coordination of an older man. He could envision the face of Natasha's mother in his mind, her memory. His own vulnerability and embellished temptation fought with each and every decision that he encroached himself with. A wide-eyed woman tried capturing a demented and bored beast within him; she began speaking with an overly brooded voice. Once again, the image of Natasha thrashed to his mind. He could hear her mother's voice. "She went to the coast, and she's going to have fun, and you, Julian, aren't going to stop her."

Once again, the lucid eyes of the prostitute woman tempted his premonitions. He mentioned the words "Hello, how do you do?" and quickly "Goodbye." A barrage flow of guilt paranoia controlled his steps, and he began traversing across the archaic-looking dance floor with an astute bravado that supported his frailties and monumental tasks. And without warning, a foreclosure of cultured divinity stared at him directly into his face. It was the feeling of familiarity coming from the public eyes who sat at the old tables. This made him feel at home, as if the environment had gone through a custom's etiquette, a border check. Mexico was in the air. Mexicans were everywhere, and the chameleon-like character of an alienated kind grasp at Julian's idea of coterie and colonial vagabond existence. He stayed far from the majority of characters; he kept his distance, his personality, so it seemed, at a sacrosanct flavor.

There was a group of card players toward the very back of the room, none of whose faces he seemed to recognize. All for the better, he thought. And like all bar hangouts located on this street, most of the card games were always controlled by these field workers and some lifelong residents of the community. His curiosity began begging the question, literally, and his courage approached several of the members who waited for their turns at the table. They confided in his curiosity, his loneness, and aloofness reprimand which carried itself into their *soledad* worlds and happy-go-lucky characters. Their doldrums and their secret personalities lie open away, a haven, for Julian's novical idea of his own ritual. He decided to stay for the evening. One or two beers would be his social limit. After a few witnessing acts at seeing the tumultuous and variety interplay of the card players, he solemnly walked out, bored yet dignified of the shortcomings and passed-up opportunities. His robust character had made them believe he was a medical doctor. That precisely hadn't changed over the past two years.

After exiting the door to the bar, he unleased and unlocked the chain that held his bike to the sewer porthole. And without wasting time to notice anyone around him, he raced down the street to a phone booth. He picked up the receiver and called the hospital. He was determined to return to work again that night.

"Hello…that's right! It's me. Julian Solbriozo. I'm available for working on the graveyard shift tonight. Can you use me?" Julian's voice paused, and so did the supervisor's voice at the other end of the line.

"Good! I'll be over at eleven. Goodbye," he concluded with an austere reclamation.

Now, Julian would head back south, across the freeway, and to the direction of the hospital. He pedaled back to the direction of the ranch house, where he long awaited the stay in his room so that he could catch his breath and sober himself. The mechanic and the college instructor were asleep. The only creatures alive and making any remnants of sound were the dogs and a few stray cats who were daring enough to approach the yards at night. Julian was good at approaching the yard on his bike during these nighttime hours.

Here was one dark figure of a beast who protruded every corner of this labyrinth, this secluded yet chaste area behind the grounds of the hospital. Much to the recognition and domestic familiarity of those stray cats trying to stealthily create silence in the dark without waking up the adamant residence of the house, Julian would find his room in the darkness of the hallway. Turning on the lamplights, he changed his clothes and dressed himself into his white outfit. He opened the curtains to the window, and the black night stared at him. Those not-so-far-distant lights from the hospital were made visible through the walnut orchard that lay between his room and the hospital grounds. Closing the door gently, he made his way out of the kitchen and tried not to stir anyone's content. He began his quiet walk down Golden State Boulevard. With the image of the lowly, gauntlet faces of the people from the bars, his memory began alluding him, and now the faces of Natasha and her mother were barely visible in the webs of his mind. Margaret Farrington's complexion hadn't changed any since the last time she had spoken with Julian. She had told him about her recent proposal of being engaged with a northerly man from the area nearby. Julian wasn't at all interested in hearing about her recent love affairs and infatuations. Everyone on the medical floor welcomed him with sureness and lividness, a familiar cast. Aside from their knowledgeable demeanors and first-hand reports of US Highway 99 rumors, no such rumors were any different at any such time.

"Eager to work tonight, Julian?" The flagrant statement came from Margaret's voice box.

"That's pretty good, boy," mumbled one of the other nurses who was talking to the medicine nurse for the night. "The man goes into town, has a few beers, and finally, casually, comes to work as if nothing's happened."

"Nothing has happened. Can't you see?" said the medicine nurse, who was one woman who would always publicize the fact about her marriage to a fairly successful practicing psychiatrist. She would bore everyone about her marriage, as did most nurses, Julian could recall. This eccentric orderly would entertain himself by standing close to her as many times as possible. She was built like a tank and showed the most cleavage from her large breast than any other nurse. Everyone knew the fact.

Everyone there knew that nothing would happen between him and many of the nurses, as nothing consequently did happen. During these nights, there were times that he would hide himself in the frenzy of the patients' rooms, cajoling with the patients and entertaining them the best he knew how. These nightly visitors of families who would arrive would confront him. He was becoming a well-cooked mascot and revered himself to be so as he disciplined his high ebb for quick arguments and competition. And so it would seem that he should remain at the bottom of the totem pole for sacred reasons of privacy. There was no such a word.

The smell of mercresin and alcohol polluted the hallway with a mercantile stench of clinical friendliness. The night had shown an opportunity for infringing on Natasha's rights. Instead, the hospital had called him to do some double duty at the mental care ward, a not-so-familiar place located next door to the medical floor, a place where Julian had settled himself within the habitat. The supervisor of the night allowed him to wear plain clothes; no white clothes were necessary. A week later had passed, and his distinct attitude had changed. He succinctly aborted the visit to Natasha and decided upon devoting more time at the hospital. Reporting time was at eleven o'clock as usual during a night shift.

"Where in the hell has the nurse gone to, anyway? God bless this place. God damn these people!" yelled the voice from one of the rearmost rooms along the north hallway. Julian sat at the counter within the nursing station and began paying tribute to the sounds of the heavyset voice as he no sooner than placed a marker deep into the binder of the book he was reading. The book was entitled *La Vida Religiosa Entre Medicina*.

"Nurse. Nurse!" came the words again, echoing down the pathway. Julian rushed his movements as he entered the patient's room alone and at ease. There were no other persons on the floor at that particular time after which the midnight vitals had been taken and medications had all been administered. The charge nurse had stepped out for several minutes to speak with some personnel in the other ward. Julian was alone as his shadow approached the room.

"What seems to be the problem, sir? Is there anything I could help you with?" consoled Julian with a soft yet tangible voice.

"Hell! Damn it! I don't mean to be so loud, but where in the damn hell is the medicine nurse?" he stammered again with his voice and struggled in his bed. A big, obese man of latent middle-aged character, with a cigarette tucked away in his mouth, tried relaxing as he placed both hands in a casual life-of-Riley position behind his skull with a repose and a smile forced upon his face.

"It's my back. My back is killing me. I just had an operation recently, you know! Yesterday! And they are sons of bitches! Believe me," he said.

"Here! Let me help you be more comfortable," said Julian as he approached the bed with the usual eagerness.

"Comfortable? Hell! You people don't know what feeling comfortable is all about," he said, delivering his statements with an incumbent thirst for advice.

"Hey, man! We try to do our best here, you know? We're not gods who walk around these halls all day long, trying to please everyone," defended Julian. "We're ordinary people too, you know."

"Ordinary people? Shit!" exclaimed the man as he tugged at the cigarette away from his mouth and began pulling down the nostrils on his nose. "Boy, so what does that mean anyhow?" An ingrate smile, unkempt yet wholesome, slowed the avarice that Julian beheld.

"Look, man! I just work here."

"There's nothing to look at, buddy," he interrupted.

"Well! That's your problem, not mine."

"Look! Amigo. Just get me the nurse, all right?" He was putting out a hand in a gentle motion. The appeal of a warm handshake preached out to Julian. Julian took hold of his left hand and shook it.

"How's it going, compadre?" he said. "Boy, you look like you could use some sleep yourself, a street-clothed guy like you. Who are you anyway?"

"Julian, Julian Solbriozo," he said to the stranger. "They let us dress like this once in a while."

"You mean, they let Joe Blow Gonzales dress like that once in a while?" he stammered haughtily, changing the tone in his voice. "Hey, friend, don't get mad. Your white outfit, where do you keep it anyway? What's the matter, you tired of trying to be somebody special?"

And with those words, Julian backed off and moved himself some distance away from the bed. *Why should I care about this alcoholic slut?* he thought. *Hell! He's just another slut, some passerby who's making good some time here at the hospital. Doctor, perhaps I myself should speak so loud as to think of my own hazardous position.*

"So what the hell do you do for a living?" he reproached the bedridden man's character.

"Oh…shit! You'd never guess in a million years exactly what I used to do for a living. I'm retired now. Thank God I'm retired now." He paused a few moments. "Boy, but can you stand these politicians, all these bastards who sit on their big fat asses up in Sacramento?"

"And?" asked Julian.

"What do ya mean *and?*" replied the stranger. "Hell! They're always allocating money to some poor, dumb *culero* who comes from a halfway upper-middle-class family and who goes around smoking pot and taking drugs like any regular dumb fuck who doesn't give a shit about putting the money to good use."

"So what does all of this have to do with what you do for a living?" asked Julian. The stranger inhaled with a slow drag from his cigarette.

"What do ya mean what does it have to do? Who are you anyway, and where's your white outfit? Hell! All nurses wear white outfits."

"Sorry, mister, I'm not a nurse," replied Julian.

"So what the damn hell are you anyway?" he blurted out. Julian remained silent and brought forth on his face a redemption of negritude and austerity, as stunned eyes replaced his facial expression so flushed.

"Listen, I haven't even touched you tonight, your territory or whatever it is you want to call it. What makes you think I've done a terrible thing as that anyway?" Julian's temper was becoming aglow in the murky-lit room.

"You know something, speedy Gonzales, that's your problem," the stranger catapulted and began defending his own personality with a blankness of intrepidation.

"Hell!" He shook his head. "Guys like me deserve a kick in the ass, but guys like you, boy!" he mustered his broken sentences and rallied with a few consecutive puffs on his cigarette. Now he appeared to be as a man who had recently been fired on a discreet pardon from penitentiary life, a man gathering his thoughts and readying himself for an "e pluribus unum" speech. His tired, dark eyes turned into a swarthy, deep, red picture of relaxed heaven, and he showed no excess signs of strain nor discomfort.

"Boy! What I'd do to go back into time just to have made a different kind of a living for myself. But that's all over with now. I've spent my money unregrettably. I've given myself to the maximum, pleasing both the companies and some friends I've made along the way. I performed enough acts and acts to follow. I've covered up for both people and still more people along the same road. I've had fun: I've done some gambling, not knowing that I should have gambled or not. I've had my share of women, not knowing which one really loved me or not. I've had my share of living, buddy, fun and drink, whatever you want to call it." His voice beckoned to that of a broken tape recorder as Julian listened to the verbosity.

"So what are you complaining about?" asked Julian while his own blood began to run at a more vivid, warm pace throughout his own body.

"Hell! You would know, compadre. You of all people! Shit! You've got it made. You've got everything set out in front of you, don't you?" he posthumously asked with less discreetness.

Julian shimmered somewhat with a beguiled smile; he nodded as if to signal some horrid character within him. Secondly, he began breaking away the feathered formation of smoke that began getting in the way of his eyes.

"I'm happy with myself, mister," said Julian with a serene rebuttal of nonconformance.

"Why in the hell aren't you a nurse? You lazy or something?" he asked.

"I really did get into it at one time, but my interest led me to other areas," answered Julian.

"You mean women!" he stated. Julian blushed with a flippant expression at the statement.

"Hey! I bet you find a lot around this hospital, hey, kid?"

"Oh! I can say I know a few women around this town."

"You mean nurses?"

"Not in particular."

"Yeah! Sure! Some of these nurses are really good-looking women. Then you never know about nurses, do you?"

"Like I had told you earlier, the charge nurse will not be back. She's busy!" said Julian.

"Yeah! Well, I guess I'll make out all right after all. Like I said, I've had my share of wagon wheels and hangovers." The stranger appeared in a daze for a few seconds. He'd look to the ceiling and not move an eye.

"So…what did you do for a living? You a bartender?"

"No!"

"A truck driver?"

"Nope! You'll never guess."

"A taxi driver?"

"Hell! I took a damn taxi all the way over from Frisco to this hospital. Two hundred and eighty-five dollars is what the bastard charged me. Can you believe that?" he stammered.

"You paid a taxi driver that much money to come all the way to this hospital?" asked Julian in a sarcastic jest.

"You'd better believe it. Hell! Those damn doctors in San Francisco belong in San Francisco with all those flutterers."

"So what the hell is so wrong with that? I can't imagine why somebody would travel that far to a small-town area along the US 99 Freeway."

"Man! Where have you been anyway, boy? They have some pretty hot stuff here in this place. You ought to know. Nah! Hell! You wouldn't know…Nah! You'll never guess what I did for a living."

"You're an insurance man…right?"

"Shit! Insurance man, ass," he rescinded with a meaner tone in his definite voice. "Hell! I was better than an insurance man, boy! Don't you know anything?"

"I know some," said Julian.

"Ya ever heard of Steve McQueen?" he asked.

"Sure! He died in Mexico. Why all the names of these movie stars?" exclaimed Julian.

"Movie stars!" he gasped as if choking for air. "Hell, I have worked with plenty of movie stars and the like."

"Really?" said Julian with a rise in his curiosity, which brought forth a change of enthusiasm in his dialect. "I'm one of the guys who goes around in the movie, trying to make these characters look good. Don't you see?"

"You don't act or talk like a writer or director."

"Writer? What do you know about writing?" he still plundered with a forward march in his voice. "Did you ever see that one guy who falls out of the tall building in the movie called *The Towering Inferno?*"

"You mean the guy who's on fire, and he's burning up on his way down to the first floor."

"Yeah! That's it," said the man with a sudden chill of enthusiasm in his voice. "You see, the guy that's falling off the building happens to be me."

"You?" exclaimed Julian. "You're the guy on fire?"

"That's right."

"So you're a stuntman?"

"That's what I do for a living. I'm a stuntman. You'll learn to get smart before you learn to be damned."

"I'll be damned!" said Julian.

"I've been around, kid. Hell, I've worked almost side by side with Steve McQueen. I've appeared in a few good movies. Nobody ever knew who I am. It's a quick fill-in-type job, no glamour nor recognition. You know. Just work! The type of work which fills your day from sunup to sunrise. It was sure a hell of an interesting experience. Plenty of work was involved, and the pay wasn't bad. Hell! It was good enough gravy to enjoy myself. I survived. I managed. I covered up for plenty of people. I made them look good. I didn't get rich, but I sure in hell made plenty of people look good— all of those faces, all of those remembrances."

"You let it get to ya, uh?" said Julian. "The booze, the drink, the money, and all those good times."

"That's not the reason why I'm an alcoholic. I'm the one guy that got to those people. Most of them lose track of what it means to be a human being anymore. All of those sorry souls, hell! If it wouldn't have been for me, there's a good number of people who wouldn't have won their awards and recognition and all of that bull that goes along with it."

"You mean the money?" asked Julian.

"No, just the bull!" he said.

"I don't understand you, mister."

"You don't understand. This is what I've been trying to tell you all morning. You don't understand. You take everything too serious. You don't know how to flow along with the stream. Easy! Why fight it?"

"Fight it?" questioned Julian with a crescendo tone of poise and epic in his voice. "You're the one who fought it, mister. You're the one who took the entire joke too serious. You're the one who hid behind all those disguised faces, those daredevil attitudes. You're the guy who fell flat on your face when you had to, and every time someone decided to jump to the side, you ventured over a cliff somewhere. That's all too lonely for me, mister."

"So what are you trying to prove?" he contented himself with a maligned face, empty and defeated to argument. Julian gulped with a tenacious swallow. He hesitated to say anything after the stranger's lengthy discourse.

"Why don't you put yourself out before it's too late?" He raised his voice again. "You're burning up, kid…you're burning up…up." Now his voice faded into a mixed gurgle and repented cough. He moaned and tried sullying himself with a familiar clinical groan that one hears coming from most alcoholics who find haven in a local hospital.

Julian repealed himself to answering the question. He stood there, frigid. Next, he would begin adjusting a stethoscope around his neck. Finally, he would pretend to clean the washbasin near the mirror.

"Hey! Don't go away, compadre! You're all right. You know that," said the stranger with a residual smile.

"Don't worry, mister. I'll be here all morning. You can count on that," Julian replied with a chivalrous look on his face and constantly ignored looking at his own image in the mirror.

"Say, Julian, how about another glass of water? I can't reach my jug." Julian slowly moved across the floor and inflated himself with heavy breathing. He handed the jug and an empty glass to him.

"Here! It's all yours," he said.

"Thanks!" the stranger replied, appearing to stare Julian in the mind.

"The name's Alan, Alan Torrezano." He woke up. They both reached out and shook each other's hands.

"Well! I can't say it's been a pleasure knowing you. And then again, I can't say that it's been a pleasure not knowing you," said Julian.

"Hold on, buddy! You gonna leave me already? What's your hurry, big boy?" asked Alan.

"I've got to go down the hall. There are the other chores to be done. There's plenty to do in this hospital. Being that I'm the only one on duty tonight, if I don't get anything done, then nothing gets done. It's as simple as that," said Julian.

"All right, all right! I get the picture. I've heard everything," he resigned as he gasped for air; and the turbid cough became the main thrust for the night.

"Go ahead! I understand. Go ahead and tend to your turkey farm, mister.

Sure."

"You know something, Alan?" asked Julian as he approached the entrance to the patient's room.

"What's that cowboy?"

"For someone who's been a professional stuntman, for a man who's been around places and has seen plenty of action, you really don't understand the way things are seen around here. Are you like other people who come here and decide to spend their money because they want to and not because anyone is forcing you?"

"Force?" The jaws of his palate froze with an incantation of solid nerves. "What the hell do you people in these hospitals understand about force anyway? Hell! It takes a lot of work to pull a good stunt."

"Does it?" flagellated the voice of Julian.

"Let me tell you something, compadre! Boy! If I were your age, I'd be out hunting pussy and having a good time instead of trying to play Dr. Kildare in some monastery," said Alan.

"Shit! They used you, and you know it, don't you?" cried out Julian. "Eh! Look who's talking about getting used. What a waste!" stammered the elderly man with a peculiar vengeance.

"A waste, Alan?" questioned Julian with an astute bluff of termination.

"First, you talk about why I'm just a common below-the-line grunt of an orderly. Next, you're knocking me down by telling me that I shouldn't waste my time upgrading a nursing and medical attitude. Instead, I should devote my energies to chasing women and laissez-faire activities. Alan! People like you are just too common. You come in, and you leave just as soon as you're in a position to play the maternal role of daddy. I certainly hope that what you're speaking of is not your idea of a stunt. Why don't you come out of it and admit you've failed your most daring of all circus acts."

"Which one's that, Socrates?" he stated with a Morse mumble in his voice box.

"Being yourself, mister! Just being yourself," said Julian. The heavyset man repeated sucking on his used cigarette and laughed without any grace whatsoever.

"No way, compadre! That's where you're wrong. Dead wrong," he said.

"You see. You're the one who's afraid of being yourself. You're the one who's afraid of getting out of this place. Not me!" repeated Alan.

Another voice could be heard at the entrance of the room. It was the voice of a female, innocent of any conversation taking place within those octogenarian halls. Perturbedly, inconsequentially, an acoustic acquiescence.

"Well, well, Mr. Torrezano…I see you've pleasured yourself in meeting our new help tonight," spoke out the tall female nurse who had a supervisor's tag pinned on her white lapel.

"So speak of the devil," cried out Mr. Torrezano.

"The devil, Mr. Torrezano, has long since lost his appointment with any of us, I'm afraid," spoke the nurse in a reassuring voice and character of high-minded clinical endeavor.

"Listen, sweetheart! All I was asking for were some medication tablets," pleaded Mr. Torrezano.

"Oh, but you look fine to me, Alan. Perhaps Julian must have left a kindling spark somewhere in your heart," she said.

"Julian's a good man. I like him plenty. I really do." replied Mr. Torrezano.

"He's misty, but I like him."

"I'm glad to hear that, Alex. But for now, it's getting late, and you need some rest. And for heaven's sake, don't worry about your medication. I'll have Julian give you a pill here in a minute." She stepped out the door in a frolic and held her pace for a few seconds. She gasped for her extra breath, "Oh, and, Mr. Torrezano, was that for pain or sleep?"

He hadn't answered. He seemed to have slipped into a daydream, a euphoria. His eyes appeared in a nemesis.

"Say, Alan! What'll it be? A Mickey Finn or some Demerol," she spoke out in a louder tone of voice. The bedded man moved his head and his eyes, and his body began to come alive. With one sudden movement, he spoke up in a melodious genteel of words.

"Say, nurse, I can hear ya. That's all right. That's okay! Forget about it. It's nothing. Everything's fine now, nurse," spoke Mr. Torrezano.

"You what?" she asked.

"You heard me. Just let me be, would you?" he repeated.

"Oh no you don't, Alan. It's not that easy. I'm not going to let you get away with it just like that," she excelled her authority and dismissed his disposition with her rivaled forcefulness. "You people put me through too much hell for me to allow that to happen."

Mr. Torrezano's voice faded out, and Julian was sitting at the nursing station's desk, where he continued reading about religious faith in community health. The halls were quiet, and the second hand on the wall clock continued turning over into the night. A paper moon shone brightly in the distant sky as one flew over the cuckoo's nest.

The traffic on US Highway 99 was as adamant as ever and wore a lowly face of vehicular frenzy, which hadn't changed any since the time that a redheaded nurse named Katherine had taken a drive with him to his hometown. It was at this time that the bleached red-handed Italian woman named Natasha was sitting next to him as his pickup traveled southward along the old "has been" of Camino Real.

Most young men, the early middle-aged echo type, could only imagine of having a make-believe wife. She sat next to them and coaxed their presence along their personal profile and valley-crotched driving habits, they moved between the number one and two richest agricultural regions of the world. This, however; did not seem to set the prerequisite retort of masking a woman to that of a deleted concubine. If a woman had grown up in this valley, she would always be a valley girl no matter what route had been taken. And for all of this sanitized debut which groped Julian's nearest ambitions as well as ambivalence concerning his own personal performance with women, he decided that taking Natasha to dinner outside his hometown would not only convince her of his own credibility for being this kind of valley boy but also convince himself of his own integrity and resoluteness, which recompensed the paper-moon image of his own demeanor. Julian felt he needed to be reassured of his personal suspicions as far as the song would go about the virility of women and pride of his own manhood. Natasha conceded to his untimely invitation: another view into the bottom lure of memory, past, and one last look into a grain of nestled and forgotten courage.

"I told you, Julian, I'm not hungry," she said. "Why don't you just turn the truck around and take me home?"

"You know something…The reason why I'm so quiet is because your level of sensitivity is so high that whenever I say I like you or mention anything concerning your own personal attire, you take it as though the world were coming to an end," he said.

"The end is nearer than you think, Julian," she answered. "How can anyone make waves while walking over rocky ground?"

Julian sat still. "We're too far past Raisintown now. We're going to go get something to eat, because my stomach is growling," said Julian.

"Your stomach! That's all you ever think about is your stomach," she said.

"You're better off being a quiet man, Julian. My husband was a very quiet man. He was even more quiet while listening to classical music. You know? Modern pop."

"If you want to listen to modern pop, I'll turn the radio on to the more serene channel. Then you'll be speaking to me as if I were an older man, an older man like your husband. Perhaps an even older man," he said.

Julian veered the vehicle off to the side of the road and entered an overpass crossing. It was the ten-mile avenue that cut across the eastern countryside vineyards and led to his hometown. He directed himself to increasing the speed of the truck to a faster and unusual velocity, as he tried nursing his conversation to a lengthy description of the pastoral view.

"I'm well aware of that, Julian. I've traveled through your hometown in the past. I can't really say I know the area that well, however," she conjectured with a less familiar reply.

"How long ago has this been?" he asked.

"I don't remember now. It's been some time, I'm afraid," she replied.

"While we're there, I think I'll stop by and visit old friends of mine. And since you're with me, I know you don't mind, will you?" His voice lowered in a secure tone of confidence.

"No, I don't mind," she answered in a snobbish, short burst of clause.

Julian looked to one side of him, and he suddenly felt a coalesced feeling of security.

"Good!" he replied.

"Good?" she asked. "Is that all you can say?" she spoke up again.

"Don't tell me that you're still mad at me for what happened last week at the playhouse," said Julian.

"No…not exactly," she said. "It's just that sometimes I feel that your plans are too rushed, too hurried. For some funny reason, they're not real. For some reason, they don't seem like plans." She began massaging her throat with her hands and finally ended the movement with wild strokes across her chest, as she fidgeted in a delicate, truncated manner.

"So what are you trying to tell me?" Julian asked in a trying manner as if to hide his feelings of irrational behavior. He remained at a loss for words.

"I don't think you actually care about what you do. You don't give a damn about planning, about early minute warnings, about other people, about anything or anyone, including yourself. You just don't give a damn about anyone, do you?" she said in a vivid display of sharp character and an abrupt intrepidation. Julian's face turned blush red and launched his guilt with his body slowly sinking into his chair. Vivid pictures of years gone by had sprinkled thoughts of precise spoken words mentioned and a conscience of a benign quietude. She too had become quiet.

The summer basket and serene weather had engulfed the green and emeraldness of the countryside with all the fruit and raw products of agricultural offerings shining in the soil. The first and second harvest were in the making as the premiere picking of table grapes awaited. Several field workers were always visible during these afternoon drives. One could always see the tall aluminum ladders crouched in between the plant's bushes of these orchards. A domestic reunion was always in the plight of the late summer's rehearsal, a reunion with familiar faces and extravagating foreigners from south of the border. Julian felt he had something to offer them, and if memories were all and everything he could conjecture in his mind entrenched and entwined, then she, he felt, would understand.

The vehicle rolled through the city limits until she came to a rest on a small neighborhood street where Julian could recall some of his boyhood antics and playground efforts in growing up. The streets there hadn't changed any, nor did the shanty profile of the neighborhood. There was a group of Mexican children playing to one side of the avenue. Julian recalled where the home of an old friend reminded him of busy nights and flustered days of puberty. A small town had only so much to offer a man. And if puberty has the mainstay of a small-town ministry and duty, then a small town could offer a man a place to live and grow up on the corner and down the road. All this was going through his mind constantly.

"You wait here, Natasha. I won't be long," resided Julian in a different effort to embalm Natasha with husband-like commands. She played alongside of him.

"Very well! I'll wait right here," she responded with an astute sense of dignified confidence as if a wife would to her husband. Julian played along with the idea, and Natasha waited patiently. She watched him as he crossed the street with the maternity and the eyes of a mother, less formal but showing a devoted interest in Julian's decisions. As he approached the old house, two of the children playing walked up to him. They asked him what he wanted.

"I need the telephone number to your older brother's address. You older brother Alfonzo, the one who lives up north, near Santa Cruz," said Julian. The children rushed into the house, and one minute later, the mother, an elderly woman, walked out from the house, carrying a phone number and address written on a piece of paper.

"Thank you! Thank you very much," replied Julian. He and Natasha both left the neighborhood and drove through the northern section of town. There, they came upon a large-sized city park that situated itself next door to the hospital. The park contained an old swimming pool and playground for children's use from the community. Old green-painted benches and barbecue stoves lay hidden within the base of some of the pine trees. Both Julian and Natasha sat down on the grass next to some greenery that hung from one of the low-lying branches of a pine tree.

"So this is your hometown, Julian?" she asked with an educated, sarcastic statement. "It's quiet. I like it."

"This park brings old memories to me," spoke out Julian as he lay himself down on the grass, some dried blades and green traces also.

"I should say so," said Natasha. "Anything in my hometown would bring back memories." She stretched herself out comfortably on the green in a pose that reminded Julian of several old photographs shown to him by his mother, photographs from an old family album.

"So tell me, Natasha," he asked. "What do you plan on doing with yourself, you know, in the years to come."

"I don't know for sure. I suppose I'll move away, somewhere far away. My daughter is a sophomore in high school, and I'll have to wait till she turns of age to care for herself, possibly a year or so." Natasha was relaxing herself more with her conversation as the minutes passed on. "Why do you ask anyway? I already told you that I'm too old for you. Can't you ever get the point straight?"

"Yeah. I already have it straight. We discussed it once, remember?" said Julian.

"Who can forget when someone like you keeps coming over all the time like a pest without control," she stated. Julian looked the opposite way for a few seconds. "And so what do you plan on doing with yourself anyway?" she continued speaking. "Don't your folks realize that you can't even afford to feed yourself sometimes?"

"Sure. That's why I live with them," he said.

"I mean…aren't you getting a little too old for that?" she asked again. "I have an idea. Why don't you buy my trailer house? You could afford it on monthly payments, couldn't you?"

"Maybe," said Julian. He mummed a few words to rifle and strafe the time. "If you did that, where would you live?"

"That's no problem. I plan on buying a new trailer house."

"I'll be the one to live in," she said.

The woman had not at all shaken Julian's intellectual montage, and her statement had not left him sundered nor moved. The word *trailer house* had taken on a structured litany of required moray with a menial note of self-prudence. The importance of trailer houses had not yet registered into the puzzle of pastoral syntax or perhaps someone in the past he dreaded. However, not matter to what place he would socialize with the curious lure of the valley folks, most people agreed that trailer house living was a matter which well became fitting for derelict members of a pansy "sissy" community, a community which most often received its own way the majority of the time. No matter what the cost in any of these issues, Julian decided on staying to his own guns, neither deviating from his proper of living nor spending uselessly on the causes more demanding to his own character.

"No thanks! I don't think I'll be needing a trailer house so soon," he replied in a soft answer.

"No? I should say so! You never need anything," she rifled back at him so loud that even the birds in the park were becoming startled with the couple's conversation. They sat there on the grass for a few elongated moments of recollections. Julian then decided that they would leave to see other friends in the area. Natasha agreed only because he was doing the driving. She picked up her purse and slung its strap over her right shoulder blade. The afternoon sun zeas drifting further down into the western horizon, and the day seemed to be half over. Julian hadn't actually decided on where he should take her in this semi-ghost town appearance of a neighborhood he had at one time come to know so well.

The neighborhood, Weathering Heights, sat as placid as ever, northwest of the town. And in a common turn of events, as before, many times Julian drove Natasha down the street to where he had once lived before. He stopped the vehicle in front of the next-door neighbor's home. They both noticed two large glass jars implanted on the front lawn.

"There must be plenty of dogs in this neighborhood, Julian," said Natasha as she also insisted on using the sidewalk leading up to the front door of the house.

"I don't know, Natasha, it's been years since I've come over this way," said Julian.

"I don't believe that, Julian," said Natasha. "Years for you means months only, many times. You don't mean the words you say. And for a guy that's dying of hunger, you certainly have taken on a different mood for saying things."

"Okay! Okay, Natasha! Let's find out if anyone's home. There's a light on," said Julian, pressing on the front door bell button. "There's someone coming to the door."

Julian could only recall the many times that the woman next door would always be so curious as to show her face in the garage where he used to do some of his paintings and stand countless hours kneading at the weeds in the backyard. Her husband was a barber, a small-town jewel of a barbershop hound and a reserved family man who kept away from anything that meant being popular. He was a gigantic posture of a heavyset man who had once reserved himself as one of the local high school football players. That's the way he remembered him the last time.

"Hello, Julian! How have you been? Gee! Come on in," said the woman who appeared rather surprised to see Julian in the presence of a female. She invited them both into their kitchen. Salutations were always hurried and rushed occasions of getting to know one another, and the pattern that Julian laid down for himself gave him no time for intimate replays. Her husband, no sooner did he walk in, offered both of them beer and some spaghetti. "We'll have to turn the offer down. We're on our way to one of the local restaurants for dinner," said Julian.

"Think nothing of it," spoke the husband. "Grab seconds on your way out." Both Natasha and Julian stared at the food that was laid out on the table, and a mesmerized refusal of their leeched stomachs held itself forward to the hospitality.

"We're really going to have to be leaving soon. It's getting late," pleaded Julian while sitting in an interrogated manner with his head turned toward the television set. The shyness and embarrassment of his coaxed character protruded Natasha's presence as she as well tried bringing herself down to a younger novical level of thinking. Soon afterward, the questioning period enveloped from the husband and the wife.

"So tell us, Julian, where did you find her anyway?" asked the woman as her husband appeared to be involved with Natasha's facial beauty in a hypnotized enthusiasm. He appeared to be staring into her eyes.

"It's a very short story," said Julian. "We ran into each other at the community hospital in Winetown. Then I had asked her if she wanted to pose for me. You know…like models do?" His voice ran up an effort of a solace tenor.

"You ought to keep track of her and not lose her," said the wife. Natasha interrupted with an elderly authority.

"He's too overbearing. He just won't leave me alone for one night. He's almost a good burglar."

"I think we'll have to get a German shepherd to guard your front doorstep," said the husband. Julian mumbled with a discreet shyness, and Natasha blushed about a bleat cynicism.

"With this guy coming around the house all the time, a person needs a mountain lion," said Natasha, reinforcing her domestic role. Everyone laughed at her reprisal; even the sons of the house were laughing. However, the company made for a good reunion at filial memories. These precise memories and feelings took Julian back to early years when he remembered living as a boy next door. The face of the barber was becoming more visible and raped with former wrinkles of those early years. Julian hadn't really taken to heart his exact role of acquaintance with Natasha as far as showing his old friends who his girlfriends were.

"What's your hurry anyway, big guy?" said the barber. "You've got all night to eat, man!" Julian was feeling anxious and hurried his rushed attitude about showing Natasha the hometown. Natasha blurted out.

"It's exactly what I've been thinking about, getting my own daughter."

"You don't say!" said the wife. "Come over to the backyard. There's still some sunlight left outside." Everyone stood up to leave to the patio through the back door. Julian conceded and said nothing contrary to the occasion. He picked up his beer and followed the homely crowd out to the backyard. Standing next to the high-rise rubber pool, he gulped on the beer bottle. Natasha spoke with the husband about prices and some common words. Julian looked on with uncommon caution and attention beyond what any uncanny motive may offer.

"Well, shall we go, Natasha? It's getting late, and my stomach can't wait." The husband's eyes veered over to one angle, and his head moved to one side. His eyes were red, as if some potion of glamorous mystique had cast into his profile and personal posture. *He's probably falling in love with her already*, cast away Julian's thoughts as he waited in a courtship fashion with the courtesy of a gentleman. Ten minutes had passed into the night as her conversation ended on a high note of youthful enthusiasm and gratitude.

And so they left the home, the neighborhood, the city limits with ever so friendly goodbyes and mixed emotions of sacred futility. The truck passed beyond the city limits, and soon the dark country sky appeared before them in a nocturnal flash with the orchards tracing passed them. The minutes themselves raced passed their starved faces, and the murk and glimpse of the tandem hills could be seen from the roadway. The shock absorbers flexed, and the chassis rumbled to a slight rear as the truck crossed the Santa Fe tracks that intersected the roadway in a northwest and southeastern direction.

"What did you say the name of this small town was, Julian?" asked Natasha, stirring up a silenced commotion within Julian.

"Sultana…Sultana. You know?" he hammered out the words.

"Oh! You've heard of it before, Natasha. You're pretending. I know you're pretending, Natasha," said Julian as he turned with a friskiness to look at her.

"No! You're wrong, Julian. I'm telling you that I don't really know this area that well," she answered. "You're impossible, you know that?" Julian shrugged his shoulders and kept an unkempt silence as he turned the car over to one side and onto the parking area of a restaurant that sat at the intersection of the only stoplight in the area. The Redwood Inn was open that night, and the neon light flickered a predominant sure of flame about the street. Julian parked the truck and stopped the engine with a twitch of the ignition switch.

"I don't know about you, Natasha, but I'm starved," spoke up Julian.

"Well, okay. Let's eat," said Natasha. They both entered through the side of the bar where all the lights glistened in a sanguine halo inside the rug-laden environment as well as the outside.

"Well, here we are," said Julian as they both walked through the bar toward the direction of the dining room.

"Hello there," came a voice from behind the bar with every step they would take. One of the bartenders directed them to the drinking area. They quickly agreed on a choice corner in which to have their dinner, which consisted of two large dishes of Chateau Sauvignon with potatoes and whipped sour cream, a salad, and some slices of French bread. The two large glasses of wine matched the elegance of the napkins, tablecloth, the silverware and the shimmering glare of the bright chandeliers which hung from the ceiling overhead. Not more than fifteen minutes would pass that Julian finished his plate in an arduous rush of impatience. Natasha looked on with timid comedy in her eyes.

"You don't have to kill yourself, Julian," she blatantly yelled out in a mediocre whisper of mockery. "The dinner cost enough, you know."

"I want to get all of my money's worth," said Julian. "Tell me, Natasha. Exactly. What is it that you do at the olive plant in Winetown?"

"Oh! It's nothing, really. I work on an assembly line where we process olives, can them, and finally, we prepare them for distribution," she answered, this time placing the large white silk in a formal drape over her thighs and knees.

"It all sounds interesting, Natasha," he said. "But exactly what is it that you do?"

"Well…you see, I stand next to a conveyor belt."

"You stand, Natasha?" he stated.

"Well…sometimes I'm sitting down when the olives pass by."

"You mean you sit down on your royal behind when the olives are passing by on the conveyor belt?" he blurted back at her, licking up his plate.

"Well, it's actually a lot more than that. What I mean is that there is a lot more involved than simply separating olives on a conveyor belt."

"Is that right?" he bottled up his voice while putting a last piece of steak meat into his mouth.

"That's right! Hell! We work our butts off at that factory, day and night. The loads of olives are brought over in wooden boxes from the fields and dumped into large digesters" Instantaneously and from the rear of the diner, a voice came out of the dark-lit corner of the room.

"Will that be all? Is everything all right?" added one of the waitresses.

"That's fine. Everything is fine," said Natasha. Julian agreed, and they both waited for the stub to fall on the tablecloth. The waitress left the room; Julian left a tip of two dollars on the table. Soon afterward, they both stood up and walked out into the muggy temperature of the night.

"Well! Where to? Any place in particular, Natasha?" his voice drought on.

"No. Not really!" she answered. "Whichever way you'd like to find your way back home. You're the one who's driving, not me."

"We'll take some of the back country roads. I know of a great spot to stop at not so far up into the mountains, southeast of Fresno," he said.

The vehicle passed along the eastern side of the mountain that resembled a naked women lying down on her side. And through orchards of oranges and vineyards of old memories past, the wheels raced through a small town called Orangetown. Julian continued his explanations of entertaining Natasha with his gaunt experiences of boyhood life.

"And you know something, Natasha, after going to that police academy in Almondtown, I met an officer from Orangetown, the only black police officer in this entire area. They work him to death out here for three dollars and twenty-five cents an hour. Can you believe that, lady?" he stated.

"Oh my god!" She gasped for air and remained silent for a few minutes!

The vehicle entered the darker area of the countryside and began a slow ascent on the foothills. The mountains were nearby.

"I can't say I know this area like an eagle in the night, but I have been a traveler through here many times as a kid, as a teenager on dates, you know. Why, I even used to work up here before going into the US Army," said Julian as he swerved the truck through the rolling curves up and down the slopes.

"What did you do up there, Julian? You know, the work?" she spiked back with her own question.

"Not anything to brag about, actually," he replied.

"Well?" she stammered.

Julian paused. "I used to build trails for the Department of Interior."

"And…what else?"

"I drove a garbage truck."

"Anything spectacular?" she asked. The truck neared the main road leading to the Sequoia Kings Canyon National Park, a main highway.

"Well, we used to build garbage cans which were bear-proof."

"Bear-proof?"

"Yeah! You know? We would paint them and set them on large heavy slabs of concrete tied with a chain and a post."

"I see!" she stated.

"Interesting or not?"

"Well, if you had to work, you had to work," she said with a calm enunciation. Julian mumbled his words and brought the truck to a halt at the edge of the main highway. Turning the vehicle in a right direction, Julian came to a stop alongside a turnout that overlooked the night's profile of the countryside. The air was still, and all around them, the quiet song of the evening played a familiar tune to the hillside and melodic stance of the manzanitas. Julian and Natasha opened their doors at the same instant that this certain tranquility captured their curiosity for the night. They both walked to the rear of the truck and stood a few moments staring at the vast view of a black starry sky. Julian grabbed Natasha by the hips with both hands as if to help her onto the back bed of the tailgate. She refused the assistance and climbed aboard herself. Julian stood by with a timid response.

"She's beautiful, isn't she?" mumbled Julian with a spiteful look of almost unsure regret in his eyes so wide.

"Oh my god! But she is a beautiful sight, Julian!"

Julian began pointing out to her several of the cities in the distant blanket of lights embedded in jeweled orchards of a checkerboard menagerie. Almost explaining his professional opinion of the valley area, which showed itself with valor and brightness, he spoke, "Right there… over there, Natasha. That dark spot next to the mass of lights. You see it." His hand began pointing to the direction of the restaurant of where they had just eaten.

"I've been up here many times myself, Julian. I've just never seen the view from up here at night. It's so great. I really think so, Julian." She motioned out bluntly. They both gazed into the distant shore of lights below, and a sudden chill of boorish and contemplative fervor swept across the ideas of their minds and wishful-thinking dispositions.

And with a further timidity and reproach, Julian angered himself. For not being able to show enough fortitude and courage to put his arm around her and follow the motion with a kiss so rare, he angered himself. His body stuck to the red metal of the truck ever so daring and tightly.

"Here! I'll show you something, Natasha!" he blurted out once again. He aimed his arm and diligence to a different direction on the obscure map of glazed jewelry.

"Right there…see! Right there," she said.

"What is it?" she asked, and her face turned toward him for a rapid second.

"You see those lights there below the town, and there's smoke coming from a large burner. It looks red."

"Red?" she asked again.

"Oh, come on, Natasha. Don't stand there and tell me that you can't see that bright reddish light? Have you become color blind all of a sudden?" he insisted with the sexuality of a reserved salesman. "That happens to be the burner of a large sawmill where my father used to work."

"Oh! Really?" she pretended to show an emphatic exultation of surprise.

"That's right!" Julian continued with his onward insistence. "My father worked there for about thirteen years. That's a long time to be staying in one mill, wouldn't you say?"

"But of course, Julian," she answered back, and soon she would bring her arms up to her chest and folded them on top of each other. She stammered herself a few seconds of pause before committing herself to some more rhetoric.

"A funny thing too."

"What's that?" asked Julian with more inquisitiveness. She waited until he interrupted no more.

"Oh! Well…what I was going to say was that even my own father did nothing but work. That's all he ever knew."

"Um!" mumbled Julian. "So did mine. He worked feverishly, and then he would simply give everything away."

"What do you mean, give everything away?" she asked, retrograding Julian's statements.

"He wasn't too bothered in saving for people's problems other than his own family's. He would work and spend everything as he worked. Why live for tomorrow? Why not just live for today's sake? That's the way he was," answered Julian. He knew many things, and then he buried himself in a lumber mill.

"And give away everything he knew, right?" she interrupted one minute—a lasting moment—before opening the side door to the truck.

"What's your hurry anyway, Natasha?"

"You still think you're the only one, don't you?" she sharply answered, and, then, she stepped inside the truck and shut the door. Julian left the orgasmic view and entered the pickup to fire up the ignition. He turned the vehicle around and headed downhill toward Fresno. They were both quiet at first, and no words were spoken. The only real evidence of any kind of communication shown was the mean, wicked expression on Natasha's face. Julian perceived it at first as a personal thrust to his own conversation.

"And then once a year, the company would always have a large picnic nearby at one of the local ranches. Why! There was even a small lake in back of the dance terrace where all the families would meet."

Natasha had more important issues on her mind rather than to listen to Julian's voice anymore. After passing by a remote nightclub called the Collegetown Inn, Natasha begged him to stop the truck so they could have a few more beers before driving back to Raisintown. They entered the front door and fell prey to the country-laden-style atmosphere of wooden benches, tables, and wall with a display of horseshoes and oxen girdles. The diner was practically empty, and the bar was as stolid as a museum.

"I'll take two beers," Julian asked the maid. Natasha had no problem with dawning the glass of Budweiser. She giggled smartly and held her thoughts separate from Julian's pretense about his own local rural history. Natasha could only laugh at him as if he were some kind of rustic, pastoral, clownish character of ashamed negritude.

"I think we'd better go. I really have to be going now. Really, I do," said Natasha.

"If you need to go, I'll take you home," Julian replied with a sluggish somberness and lackadaisical genteelness that stemmed from the spirits of the beer. He moved Natasha's stool aside and left a twenty-five-cent tip on the counter. That morning, the truck passed through Raisintown by way of the air terminal. Natasha at once placed her head down upon his thigh with a soporific appeal.

"Your leg. It's so hard. I like it," she muffled out the words. Julian awoke her upon entering her mother's driveway. The time was well into the early morning hours. The pickup came to another halt, and they both sat there for a few minutes ever riding out their intentions and assuming greater temptations. The similar light appeared to flicker from her mother's porch, and its effervescent character glowed with a prism around Natasha's profile. Her hair bristled in the cab's darkness. Julian removed his Pendleton and covered Natasha's bare arms and neck. He then threw himself on top of her thighs in a random fashion without giving her any warning or chance of refusal.

"What are you doing?" she squandered in a high-pitch voice. Julian wrestled with a tandem frolic and motion on her knees and resumed to lying there almost lifeless.

He spoke up, "Oh, Natasha, Natasha…Natasha." His voice was mellowed out to a lure of yearning for forgiveness.

"What now, Julian?" she quickly asked with a funneled sarcasm.

"Please be my pillow. Won't you please be my pillow?" he gagged with an unusual resounding complexion. Natasha did not hesitate in pushing his head off her knees. He rolled down onto the floorboard, and the Pendleton covered his face after she threw it on top of him.

"Well, I'd better be going now. My daughter is leaving early in the morning. I'm going to have to drive her," she stated.

"But wait a minute!" blurted Julian.

"I'm sorry, Julian, but I already told you. I'm too old for you. You're a nice person, and I don't want to hurt you. Now you don't really love me! All you want is to take me to bed."

"Oh! But you know by now that is not true," he said.

"What are you…a queer?" she asked.

"No!" He paused a moment. "But of course I want to go to bed with you. Isn't that the natural reaction to do?" he stated.

"I told you, if that is all you want to do here, then I don't want you coming over ever again." She quickly stepped out of the pickup and walked around to Julian's side. Approaching the window, she came upon Julian's face within so many feet of his position.

"Well, don't I even get a small kiss? After all, I took you out to dinner. We had several drinks and passed the time."

"What!" she exclaimed with a surprised expression of unladylike on her face.

"Just one friendly good-night kiss. One friendly kiss?" he begged her like a spoiled child who neither bothered hiding his insecurities nor inexperience with women at this time. Her eyes opened wide, and a coercive, lustful appeal droned from her womanly features.

"Okay! Just one small good-night kiss, and then I'll have to be going inside. All right?" she mottled out her sentences.

"All right!" answered Julian, waiting patiently. He stuck his head out the window to reveal his somewhat chapped line in character. She kissed him hurriedly on the cheek and said, "Good night."

C H A P T E R 5

The Death of an Artist

"Oh, how I wish my father were alive."

The summer once again showed her seasonal age onto the early August days and surface heat in the valley. It seemed as though an unchanging and adamant coterie of seasonal lure would bring nothing newer to Julian's taste or demeanor. However, even though many previous seasonal ages have surmounted to glorious stockpiles of husbandry and nursing to various empires, what was conducive to being constructive projects have also been stymied by natural disaster, human error, and surprise attacks. It was the late July morning that Julian had not so much entered his mother's kitchen door that she sat there waiting for him to receive her message that Clark Stevenson had called early that same morning, asking that Julian return a call. "Something important," his mother had said to him.

"Something about going with him back home, back to Oregon!"

"Oregon?" exclaimed Julian as he sat down on the dining room chair. He quickly dialed the number and talked to Clark for several

197

minutes before deciding to take a nap. Julian's mother had coerced him to go, recommending that he leave the area for his own mental good. He was surprised to see his mother giving him such elusive advice as if she were sending him off to a make-believe paradise, a nemesis for soothing his chip on the old shoulder. Clark was already giving his instructions to meet with him in Raisintown so that they could better discuss travel plans. That same afternoon, Julian woke up to find the house empty. He left for Raisintown and made a quick stop at Natasha's home to find her mowing her uncle's lawn with a gas lawnmower. He approached her from behind without her knowing it and oblivious because of the noise the machine was producing.

"Oh my god, it's you…what do you want?" she yelled out.

"I came by to say hello. That's all!" he yelled into her ears.

"Hello!" she hammered back at him. "Now go away. Leave me alone. I'm busy."

Julian backed off and stared with an unsure recognizance about her disposition. He felt it better not to tell her anything about his going to Oregon. Waving his hand, he walked away from the scene.

Thirty minutes later, he arrived in Raisintown and mustered his way to Clark's apartment. The sun was beginning to shine despite the early morning occurrence with tangible clouds still evident over a light-colored lavender sky. He neared the door to Clark's apartment room and knocked against the wooden paneling with his fist. The radio could be heard playing on the inside, and there were voices. The door opened, and Clark appeared.

"Julian…Julian! Hello! Come on in," went Clark's voice. "We were just talking about you. Come on in, buddy!"

"Hello there!" said Julian. He turned to glance at one of Clark's girlfriends, someone with whom he had been going to nursing school and training at the medical center. Her name was Carol.

"So have you decided upon leaving with Clark to Oregon? It would be good for you," she said. Julian took some deeper breaths and stared at the Chicana a few moments before answering.

Hell! But what's in it for me? he thought. "I have to go to work, you know!" he shot back before accepting a beer from Clark.

"We know! But you're not the only one!" she spoke onward.

"Um!" Julian looked on with almost a silent revenge in his eyes.

"You should go with him, Julian. It would be good for the both of you to get away," she spoke onward. Julian sat himself down with a slow appeal on the large sofa where he always slept when coming over to visit Clark.

"Well, I'm going to have to be leaving now, you guys!" said Carol.

"Yeah! I know…you have children!" said Julian. Clark laughed. He stepped over toward the refrigerator.

"That's very good, Julian," blasted out Carol with a sneaked-up sizzle of sarcasm. "But I really do have to be going. If I should—and I should—I'd simply call up the hospital and tell them that my grandmother died. Something brash! You know?"

"That's it!" cried out Clark. "Julian! Call up the community hospital and tell them that you can't go to work for the next two weeks."

"For god's sake, Clark! Why?" shouted Julian. Carol was overcome by her own comical joust.

"Because your uncle died, and he lives in Mexico," answered Clark.

"I suppose I'm going to Mexico now?" asked Julian.

"That's right," answered Clark. "You'll have to go to Mexico for two weeks."

Julian exhaled with a demeaning breath and began running his fingers through his dark hair. Carol picked up her purse.

"Well, have a good trip, fellas, and don't collect any wooden nickels in Mexico!" she said while closing shut the door behind her. Julian and Clark remained staring at each other with demented smiles.

"There's the phone, Julian," stated Clark.

Julian headed back home, back to the large house behind the hospital. He gathered his clothes together and packed his .357 Magnum and .38 pistol in his suitcase. He wasted no time in finding the various items which he needed—ammunition, gun-cleaning kit, and a book about eschatology, which was given to him by Natasha's mother. For a great, regarded, unmistakable reason, he called up Natasha's mother for a few minutes. He told her that he would not be able to make his scheduled appointment to meet with her and they should choose a more convenient time to meet. He was very formal about the telephone call and spoke as if he were an older, aged man telling his wife that his departure for leaving town for two weeks was a necessity and a very important engagement. He hung up the receiver and began his walk to the greyhound bus station, a small building situated along the main drive of the city.

Walking above the highway on the overpass near the house, he climbed down the east embankment and strolled himself onto the railroad tracks, where he continued north along the US Highway 99. A strange figure he became while walking alongside the railroads tracks. He carried two old luggage, something his grandmother had left behind for his own personal purposes. The pistols could be felt with the cargo and proved to be heavy with extra weight. His feet paced faster. Twenty minutes is what he had given himself to reach the northbound bus that carried Clark. Julian would have to hurry his pace. The whistling from his vocal cords were making the minutes go by faster as he passed the hospital that lay on the opposite side of the highway. And with a sudden pillar of smoke and diminished sounding of an old muffler, an old battered truck pulled alongside of him. There were workers sitting in the cab, and they yelled at him to climb into the back of the vehicle. Julian did not hesitate in accepting the offer. His chances of missing the bus would have been much greater with the fast walk into town. His hair blew wild with the wind, and he clutched onto his one briefcase that carried the pair of guns.

"Gracias…muchas gracias," he told them as they stopped in front of the Greyhound building. He waved his hand goodbye, and they also waved with hands and contained grimly smiling faces. They were field workers from one of the local labor camps.

"I'll take one ticket to Central Oregon, please. Madras, Madras, Oregon. Make that one a round trip," Julian said to the older woman who stood behind the old rustic-looking counter. There was hardly walking room between the stacks of boxes, boots, and old hats piled on one another and giving the waiting room the skirt appearance of a J. C. Penny's department store. The woman appeared curious and suspicious, and she concerned herself with Julian's presence as she backed away from the counter a few feet. The next moment, one of the laboratory phlebotomist from the community hospital walked in with some containers of blood and laboratory utensils.

"Hello there, Julian. Going somewhere, partner?" he said.

"Yeah, I'm heading down to Mexico. An uncle of mine passed away. I'll be in the south for about two weeks," replied Julian.

"Oh! I see. Well, have a good trip, and we'll see you when you get back," he said as he walked out the back door of the waiting room.

"Sure thing, buddy," said Julian with a nonchalant, reserved grin on his face.

The counter woman handed Julian the ticket, receipt, and some change. Her face turned into a sanguine, distilled appearance, somewhat embarrassed and shocked. She remained reserved.

"Thank you. Thank you, very much," said Julian.

"You're welcome, young man," she insisted and continued about her business. Julian set his luggage down next to a door of a telephone room and quietly sat himself on top of them. His heart pounding, he remained impatient for the bus's arrival. A person stepped out of the phone booth and quickly sat next to him in a semi-squalid Indian squat. He was dirty-appearing and scrounge-looking, and his face appeared to be sprinkled with dust and pasted with dry sweat. His hair was thrown around and covered his eyes and forehead. His T-shirt and jeans matched his barefoot appearance.

"How's it going, partner?" he exclaimed. Julian hesitated to say anything at first. Not knowing what to think because most people had been using the term *partner* and *buddy* for the past eight hundred hours, he kept his social distance from people for his quote.

"Pretty good, I suppose," replied Julian, turning to glance at him only for a moment at spurs.

"Man! I'll tell ya, buddy, you can't get clear to anybody these days. You know that?" said the young white kid who appeared to be in his early twenties.

"What do you mean?" answered Julian, hoping to end the conversation. "I mean you can't get away with anything these days, you know?" he said.

"I think I know what you mean," replied Julian, yearning to see the bus drive around the backside of the station.

"God! I swear! These highway patrol officers don't cut slack with anyone. I guess I'm just lucky to be here and calling on the telephone."

"Hell! Just yesterday, I was hitchhiking south of Bakersfield when suddenly I got this ride. See. Well, anyway, it turns out that this guy I'm riding with is being wanted by the cops for stolen vehicle charges. So here I go riding down the freeway, not knowing this car's been stolen. And the next thing I know is that there's a red light on our tail, some California highway patrol officer telling us to pull over to one side. He comes up to the window and tells the guy to step out of the car. Next thing, he's putting handcuffs on him and telling me to step out of the car. Hell! I had nothing to do with it. Honest! Anyway, the officer gives me a ride to Raisintown, and for some strange reason, he drops me off." It seemed as if his voice would never end. Julian bore along with the conversation until he could hear the air brakes of the bus hissing in a tumultuous halt in the rear driveway of the station. His bus had arrived.

"This is the bus to Oregon," said the counter woman.

"Well, good luck there," Julian told the young stranger. "I have to go. My bus is here."

"Hey! That's my bus too. It'll usually make a quick stop in Hollister. That's where I'm headed," he said.

"Well then," Julian reinstated himself. "We'd better be going." He could see Clark from the outside of the bus, his face sullen and tainted by the shaded windows. He was bobbing around on the inside between the aisle like a monkey in a cage. He waved, and Julian waved back at him. The line was small, and Julian had no problem in climbing on board as soon as the driver took his ticket.

"This is the express, right?" Julian asked the uniformed man.

"This is the express, all right!" he stated.

Julian walked down the aisle with the luggage jutting out in front of him. He came up to where Clark was sitting. The seats of the bus were almost empty, and there was plenty room everywhere.

"C'mon, Julian. Sit here, next to me, anywhere," said Clark while pointing his fingers to the empty seats across the aisle. Julian placed his luggage on the overhead rack and wasted no time in sitting himself down.

"Believe me, Julian, you won't regret this. You'll be glad you're leaving this place. When we get there, you won't want to come back," spoke up Clark with amazement at Julian's presence.

"Okay, Clark. What more do you want? I'm here. Isn't that enough?" blurted out Julian!

"I'm sorry, Julian," replied Clark with a cynical chain of comical expressions. People were climbing aboard steadily, one by one.

"God, this station was empty just a few minutes ago! Where did all these travelers come from?" questioned Julian, directing his activity toward Clark, who appeared to be looking out the window inattentive to Julian's words. Then he spoke up.

"Well, it's like this, Julian. Some of these stations—actually most of these stations—are unpredictable," he said, turning his face back around so that it was visible to Julian's eyes.

"Yeah! Tell me about it. You take these buses like as if they were going out of style," said Julian. Next, the stranger whom he encountered earlier in the station sat down in front of him. More people were pouring in now, and seats were no longer empty. Clark insisted that Julian move over and sit next to him in his bunk. Julian didn't argue.

"Well! Here we are, Julian. Relax. We have a ways to go yet. This is another great adventure for you, Julian," spoke Clark as the wheels began to roll.

"I don't know about you, Clark," said Julian.

"Now what, Julian?" replied Clark.

"It's the way in which you talk. Sometimes you come on like an eccentric, pompous travel guide who's recently lost his position as master of ceremonies."

The bus began leaving the city, and the flats and orchards were all that lay in their line of vision. They tried making themselves more comfortable and adjusted the angle on the backrest. Clark showed a bottle of Smirnoff vodka to Julian, and he would tuck it back on the inside of his coat where a secret pocket held it in the storage.

"When we get to our next stop, Julian, we'll buy some 7 Up and make ourselves a drink," said Clark.

"That's fine, Clark. You take your chances, but that sure was a dirty, brash move you and Carol did on me back in Raisintown," exclaimed Julian.

"Dirty move? Hell! You're the one who did all the talking," said Clark, nestling his hands deep into his jacket's pockets. "Don't worry about it, Julian. Hell! Enjoy these next two weeks. You won't be sorry you came. Believe me."

Clark's insistence could not be matched by Julian's appeal to pity.

"I hope I'm not sorry that I should have remained in Winetown," spoke Julian. Clark looked on with encroaching eyes, saying nothing whatsoever.

Julian reached toward the overhead rack and grabbed the paperback book strapped across his luggage with a four-foot-length piece of light material rope. It was the book about eschatology, the book which Natasha's mother had given him earlier for lesson purposes. He turned the pages until he arrived to where the marker indicated.

"Literature, Julian?" asked Clark.

"Just something I brought along with me on the trip to feel my empty time," replied Julian.

"Am I that terrible of company, Julian?" said Clark as he reached for the bottle again, grasping it with a proffered touch and in a genteel fashion.

"Can't you find something else to talk about for heaven's sake, Clark!" said Julian.

"That's a deep subject matter, Julian," said Clark.

"What's that? You do mean *booze*, don't you?" asked Julian, slouching further back with the inclined seat. "No. I meant to say heaven, Julian," said Clark, and Julian appeared at a peak of being uninterested.

"I think I have something better, Clark!" clamored Julian.

"You mean you bought yourself a bottle of liquor before getting on the bus?"

"No!"

"I know! You have it stored in your luggage and—"

"No! It has something to do with the study of eschatology."

"Escha…what?"

"Eschatology! Haven't you ever heard of eschatology before, Clark?"

"You mean, scientology? You mean, all of that garbage about spirits and leech-ass money-hungry social workers? Rosicrucian hogwash, Julian?" blasted Clark.

"Call it what you want, Clark. I particularly think it's interesting," said Julian.

"Julian, you're wasting your time with all of that, you know?" he questioned Julian's interest.

"The girl I told you about that time—"

"What girl?" asked Clark, interrupting with a lewd, mischievous gait.

"The Italian woman I made contact with, crazy. You know, the one I became involved with?" insisted Julian.

"You made contact with an Italian woman, Julian? Was it serious?" blurted Clark.

"Mister, this is no time for blasting away at me with jokes of any sort. I mean—"

"You mean that book belongs to that woman…Julian?" Clark's eyes opened wide with an irrevocable claim to providence and leaned in toward Julian's visions of solace and homespun grandeur.

"No! Now would ya listen, Clark! This book belongs to her mother," said Julian.

"Her mother?" shouted out Clark. The people sitting in front of them were becoming restless and less amiable to all of the yelling.

"Say, could you guys hold it down, please?" came a voice from their front profiles of the seats.

"Sorry, mister! We don't mean to be rude," said Julian, clearing his throat and aligning himself in his seat. With both his arms and feet, he shoved himself upward to a position of where his hairline soared high above Clark's.

"Julian, what are these people going to think of us?"

"They already think of us, buddy!" answered Julian.

"What are you getting out of that book anyway? It's all nothing but bull. You know that!" said Clark.

"Did I ever criticize your taste to the intellectual arts? You know? Literature! Do I ever make fun of the books you read, Clark? Those horrid, elusive, cantankerous collection of outrageous ingenuity."

"Outrageous ingenuity?" shouted Clark.

"War stories! Survival magazine, *American Rifleman*! *Gun Digest* upon *Gun Digest*!" burst Julian. "That's the most ridiculous thing I've ever heard, Clark!"

Clark eyed Julian with a tangent interest.

"Look. Look at this. Let me read it to you, mister!" said Julian, unfolding the marker and pointing to the top of the page. Julian next read the words out loud, carefully and very slowly, "For Engineers Only. And there is nothing to fear of in this world, no insecurities to struggle with, because when love is true and real, true love, then there are no worries."

Clark hid the bottle inside his coat again. "That's nice, Julian. I like that. But there's only one thing wrong with that entire title, chapter, and phrase," said Clark.

"What do ya mean?" asked Clark.

"Hell! Shit! You know, blood! Love is blind, and it sure in the hell doesn't pay the rent, engineer or no engineer!" said Clark.

"There you go again. You and your militaristic ways!" surmounted Julian.

"Julian! Here's your self-respect, man! I think this woman is taking you for a ride!" stated Clark.

"A ride?" asked Julian with an anonymous guilt well exposed.

"Yeah! Man!" he expressed in cool flavor. "The woman is gonna literally rip you off. Scientology! It's all the same."

"So are *Gun Digest* magazines," explained Julian. There were no more words spoken for some time after that. And they both sat back in their seats, casual and content with each other's revelations about hometown experience. The bus rolled past Stockton and was coming into South Sacramento, a larger section of the state capital's city limits. Clark began pointing his fingers toward separate buildings.

"And just what in the hell were you doing here in Sacramento?" asked Julian as he cleared the dried, sticky materials of his eyelids.

"Believe me, boy! I sure in the hell wasn't studying scientology," replied Clark. Julian merely shrugged his shoulders and blew off some breath to his left side. He chuckled somewhat.

"Have you ever heard of Old Sacramento, Julian?" Clark interrupted his comical potpourri of character.

"Not really! But I've heard of the name mentioned in a song at one time," replied Julian. The bus was entering the more recent downtown area, which was the state capital and the federal buildings. One could conjecture in his mind what was in plain view. The metropolis woke them both from their verbal stupor and lackadaisical conversation.

"Let's get ourselves down and get a bite to eat." Clark yawned, swiveling his head with a backward and forward motion. Julian stretched himself as some of the passersby had already begun to stand on their feet. The bus driver, bringing the large shining omnibus to a roaring halt, signaled over the interior's speakers that he would be at rest for about forty minutes until the next departure. The wheels had stopped at a central station.

"It sounds good to me, Clark," said Julian, standing himself into a cuddly fashion and clearing a path in the crowded aisle.

"Okay, Julian…okay, ole buddy! I'm coming." Clark gasped, brooding over his own uncomfortable position and posture.

Clark pivoted his way behind Julian, and suddenly, an almost hidden stench of foul-smelling hue quenched the interior of the bus. The smell of popcorn and sweat engulfed the olfactory stupor of passengers. Julian waited a few seconds for the presence of Clarks' steps off the bus, and the cramped hoard of passengers filed passed him. The Sacramento station was by and large an inside terminal, indoor, which represented the largest bus network of the state. The smell of oil, carbon monoxide, and tire rubber was evident. Evening had set in the Sacramento entourage.

"Well? What do ya say we grab a hamburger over at the Carl's Junior inside the lounge?" garbled Clark, coming back to his usual sobered sense of being.

"I'm right with you, compadre," stated Julian. Upon making their way to the chow line, Julian lined up behind Clark and was approached by a ragged character. He was a young black man wearing a baseball hat and parading yellow cards in a solicitous manner. He seemed to be receiving a quarter for every card he managed to give away to his customers. Julian, with large obelisk sympathetic eyes, turned toward the direction of the dark salesman who spoke no words. Julian grasped the yellow three-by-four-inch card and proceeded to read it. The card was a cry out for help from one who claimed to be deaf and dumb. "Please contribute," it read. On the opposite side of the card was phonetic alphabet for deaf and dumb people. Julian grabbed for the inside of his pockets and pulled out a quarter. Clark was viewing the exchange by this time and remained reluctant to mention anything.

Julian was finished with completing the transaction. Upon taking the contribution from Julian, the young black man bowed with a grateful gesture and walked away from the line in search for more coins. The silence at first trickled away into the hamburger line as soon as the black man disappeared from view. Clark looked on with a cold, withdrawn stare at Julian for the moment. Julian felt a streak of fear, and a false humility ran down his spine. He was surprised and disillusioned by Clark's advances.

"Julian, what on earth did you do that for?" Clark frowned and chuckled. "What does the card say, Julian? Hell! That dude just took you, boy!" he interrupted, with chastising enthusiasm bent upon bringing out Julian's insecurities. "Hell, Clark! How do you know if he can talk or not? Shit, boy, these characters come in all sizes and colors in these bus stations. You can't believe any of them!"

Julian shook his head, swallowed, and rationalized a grim of retention and sudden defense. They both stared at each other as the line closed itself to a shorter chain.

"I know!" spoke up Julian. "It's your good deed for the day."

The Smirnoff vodka had a depleted reserve and traces of the potent container had dwindled to nil. Julian was not yet finished tipping a plastic 7 Up soda cup, as the wheels of the bus air-streamed past the moth face of Mount Shasta. The peak of the mountain billowed high against the early morning hue of a white pale background of sunrise. The ground stared at the cut and curvet of the freeway in an eerie of blue color and frozen lavender of sheeted ice and snow. Clark lay fast and innocuous as in a deep sleep. Julian pushed and tugged, this time against Clark's somnambulistic and drunk character.

"Clark! Clark!" whispered Julian in an abated persuasion of cynicism.

"Would you check it out, mister? Why don't you tell me where we're at, for heaven's sake!"

Clark slumbered over and appeared to have been drugged, opened his eyes, bloodshot, and his face red and pale.

"What's up? What's happening?" A pause came through his voice. "What now, Julian?" he stymied off his coveted enthusiasm.

"Hey! Where in the hell are we, if you don't mind me saying so?" squawked Julian. Clark peered over to one side and caught his own glimpse of the trenchant-made horizon of the sun's rays. "Oh, hell yeah, Julian! We're not too further away from the Oregon border this time. You'll see partner. Soon, we'll be coming upon a low-elevation tundra, almost like flat lands, before we come upon the mountains and the higher elevations and forest," he dictated with an awakening alertness while he rubbed both his eyes.

"Now you're starting to sound like the tour guide," said Julian.

"Well, Julian! That's because I'm a tour guide. I'm used to this scene, mister!" replied Clark.

"It seems so," stated Julian.

The bus reamed through the Shasta pass and approached the fast and oncoming low stretch of flatland that appeared in the northeast. The mountain ranges of Oregon were becoming visible. A low morning fog crawled over the roadway and began entrenching itself upon the brown grass-barren hills. With every mile that rolled across the odometer, trees of oak and pine began to spruce upward. A spellbound lure of curiosity eluded from Julian's inherent image of Oregon acquired from watching television programs and reading from hearsay approaches about the gateway to the Big Valley and Ponderosa relics established on the long-standing successful series of bonanza.

"That's right, Julian!" hammered out Clark, sitting erect in his seat this time with his chest protruding and his chin tucked into his neck.

"Shit, boy! This is where I grew up. This is where I hunted. I didn't show you this mountain where I killed my first buck."

It was indeed a tall countryside with pine forest stretching out for miles and miles, and high above, white clouds billowed about the open fresh, smelling air and blue sky. The environment resembled the pictures of a *National Geographic* magazine.

Central Oregon was a combination of mixed scenery and innovating communities far flung from notions built up by Julian's curiosity. The bus had arrived in Madras that day in the after-lunch hours. The wheels rolled through the main street of the small-sized central Oregonian town, which lay obscure and placed inside a valley away from the main road that led from Three Sisters. The environment had not appeared anymore modern nor archaic-looking than Julian's own hometown in central California.

The numerous figures of dark-skinned persons nursed his premonitions about good ole Oregon white homespun characters. Julian took a closer look at these dark-skinned people. They were Indians. And to one's surprise, there were even traces of Chicanos walking about with several of them wearing graffiti T-shirts emblazoned with "Chicano Power" writing across the back. There was a celebration going on, so it seemed, near the bus station, as the bus came to an abrupt stop at the intersection's corner. The people were wearing red and white outfits with head gear resembling an Indian's feathered crown, common, simple, and homespun.

"Well! Here we are, Julian! I'm sure I saw my folks standing on the opposite corner from where we're parked."

"You have good eyes, Clark," said Julian as he yanked on his clothes, bag, and luggage. And again, they both crowded into the center isle and tugged and pushed on their luggage, and the isle was crowded, and people were anxious to get off the bus. Julian propped up the bags to his knees and upper legs and led Clark on the way out of the bus. There wasn't a very large group of persons waiting on the sidewalk, so barren, as the bright sunlight blasted its confidence over the valley. The sullen characters each aborted their ride, and so Clark and Julian found themselves staring at an elderly couple who stood against an old brick-lined cafe for the incoming bus people.

"Well! If that just doesn't suite me fine, boy! Were we ever expecting you, Buck!" said the woman dressed in a petite outfit suited for something more edible to barn dancing. She had red hair worn up in a curl, wore glasses, heavy red lipstick, black shoes, low heels, and would remind you of an Oregonian Minnie Pearl, without the price tags.

"How are ya, Buck?" said the aged man leaning against a walking cane; he would gingerly hold the oak-formed pipe in his free left hand. "Welcome home, son," he spoke with a revered casualness typical of an elderly Anglo Oregonian, as the impression was becoming ever clearer to Julian's mind. The age of Clark's father could have had some bearing on his quiet behavior, of course, for he seemed the least surprised and not a yard moved for taking on Buck's arrival. Nevertheless, he was complacent enough to shed a warm greeting, wearing a large ten-gallon beige-looking hat and a cowboy's vest of imitation rawhide. Clark turned a different color, homespun and boyish, all of a sudden.

"Well, Ma…Well, Pa! This is my friend I was talking to you about who lives near Raisintown. This is Julian," said Clark as the crowd began making its way down the sidewalk, down the street a distance to where the folks' car was parked.

"You can call me Ira, Julian. Clark's my husband, so you could call him Clark," she spoke with almost excuse and a reduced apology to her tone of voice.

"It's a pleasure being here," stuttered Julian's voice. He remained quiet all the way to the car. They carried the conversation to the entire way to the Dodge, which set parked. "We had expected you earlier since your last call at the bus stop," spoke Ira. "You mean our most recent bus stop in Three Sister?" asked her son, Clark.

"Well! Are you boys ready to go home so we can fix you up with something to eat? You must both be terribly tired!" she rambled on with anxious overtones. Julian turned to one side to look at her. She held a cigarette in one hand and appeared nervous and jumpy. "Heck, no! What I mean is that we slept most of the trip over here," answered Julian as they approached the car. Julian made himself convenient and aided in assisting Clark's father into the vehicle. He almost grabbed the cane away from the old man. "Here! I'll take that, Mr. Stevenson. Let me help you."

The day was not hesitating to undress her temper and moderately warm weather. Suddenly, the mystique and foreboded ancient delight of the Oregon topographical weather began to disappear from any seething institution or expectations. And it could have been only a few taken-for-granted minutes that Julian could have sworn he was back in the San Joaquin Valley. Here, he gestured himself going through just another routine ride through a small town, casual, complacent, and anachronistic in every way. Where Clark had grown up was no less surprising to Julian than to discover that an old wooden ranch-house cottage sat on a slope located south of the city. There were ranches and horses in every direction adjacent to their property. This also was not as becoming to excite Julian's conceptions of Clark's hometown.

The warm August day allowed a bountiful view of all and anything one would want to glance at with a bird's eye view of this cataclysmic hoards of rural checkerboard. Once they entered Ira's kitchen and had taken a respectable table position in rejuvenating the old times and constant household memories, the fact that an old, decayed garage or wooden porch with shoddy planks out of place had been trespassed onto again had not surprised the inner exploitativeness and curiosity of Julian's mind. Compared to Clark, he could now see himself coming from a struggling middle-class, modern-day family. The Stevensons lived moderately as well as modestly even though the land and horses that they owned appareled the rightness to be or become as the long-term status quo, the people who've always called themselves Oregonians.

"Your sister, Marty, called and said she'll be coming down from Portland for a few days, Clark," said Ira. "Now you can both have more company, if you wish."

"Great!" expelled Clark as he opened a can of Coors beer and handed it over to Julian with a succulent and enthusiastic hospitability. "You'll like my sister, Julian. She's a barrel of laughs." He showed some photographs of her as they accommodated themselves in the house earlier. There was a counter where Julian had set his bags down in the center parlor of the house. They began drinking the beer and soon broke the majority of the silence with some light conversation and acquaintance. However, the old man sat in the chair and mimicked very little thoughts out loud. Clark was the only person curious to know what was going on with local happenings anyhow.

"And so…Julian decided to come home with me. It took some convincing thought," spoke Clark.

"So this is your first time up here to Oregon, is it?" asked the eager and fetish woman.

"Yup! This is my first time up here," answered Julian as he appeared to be reluctant to drinking any kinds of whiskey that she and Clark had taken out of the cupboards for display.

"Why don't you show him the view of Mount Hood from the kitchen window, Clark! It's a clear enough day today for noticing Mount Hood if nothing else."

Julian stared at it once, and then the second time, it was barely visible to the eyes; she was out there in the northerly horizon. There was this old decaying barn that sat on top of the small hill in back of the house. The horses were visible from the same window.

"I'll tell ya what!" she blurted out as she puffed on her cigarette halfway between her words. "Why don't you boys go on upstairs to Clark's bedroom and put your bags and things away while in the meantime I get some dinner started?"

"Don't worry, Buck. Tonight I'll cook. Tomorrow, the kitchen's all yours." They both crossed over to the parlor and picked up their bags. Julian tugged with a slight jerk on the twine rope that held his suitcase together in one piece. He realized that the book that Natasha's mother had given him was gone. He began shaking the suitcase wildly and instantly wanted to give up the search.

"What's the matter, Julian? Did you lose something?" asked Clark.

"I'm not sure that I did or not," answered Julian. "It's that book. That one book I was telling you about."

"You mean the book on eschatology," stated Clark. "Are you sure you didn't put it inside the suitcase? You probably left it on the bus." Julian traced his footsteps out to the driveway to where the car was parked. Both he and Clark policed the outside area of the car frivolously, and next, despite their luck, they began searching the inside of the vehicle as well as the truck. After consoling themselves throughout the unsuccessfulness of their search, Clark had become more overly concerned about the subject matter than had Julian.

"We'll go back to town and look for it, Julian, if it means that much to you," said Clark, insinuating they give up the search.

"What will she do to you because you lost her book," his voice kept on and told the onslaught character of a little mischievous boy. "All you have to do is buy her another one."

"It's not that easy," stuttered Julian while looking underneath the car this time in a scurrile frenzy. "What I mean is that I'm going to have to call her up and tell her that I lost her book."

"So what's so terribly hard about that, Julian?" asked Clark, and now he could tell his voice was showing a sluggishness common to the limit of beer.

"It's embarrassing, Clark. It's embarrassing. You know what I mean?" fluctuated Julian as he gave up the search.

"Yeah! That's right, Julian," Clark whispered loudly as he placed his left hand on Julian's right shoulder with a comforting move and gesture.

"C'mon, pal, let's go inside and calm ourselves down over another beer. You can always buy her another book later on."

"I suppose you're right," said Julian in a soft residue of audible tone. "Let's go upstairs and put our gear away before we lose something else. Come on in, and I'll show you my room. Come on! You came out here to enjoy yourself, remember? Stop worrying about the crazy old book," said Clark.

Once inside the parlor, they both came to a door that was well inset to one corner next to the kitchen. Clark opened it and began forcing his way into an inner stairwell built of wooden stairs and walls. There was a pair of saddles with harness and stirrups that hung on the wall entrance of the almost hidden hallway that led diagonally upstairs.

"Come on in, Julian. It's only a short walk upstairs." Clark reached forward to pull on a string to a light switch that hung from the crooked wooden ceiling above him. After trotting upstairs, they came to another floor with three doors surrounding them.

"This one's my room, Julian," said Clark as he opened the eastside door with a gentle contemplativeness and quiet touch.

"Come on in, Julian. We'll set our bags down here for now." Julian walked in almost tiptoeing across a bright-colored woven mat that spread itself across half the floor. He slowly took curious fixated glances at the ornamentation and the various bookcases, furniture, and twenty-gallon tanks. The roof of the house sloped downward onto the only window, giving the ceiling and room an enclosed geometric shape. Nevertheless, the rustic look of old colonial house was simple and modest and touched the glare of an inexpensive lure similar to the furniture in the remainder of the house. Julian had to have been a trod of surprise to learn that Clark had indeed come from a modest background.

"So this is the room where you grew up, Clark?" asked Julian with a staunch phrase.

"This is it, amigo," declared Clark. "This is the room where I spent most of my boyhood years before I joined the marines. I would look out this window right here." Clark moved over toward the only window in the room, moved the curtains with a brief flurry of his hands, and delivered an expression on his face as to that of a man who has seen it all, who has been tainted with a satisfying source to all his lifetime curiosities—like a good loser.

"You can use this room tonight, Julian. I'll take my sister's room across the hall," said Clark. "Tonight, I'll show you some of the material I've managed to save over the years. That is if you want."

"Sure…sure, why not?" answered the other shy figure appearing to renovate his own curiosities about Clark's personal past. An emotional silence barricaded the distance between both figures. Julian's eyes began feasting on the majority of print literature, magazines, and books that covered the dressers and bookcases. Suddenly, his eyes would detect the well-arranged menagerie of soft-looking perfumes and cookware possibly from Southeast Asia. A huge array of China with smoking pipes, a sinew of artifacts, and Vietnam curios from the South Pacific Seas were visible. And in one corner, what appeared to be the butt and nozzle ends of imperial rifles were stacked in a random manner against each other and wrapped with a garbed large white sheet. Clark made a quick roundabout move and grabbed a large bottle of Christian Brother's Brandy from the top of a desk that rested against a large mirror on the wall.

"And there's plenty we can look at later on tonight, Julian. But for now, we'll go downtown. What do you say to a quick swig of brandy?" remarked Clark.

"I don't know, Clark. I'm not sure about that," said Julian. "I'm not good at mixing beer with liquor!" The quaint sound of epiglottis-made gargle a rhythm domestic and janitorial as Clark twisted back tight the fifth of brandy. The inebriated and jolly march of characters mumbled down the stairway and past the horses' saddles and mount. They were fair drivers; so they felt.

Clark drove the car to the very spot to where the bus had arrived earlier that afternoon. Julian was determined to find the book before deciding he would enjoy himself for the remainder of the stay in central Oregon.

"So what makes you so mad about anything, Clark?" spoke out Julian as the car came to an abrupt halt.

"Nothing in particular, Julian," he defended himself. "It's my folks, you know? They're getting old and senile, and well…" Clark's voice paused again to the sound of the car's engine running.

"I'll hardly call your mother an old, cranky woman, Clark," defended Julian, opening the car's door to the passenger's side.

"You mean you're still mad because she was reluctant about letting you drive her car?"

"That's right! That's right, dude," said Clark, and the car's engine burped and kicked and tugged as he turned off the ignition. "It's my father. My father's the one who is making her behave that way."

"But you just can't blame everything on your father because of his frown due to old age," stated Julian.

"Old age, my foot!" exclaimed Clark. "The only thing the guy wants to do is look down the dresses of the waitresses who work at the restaurants as they bend over to serve food to the customers." Julian chuckled and swallowed. They both frivolously searched the curb and the side building of the street corner.

"Now the bus stopped right here at this spot!" shouted Julian. "I have a funny feeling that the book never left the bus, Julian," said Clark.

"Something frightfully tells me the book slipped from the ropes. Somebody picked it up, Julian. I'm afraid somebody's picked it up."

"Probably so, Clark. Probably so," mumbled Julian. "Let's hope it's in the hands of some good person."

"Not too many good people around anymore, Julian," supported Clark. "Now you're doing a lot of wishful thinking."

"Yes! That's what the woman told me, the woman who let me use the book. She said that, sooner or later, it would fall into the hands of a good person."

"Or a bad person," inserted Clark. After several more minutes of searching and yielding to anymore hope in literary movement, they both departed their activity and decided that the thing to do was to go to one of the local bar clubs to drink a beer. Clark parked his mother's car across the street from a small plaid-painted front entrance to an old rustic appearing tavern called Club Madras.

"Well, Julian! Here she is. This place stood intact even when I was still well in my teens when I was learning how to shoot my first deer!" shouted Clark with one pompous candor of words. Crossing the street, candid and carefree, they walked in through the entrance. The long room that found itself to a rear pool-table area was almost empty to the sound conversation or walking of footsteps. Several shady figures cast their presence at the bar, and the sullen faces of some of the local individuals held onto their cue sticks as if they were spears dug deep into their clutch-like markers designating a personal claim well earned and deserved.

"The place is empty," said Julian, staying close to Clark's side.

"Gee whiz, Julian! It's one of those days, you know?" flabbergasted Clark.

"Not really, Clark," reverberated Julian as they made a slow entrance into the bar. "I really don't know."

"Don't worry about it, Julian," stated Clark, and he pointed to a place on the bar and pulled out a couple of the old, used stools that washed the wooden floor beneath them with four iron legs.

"Come on, Julian. Let's sit here. We have a long day ahead of us, you and I."

"Whatever you say," spoke Julian, moving himself up to the wooden bar counter. Clark would peer toward him with a beautiful of sordid expression.

"What's the matter with you, Julian?" explained Clark. "Ever since we arrived in Madras, you've had the worm about something only God and those mountains we passed along the way could be willing to talk about."

"Relax, mister! You're here to enjoy yourself, remember?" Julian shook his head and pantomimed several expressions of disgust and disappointment.

"For heaven's sake yourself, mister! Would you forget about that blasted book, Julian! That book! That's all you think about. Forget about it! You're not in the valley anymore. This is Oregon! Damn you, Julian!" Clark studied the bartender who stood always from their tarnished corner.

"Give the man a beer!" he yelled out. "Hell! Make that two beers. Bartender, please!"

"Hold on, boys! I'll be with ya in a moment," said the tall, slim man who had been catering to a couple of Indians sitting down on the opposite end of the bar counter. "I'll be with you in a minute, boys," the bartender repeated himself.

"And don't be so pushy, Clark," persuaded Julian. "We have a little time, don't we?"

"I suppose you're right, Julian," said Clark. "Oh! But don't worry, man. I can drive that car back home."

"Listen, you've already had enough beers for one day, Clark," rationalized the dark-haired Chicano.

"What'll it be, boys?" came the voice of the bartender as he polished and manhandled the bar's counter with both hands, flat palms, and prepared for business.

"Make that two large glasses of draft," said Clark.

"The thing, coming right up! It's a good thing to have on a warm day such as today," said the bartender. "You boys must be new in town here."

"I haven't seen your faces around here."

"We just got into town with a bus from Raisintown. Raisintown, California," spoke out Clark.

"Ah! So you boys are from the valley, are ya?" asked the tall man as he put down both glasses of beer on the counter.

"That's right!" said Julian. "Well…well, we don't get too many people from the San Joaquin Valley around here, much less from Raisintown. Tourists come from all over, but I can't say Raisintown people are more appealed to come over to Madras," said the man with a stolid groan apparent in his voice. Clark and Julian looked at each other with a reserved suspicion in each other's eyes, amazed and surprised but nevertheless not overwhelmed by any sort of bad or unwelcomed statements.

"You boys plan on staying long?" the bartender asked again. At first, Clark did not want to answer. Julian conceded.

"We'll stay a couple of weeks or so. We're not very sure about that yet," said Clark.

"There's a lot of pretty countryside to see up here. I wouldn't miss it, if I were you. No, sir," exclaimed the man. The wall in front of them was covered with relics, paintings, and antiques, among which included a long musket rifle with a barrel as long as a yardstick.

"What do you have hanging on the wall?" asked Clark.

"A Winchester long rifle. The musket is only a cover-up," said the bartender. "I'll take her down so you can both see it, if you'd like."

"Sure!" interjected Clark. "Why not?"

"I have another one in the backroom which I built myself," he muttered while stopping onto a chair in order to make easier a grasp for the rifle. With one heave up and outward, the rifle came loose from the hinges, which coupled away from the wall. The bartender stepped down to the wooden floor, which flooded the barroom with wretched creaking and loud tonnage of footsteps. He walked over to Julian and laid down the rifle on the counter.

"You like guns. They bother you, huh?" he asked.

"I keep up with them now and then," replied Clark. "I still have another one in the kitchen. I'll bring it out," said the gray-haired, tall man and slipped back into the room behind some curtains. Julian appeared neither moved nor excited because of the arms display. Instead, he began keeping both his eyes on a large Indian man who had walked into the bar after peering to the entrance for a minute or two. Clark was examining the rifle the bartender had laid down on the bar counter; the huge heavy Indian figure began examining both Clark and Julian with a strange look uncommon to the awareness since the time they had departed the bus depot.

"Here ya go, gentlemen," blasted out the bartender as he revealed himself from behind the curtain door. "Here's a babe I built when I was a young stud like you boys." Clark took hold of the newly displayed rifle and took considerable amount of time to examine it carefully. He became ecstatic about his self-propelled examination of the weapon. Julian stalled for time and appeared to avoid the display of metal rifles brought over by the bartender; he lost interest as time passed on in minutes. Clark turned to look away from time to time and realized his disinterest with the topic. Julian tipped the glass, nonchalant and systematic, and would appear lifted by a strange anachronistic touch of a hand upon his back pressing for some sudden and demanding reasons. Disturbed and shaken, Julian turned his head around to see the large hairy figure of the Indian man standing in back of him with a fixed pair of eyes that stared unto Julian's lackadaisical posture. The heavy character of braided hair and mustard and amassed complexion of ruddy olive blurted out a few cantankerous words.

"Say! Why don't you tell the man behind the counter that he has a decent pair of rifles?" Clark turned to look at Julian. The bartender was a good distance from them and was preparing some drinks for other figures who had walked into the bar. Julian appeared reluctant at first to say anything horrendous of torrid character. However, he did feel a push, despiteful and sharp.

"They're nice guns!" said Julian, speaking to the Indian who appeared a slight taut and inebriated for the moment.

"Thanks," repeated the man from the mountain region of an area called White Sands, an Indian reservation located north of the town. He mentioned other words for the sake of preponderance of any stint or elixir support.

"They're nice…real nice," muttered Clark with a soft voice very cautious and showing a steady gait of careful planning. Now he avoided a mimic of any brief confrontation of the beginning of what is the majority of barroom brawls. Clark raised his right hand with a friendly gesture of a wave. He flippantly tried showing a character of good intentions. Suddenly, the large figure moved garbling several words to himself, not near to becoming understood.

"There's no reason to become upset, Julian, but you can never tell about any of these strangers, especially here in Oregon," spoke Clark in a softening tone and disguised himself with a convenient rebuttal.

"I thought just for a minute there…that…"

"Yeah! I know, Julian!" interrupted Clark. "Finish your beer, and we'll start heading back to the house." Julian reproached the statement with a spoiled look and anticipated hastiness, not cognizant of what he should think or say in reply to this blond-headed figure of robust character. They both left the bar that afternoon and decided to do some shopping at a supermarket before taking to a southern direction turnoff out of the town.

"You'll really like it here, Julian, once we get some of our bearings straight and moving. Tonight we'll go home and drink ourselves rotten and sleep. Now I'll do all the cooking and that sort of thing," said Clark.

"That's sounds good to me, Clark. Whatever's necessary, man!" conjectured Julian as he closed the door to the vehicle and rolled down the window. Clark turned on the ignition with self-control and confident hands, as if telling Julian that he could drink and drive above any situation.

"It's all right, boy. That's what you're here for, mister." Clark kept looking at Julian with a look of calm and relaxed messages. "Relax! Have a beer. Don't worry about it," hammered Clark in a usual consoling style. "Like I said, plenty of these people are tourists. They're your everyday consumer traveler, traveler, and money spender, the type who comes from everywhere and anywhere. A good mountain of millionaires, hippie-bum type, the kind who hit and run and, after it's all over, the mess is left all over the ground and greenery."

Julian fixed on with an interested tonnage of eye contact and quick-bent attention. "Anyone else, Clark?" questioned Julian in a pretense of nonchalant and lure of inundated ignorance as he nearly stretched his body across the window and falsified the image of boredom and foreclosure.

"Sometimes, you have Indians, and then you have Indians."

"What do you mean?"

"The majority of the Indians who live here have lived in this area all their lives. The Chinooks and various other tribes. Those are, as you may already know, the first group. American Indians!"

"And the second group?" asked Julian. Clark turned. "The second group are the Indians from India. You know? The turban eccentrics, the Taj Mahal, Rapahli kind."

"I have never heard of them," said Julian.

"Come on! Sure you have! These are the ones who have controlled the icons of oil links for centuries, the ones who have escaped from skirts of starvation in India," went Clark's voice. "Think of all the starving children, Julian." Julian remained adamant and speechless. "Think of all these rich, affluent cult heroes who come to Oregon to eat and live a hippie life."

"Are you talking about the turban now?" asked Julian.

"Yeah."

"But this doesn't have anything to do with people or rather what happens in California," said Julian.

"Julian, Julian?" asked Clark with a coaxed jam of sarcasm in the way he looked directly straight at the road.

"There's a great deal of land investment involved with their drip attitude and emotionalism carried along with their so-called ambitions."

"What the hell are you talking about?"

"I'm talking about you and me, mister," answered Julian.

"And what do I have do to with any of this?"

"You're visiting up here, and I'm just another ambitious hypocrite."

"Relax, Julian. Relax! Settle down!" sparked Clark. "Don't let your attitude destroy your having a good time up here, amigo. We're going to enjoy ourselves, and that's that!"

"You're not fair. You're not being fair at all, Clark," clamored Julian.

"Look, compadre. You want to stay here or not? Just say when, and your bus ticket is still good for the ride back to California," blustered Clark.

"But we just got here, Clark!"

"You just arrived here, my friend." Clark scurried.

"Now let's just drive over to the house and forget about it, okay?" begged Julian in a refraining tone and demise.

"Now you're talking, mister!" said Clark.

Their first evening there at the house was falling fast, and the night was still long enough to allow declarations or decisions on where one should be making brash moves to overseeing the countryside. Clark had quickly dominated the kitchen scene that very first night, and Julian did nothing but a little more than listen.

"You boys are hardly ready for settling down to a new Oregon life out here?" asked Ira. Julian blushed with incessant and trying refrain as he rolled the center stage of the cooking area.

"What the hell, Ma!" screamed out Clark. "Why, this boy's going to knock down the mills in my path. I'm going places, and I have too much to do." Clark Sr. shrugged his shoulders and dealt a quaint muff of a gentle gesture as he heard those words. Ira turned a frightful half toward Julian's position and sparkled off a few sincere words of platitudes.

"He's simply terrible, Julian. I don't know what to think of him. He's a monster. I know he is." She smiled, and her glasses of drinks transformed her smiling face into a gleeful sight of hugs, open and magnifying. Her eyes glistened over and over again with her usual kindness and American-laden hospitality.

Clark handed Julian a can of Coors beer. "Here, have another one. It will do you some good." Ira chuckled as Clark Sr. lacked on with serious lain and recumbent pose.

"Well! One thing is certain. The countryside is beautiful…"

"Beautiful," interrupted Ira. "Why! You haven't seen anything that's a surprise. Why! Just wait till ole Buck here takes you around to do some sightseeing. You fall in love with the countryside."

Next, Clark Sr. would repeat the same statement in a cantankerous way to mean to discuss the same idea.

"We'll get a chance at it," stated Clark. "There's no big hurry. Be calm. We'll let him take his time."

"Do it here, Julian. We're folks who are easy to get along with."

"It's no problem there, Ira," said Julian.

"Why is he such a tense person? Relax, would you?"

She hadn't troubled Julian, as her figure sat on a chair that had rested against the wall. He sat down next to the kitchen table.

ABOUT THE AUTHOR

The Author, Jess Zepeda, currently lives and works in San Francisco. He has spent his entire living in California and concentrates on his literary resume, an active artist with the San Francisco Women's Art Group. His majority of employment as a substitute school teacher had been spread out over a period of 26 years while some images of his art appear on the ArtSlant.com international website.

www.ingramcontent.com/pod-product-compliance
Lightning Source LLC
Chambersburg PA
CBHW020110310726
48970CB00002B/559